Mrs. Pemberton

Will is the Cause of Woe

Vol. I

Mrs. Pemberton

Will is the Cause of Woe
Vol. I

ISBN/EAN: 9783337045036

Printed in Europe, USA, Canada, Australia, Japan

Cover: Foto ©Andreas Hilbeck / pixelio.de

More available books at **www.hansebooks.com**

WILL IS THE CAUSE OF WOE.

A Novel.

BY THE AUTHOR OF

'ALTOGETHER WRONG,' 'DACIA SINGLETON,' 'WHAT MONEY
CAN'T DO,' ETC.

"Evil is wrought by want of thought
As well as want of heart."

IN THREE VOLUMES.

VOL. I.

London:

SAMUEL TINSLEY & CO.,

10 SOUTHAMPTON STREET, STRAND.

1878.

WILL IS THE CAUSE OF WOE.

CHAPTER I.

NEAR to Prawle Point, on the south coast of Devonshire, there stands, at a short distance from the sea, on sloping, rough, turfy land, a small but pretty-looking cottage, belonging to a man named Miles Mason, who, after twenty years' service as a seaman, was rewarded by being made a coastguardsman.

The whole scenery around his little home is bleak and wild and desolate. Great rocks projecting into the sea, and bold, precipitous cliffs almost overhanging the house, the roaring waters, the huge black waves, breaking into a sea of silver over the shingly beach and amidst the boulders, rendering it very grand but very terrific.

The war of the elements without, for it was

a blustering, stormy night, rendered the calm scene within the house more striking. In a neatly furnished room, which was kitchen and parlour in one, close to a good fire, sat Miles Mason. His supper was being prepared by his only child and his sole companion, Cherry Mason. The savoury odour probably whetted the man's appetite, for after a few minutes' intent reading of a dirty-looking copy of the *Western Morning News*, by the feeble, glimmering light of an oil lamp, he suddenly looked up and said,—

"Isn't it time we had our supper, Cherry?"

"It wants five minutes to the hour, father," replied the girl, turning as she spoke to the large Dutch clock that hung against the wall at the further end of the room.

"Five minutes more or five minutes less doesn't matter; let's have it when it's ready. I'm hungry to-night; perhaps it's instinct tells me I shall want a good meal to keep out the cold. Do you hear the wind, Cherry?"

"Yes, father, I hear it; and, accustomed as I am to hear it, I cannot bear it. The sea is an awful thing!" exclaimed the girl, with a shudder. "To-night will be the last in this world for many. How I wish I had never known what a shipwreck was!"

"Nonsense, girl! think of your work now, and let's have our supper. But it's a bad night this!" continued the man, more to himself than his companion. "May God be with all them at sea to-night, and thanks and praises be to Him for these and all His other mercies to us," he concluded, as he sat down to the meal prepared for him, and at once commenced to do it full justice.

The storm was now on the increase; the wind whistled through the small latticed windows and rattled the doors of the little house. The rain fell in torrents, beating against the glass, and coming down the large square chimney, hissed in the fire beneath. In the distance the roaring of the murderous waves, dashing in wild fury against the giant rocks, made the young girl's cheeks to pale, accustomed as she was to tempestuous, boisterous weather. Suddenly she exclaimed,—

"Father, I think I hear voices!" and then, after listening with painful eagerness for a moment,—"I am sure I do. Don't you hear, father? Is it for help, do you think?"

"It's the voices of the wind and the waves, Cherry. Why, you look as white as your apron, and your eyes as big as dumplings. Go on with your supper, girl, and then get to bed;

it'll be calm before dawn, I'll wager, and you'll sleep through it."

"I can't eat, father, there is no use in trying," said Cherry, dropping her knife and fork, and, taking up her apron, she threw it over her face, pressing it close to her eyes. "There, again—hark! It *is* voices I hear, father; open the door and listen."

Cherry started to her feet, the apron fell back, and she stood with her large, frightened eyes fixed on the door that shook with the violence of the storm. Miles Mason rose to do his daughter's bidding, expressing, however, his doubts as to the correctness of her fears. It was not very easy to open the door; the heavy, strong wind was weighing against it with all the power of a sou'-wester. At last, when he succeeded, the volume of air that entered blew the things about in all directions, extinguished the lamp, which was unfortunately not protected by a glass, sent a cloud of smoke from the chimney into the room, and creating altogether such dark confusion that Cherry felt more frightened and bewildered than before, when, with a beating heart, she had thought she heard cries of distress.

"Oh, come in, father, and shut the door. Don't, don't leave me, father! Do you hear?

Father! Oh, why did I let him go near the door! What shall I do now? Father! are you there?"

The door was closed. Cherry knew that by the sudden calm; but she was too frightened to move. She stood shrinking up against the wall, incapable for the moment of moving, or even thinking reasonably; but presently the fire, which had been deadened by the downrush of smoke, began to send out a little flickering light, the wood crackled, and at last a bright flame showed the extent of damage done. A few broken plates were quite sufficient to cause the noise, especially when they were swept off the table with knives and forks and tin mugs, and a jug of cider.

Cherry now bethought herself of getting a light; and the lamp being only extinguished, and in no way injured, it was easy to relight it, and, adding a little more oil, she secured herself against a similar accident by placing it out of reach of harm, in case the door should again be opened with the tempest still raging. Then she set to work to put things to rights again, and in about half an hour all traces of the disaster were effaced, while the mere fact of having employed her hands sufficed to steady her nerves. She almost smiled now at her childish fears, and wondered why this night, more than any other, she should have so given way, and lost all presence of mind. She placed the remainder of her father's supper near the fire, which, burning cheerily, gave an air of comfort to the little room, increased rather than lessened by the furious storm without. Ten o'clock struck, but Cherry could not make up her mind to go to bed.

"Perhaps father will come back soon; he surely will not go to keep his watch without coming in for his storm cloak and hat, as he calls them; as it is, he must get wet through to the skin. At any rate I will wait till the storm is over," she muttered, half aloud to herself.

But the storm gave no signs of diminishing, for the sullen distant roll of thunder, now dimly heard, foretold the probability of its becoming worse before abating. Presently a vivid flash of lightning shot aslant the room, followed almost immediately by a crashing, cracking peal of thunder, that seemed as if it must by mere vibration destroy the little dwelling. Cherry buried her face in her hands, and pressed her head against the old arm-chair she was sitting in.

"Oh, if father would only come back! How awful!" she cried.

And another flash lighted up the room with
a blue, unnatural, unearthly light, and another
and yet another; the thunder never ceasing
roaring and booming, as if the whole heavens
were furnished with mitrailleuses, and thou-
sands were being fired together. Once Cherry
looked up and saw through the curtainless
window. The scene that during that moment
presented itself is almost past description.
The sea a mass of bluish frosted silver, leaping in wild fury against the gaunt, dark,
pointed rocks, and encircling them with its
boiling foam like a fringe of down, rapidly
to disappear and as rapidly return; the sky
densely black, with here and there a fleck of
yellowish cloud; the grass land that lay
between the cottage and the sea looked like a
swamp or morass, the water streaming down
it to the shingly shore. But what in that
brief moment Cherry Mason saw most distinctly was a black mass that seemed to be
moving upwards from the sea, a group that
might have consisted of some eight or ten
people, or it might be only a heap of something, perhaps a boat drawn far out of the
water and stood upright against some mass of
stone; or was it the large rock that at very
low tide and calm weather was visible?—the

folly of the latter thought did not strike her; but with all her fancies of what it might be, she believed but in the first. Some catastrophe, some dreadful shipwreck, perhaps only the dead to show what the living had suffered—for who could be cast on those jagged, sharp pointed rocks by one of those wild, mountainous waves, and live to tell it? Many a corpse lies buried in the pretty little village churchyard, which from its secure height can look down and see the havoc created amongst the young and the old, the ready and the unprepared, that perhaps had just made their first start in life, all hopeful and promising, or with years weighing heavily on their shoulders yet pressing but softly on the heart, returning home to enjoy the reapings of hard toil and labour, cut short in their career suddenly and violently, and, torn from all to whom they were dear, hastened into eternity. There lie, in that little churchyard, the bride of a day, the mother with her infant in her arms, the orphan boy, the old grandfather, and the young girl expecting so soon to become a wife—all lie there; hopes and fears, friendship and enmity, love and hatred, buried with them. All met their untimely end at different periods at that fatal spot where now Cherry Mason rightly saw some fresh victims approaching her secure and peaceful home.

The girl listened with eager ears for the sound of nearing footsteps, but in vain; it was impossible to hear anything but the howling wind and the beating rain. The thunder now was more distant, but the rumbling, growling sound, echoing from rock to rock, was still unceasing. It was a fearful night, a night never to be forgotten by any whose evil destiny caused them to witness the elements waging war against one another in that district.

Cherry Mason was no coward, yet her heart beat now with intense fear; she knew, she felt, something was going to happen; she pictured to herself a drowned man or woman being brought in; or one that might still have a spark of life left, and hers would be the hand and hers the duty to help rekindle it. She fancied an accident to her father, she fancied it might be he who would be borne in injured or perhaps dead, and then what would become of her, alone in the world and friendless? But common sense after a little came to her aid. It was next to impossible her father should have met with an accident: he knew every rock within miles: he could go blindfold without running any risk; then how could aught harm him in going down to see from whence the cries for help had come? Yet why so shaken—why so trembling? Poor Cherry! Did a presentiment of anything in the future, of events that would be the fruit of this night's work, strike fear into her girlish breast? It might be so; but of what avail are presentiments? what purpose do they fulfil? No heed is paid to them, and it is almost impossible there should be, for they are never understood—vague, meaningless, but terribly tormenting; something like good advice when unsought and undesired. Could any one have whispered into Cherry Mason's ear what from henceforth her life was to be, its aim and its end, would she have put a curb on her lips or a rein round her heart? I doubt it. Without being a fatalist, I believe that, knowing what would arise if we followed a certain line of action, we would follow it still, arguing (somewhat obstinately, perhaps, in our determination to risk doing what we know must bring us many heartaches) that if we took the other course it might be worse still—and who could tell but that it might? Live whilst you can, be happy when you may, and leave the shadowy future to work out its worst. At any rate, few of us can judge what is best for others; what may be a grief to me may be none to you; what may torment you to death may not disturb me in the least; we are all too apt to think that dispositions and characters are alike, and that what one likes so will another. And life withal is such a lottery—a game of chance played by us all from morn till eve : a careless word, an unintentional look, may turn the whole current of our existence ; golden silence sometimes making, sometimes marring us. Just as we lose all, or break the bank, by obstinately staking on a certain number ; a trifling action chancewise doing more towards the fulfilment of our dearest wishes, than a premeditated deed, in the carrying out of which all our best energies and clearest intellect have been unsparingly used, only most signally to fail in the accomplishment of our desires. In endeavouring to fashion out our future according to our own notions of what is for our happiness, we may often bring about a condition of things that becomes intolerable ; and then it is too late to remedy the evil our short-sighted finite ideas have wrought. Therefore we must come to the conclusion that it is best to leave to an overruling Power the direction of our lives, and not meddle with what we can in no way control, any more than Cherry Mason could still the tempest that was working up for her a future more stormy and disastrous than she could have ever dreamt would fall to her lot.

The young girl shuddered involuntarily as she was roused from her gloomy, nervous reverie by a loud knocking at the door. For a moment she did not move; the next she endeavoured, with trembling hands, to open it.

"Father is not with them," she thought, "or he would not have told them to knock."

Who the "them" were she had not time to think, but she connected them with the dark mass that stood out so clear and distinct in the blue lightning. It was not easy to open the door, still less to keep it so, till two men, slightly in advance of what was following, held it wide open by standing against it, and then they allowed the group to pass. Four men were carrying, to judge by their faces, a somewhat heavy load. Miles Mason was one of them.

"Get the mattress from off my bed, girl, and put it down there near the fire—make haste!" he said, addressing his daughter. "Help her, my man," he continued, turning to one of the two, who had stood by the door, but who were now inside with the rest.

They were all dripping with the heavy rain, as well as from the sea-water that had washed over them, as, clambering over the rocks, they had endeavoured to save themselves or help to save others from a horrible death.

"Is he dead?" whispered Cherry, in a hoarse voice to the man who, at her father's bidding, followed her into the adjoining room to aid her in getting the mattress.

"We don't know, miss; I think he must be, though. Lord, how he was battered about among them rocks!" he replied, in an under-tone.

The mattress was placed near the fire, and then the four men gently laid their burden down upon it. Cherry then at once removed the coat that one of the men had thrown over the face, and, without uttering a word, quickly, but very quietly, used those remedies for restoring life to which she had on more than one occasion been a witness; but never before had she been the principal one to direct and take the lead. Young as she was—she was scarcely seventeen—she yet showed herself perfectly capable; if her cheek was pale her hand was steady, no remains of nervousness were visible; indeed, it was her solitariness that had partially unnerved her. Whilst friction was being used and warm flannels applied, and the wet clothes cut away, she prepared some hot brandy-and-water, and then endeavoured to put some between the lips of the lifeless man.

It was about half an hour after the first attempt to recall life had been made, and yet no signs of its return appeared; there was no warmth as yet in any part of the body, the lips were still blue and the face of an ashy hue, the blood had trickled slowly down from a wound in his head, adding to the ghastly appearance; however, they still kept on, re-doubling their efforts as their hope seemed to wane.

"A warm bath would be the best thing, I think," said one man. "I've heard it said it'll succeed when nought else will."

"We have no bath," cried Cherry, dismally; "and if we had, he would be dead—or well enough not to need it—before the water was made hot; besides, some say it is a dangerous remedy. If I could only get some of this down his throat"; and she tried now to put some pure brandy into his mouth and rubbed his lips with the spirit.

"I think the hot flannels and rubbing quite as good," said another of the group, who as he spoke was heating a blanket at the fire and then placed it round the poor fellow's body.

There was silence now, each busy with his endeavours to restore life, except Miles Mason himself, who was piling up the wet clothes and carrying them away to a shed at the back of the cottage, and then, removing his own coat, he put on his large storm cloak and hat, and was evidently preparing to go out once again. With his pipe in his hand ready to light, he stood for a moment looking at the young man lying inanimate at his feet. It was a beautiful face, delicate enough for a woman's, finely cut small features, a slight moustache, and fair curling hair hanging dank and clammily around his broad forehead. He was tall and slight, his hands and feet small. To judge of him as he lay there, he seemed of gentle blood, and little used to a rough life, either from choice or necessity.

"Poor fellow! I fear it's all up with him. His mother—you say his mother lives near ways to this—will have a heavy heart before dawn. One of you men must go over to Sandcombe—it's there she lives, you said, I think—and break it to her."

Miles Mason spoke softly, as if—though he thought him dead—he yet might disturb him.

It is natural to all to speak gently in the presence of death, as it is to tread lightly when approaching the sick.

"You may go yourself, Miles Mason," said one of the bystanders, a neighbour who with two others had gone, as Mason had done, to see and lend a helping hand in time of need; "leastways, I won't. You could tell bad news better than I; it's the hardest thing in life to tell another of a sudden sorrow that is big enough to burst the heart; and when it's about a son, and he too an only one, why—"

"Hush, hush!" exclaimed Cherry; "listen —I think he breathes. See, his lips move! He is not dead—look, father—he lives!"

And as the young girl spoke, a slight convulsive movement was visible about the lips and hands. With bated breath the bystanders gazed at the young man, who now began in truth to show that life was yet within him.

"Thank God, he's not to be added to the number of dead belonging to that doomed ship! My master, my dear young master, you're safe! and I pray you'll never more go to sea again."

The man who spoke knelt down beside the poor young fellow who had been so unexpectedly snatched back from the brink of death;

and, now that he thought all danger was over, he gave way to his pent-up feelings, and two big tears fell down his bronzed cheeks; he brushed them rapidly away, fearing, yet hoping, none had seen his weakness; but as if he thought they might, he said apologetically,—

"You see, he's my foster brother, and I'd go to the death for Master Cyril, just as I did to sea, for I hate the water as I hate pain; but I went because he would go, and I couldn't bear for him to leave me behind. Master Treherne, can you hear me? You're safe, sir, and—and—well, I can't tell him we're all safe," he muttered to himself; "and the poor little cutter!—I don't suppose there's a bit of her left together, and he was so fond of her; but, the Lord be praised, *he*'s safe!"

"I don't think you need bother your head about the craft, when all hands, save you and I and he, are gone down with her, and they've left women and children to cry for them, and we've none it signifies to whether we be here or up there—"

"Haven't he his mother? Why, Jim, you speak as if you were like to be sorry we're not all drowned!"

"Well, maybe I am!" sulkily rejoined Jim,

turning away. " I think, master, I 'll just go out and see if there be no chance of picking up some of our mates," he continued, turning to Miles Mason.

" Well, I must go out now, too," said Mason. " I ought to have been on my way before this; not that I fancy this is a night for much of my sort of work, dearly as they love a lowering sky; this is a little too much for the most desperate of them smugglers. So we can go together if you be so inclined. But take a drop of warming stuff first, it won't hurt, after all you 've gone through, if it don't do you no good. And, Cherry, my girl, Cooper will help you to get that poor gentleman on to a bed, and I dare say he and this here friend of his will sit by him to-night," said Mason, turning to the man who called himself the foster-brother.

" 'Deed, master, I 'll never leave him, if you 'll let me remain by him, and I want none to help me; and I think, perhaps, it may be better not to let madam know of the—accident, and for nobody to go to Sandcombe to-night, since he 's like to be able to tell her all about it himself."

Mason, the man Jim, and another now left, as did also, a few minutes after, the two neighbours, leaving Cherry and John Finch alone with their charge. They sat on either side of him, each chafing a hand, and every now and then Cherry put a teaspoonful of brandy-and-water into his mouth. His teeth were no longer clenched, and he swallowed with apparent ease. Presently he opened his eyes and looked vacantly from side to side, and then a softened expression passed over his face and he fixed his eyes on John Finch, and after a few moments he said, but turning towards Cherry,—

"Where am I? What has happened?"

"You're here, Master Cyril, and it's all right; nothing's happened, so don't think just yet."

But Cyril Treherne, whose brain was still confused, and who felt as if some dozen muffled drums were being played beside his head, was, nevertheless, not of a nature to accept such a reply even in his then helpless state, and looking at Cherry—his tone of voice, though not loud, was perfectly distinct—asked where he was and who she was.

Poor Cherry told him as best she could, for John Finch was making all sorts of signs to her, which she utterly failed to read; moreover she did not know what reason there could be for not speaking rationally to a man quite in his senses, though he had just escaped death.

"And is the Marguerita totally lost?" he asked.

"She is, sir; and all our poor fellows in her I fear, but Jim," said Finch, unable himself to resist speaking out.

"And where is Jim?"

"He's gone out with the lassie's father, to see if they can hear anything of the others."

"I think, sir," said Cherry, "you had better not talk any more; and if you would get into bed, it would be well. There's the next room at your service, and it is all ready."

Cyril Treherne fixed his eyes—clear blue eyes, that looked very soft and gentle just now —on Cherry's face; he continued to watch her for a few seconds after she had done speaking, and then sighing, more as if to try if he could do so freely than from any *triste* remembrance, he said,—

"You are very kind; I do not know how I shall ever thank you for all you have done for me to-night. Yes, I will go to bed; I am sorry you should be troubled with me, but to-morrow I shall be able to get home, I think."

John Finch raised his young master up in his strong arms, and, carrying him as tenderly as a mother would her infant child, placed him down on the bed.

CHAPTER II.

But the morrow brought with it the certainty that for Cyril Treherne to return home would be out of the question.

Miles Mason, whose duties took him for twelve hours out of the twenty-four from home, his watch being alternately day and night, came back at dawn. He went as gently as he could into the room where Treherne lay. He found him sleeping quietly; and sitting on a chair near the window was his daughter Cherry, both her arms folded and resting on a little table, and her head lying on them. John Finch was beside the bed. Both were fast asleep. So Miles left them; and, climbing up the narrow wooden stairs, he went to Cherry's room, and, throwing off his coat, he lay on her bed, and in less than five minutes was asleep also. But the creaking of the stairs, the shutting of the door, not so carefully done as might have been, roused Cyril from his not over sound sleep. As he opened his eyes and looked round the humble room, with its plain furniture; the low, white-washed roof; the four-post bed, devoid both of top and drapery; the clean but old white curtains that hung at the window, the quaint little pictures of impossible ships in still more impossible positions, the two black profiles, stuck on white paper, framed and glazed, and hanging crookedly on either side of the mantelpiece, he wondered where he was and how he came there, and if the whole were not a dream.

Presently his eye fell on the sleeping form of Cherry Mason, and then he began to remember the terrible events of the previous night. He looked at her long; he did not seem to tire of letting his eyes dwell on her. Indeed, it was a pretty picture enough; one that men not so fastidious as Cyril Treherne would have thought very beautiful.

Cherry, as I have before said, was barely seventeen; she wanted a month or two yet; with a small, slight figure, *souple* and graceful, as could be easily judged by the position she was in; a warm complexion, not very much colour, but it came very easily if aught were said or done to call it forth; a soft, smooth skin; full red lips; a small, straight nose; large brown, startled-looking eyes, with black lashes, now lying as a fringe on her cheek; straight, pencilled eyebrows: and a quantity of dark, thick hair, now hanging down loosely over her shoulders. She struck Cyril as being sufficiently pretty for him to bear for a time, if need be, with his quarters, objectionable as they otherwise would be to him: and he resolved, if really unable to get home, to remain where he was with a contented mind.

He watched her so long that at last he came to the conclusion that it would almost be worth pretending to be worse than he was, that he might try the experiment of being tended by so pretty a nurse. He thought she would be worth studying. He wondered if she had the same feelings, the same tastes, the same disposition as other girls had in the sphere he had been accustomed to meet them in. He thought it would amuse him to find this all out.

So Cyril Treherne lay, innocently plotting for his own amusement at the risk of the girl's happiness to whose father and her own care he owed his life. It never occurred to him in this light. He was thinking only of a temporary diversion for himself, of a method to while a few days or hours, as the case might be, away as pleasantly as might be. He thus indulged in what is very often more hurtful to us than we ever realize—day-dreams. Day-dreams carry us rapidly on, for they are thoroughly under our control; and for that reason we rarely attempt to curb them. They are generally pleasant, so there is no desire to check them; but they are sadly harmful, sometimes to ourselves only, sometimes, and very often, as in Cyril Treherne's case, to others also.

They were interrupted at last by John Finch, who now awoke, and, looking up to see how his young master was, exclaimed, on seeing his eyes open,—

"Law, sir, to think of my sleeping and you wide awake! Do you feel any pains, sir, or hurt about anywhere?"

Treherne looked round, and answered,—

"I feel better than I have any right to expect, but horribly stiff and bruised. I fear I shall not be able to move to-day. Don't speak too loud, for you see she's sleeping," and he pointed to Cherry; "but tell me what o'clock it is."

Finch pulled out his great big silver watch.

He looked at it, then shook it, and tapped it in a way to drive any watch to go if it were possible; then he placed it against his ear, but all to no purpose—not a tick to be heard, and the hands still pointed to twenty-five minutes to seven—and he was quite aware, by the already advanced day, it must be more than that, for it was already early in the month of May.

"The water has got into the works, I think, sir; but I'll go into the room alongside this,—there is a big clock there. Never fear, sir, I'll tread so softly a fairy couldn't be disturbed."

The man did tread softly for him; but whether her ear was quick at strange footsteps, or whether the day was sufficiently advanced, notwithstanding the late hour she got to her, at best, uneasy rest, Cherry started up as Finch opened the door.

"What do you want?" she asked, instantly. "I am so sorry I went to sleep. Please tell me what you want."

"Nothing, miss; I thank you. The young master wants to know the time, that's all."

"I did not know you were awake," said Cherry, now standing over the bed, and looking anxiously and inquiringly into Cyril's face.

"I have been awake a long time," he replied.

"How sorry I am! How weary you must have felt! Why did you not call me? You will like a little tea, will you not?"

"I was not weary," he said, raising his eyes to hers with an expression in them she could not understand, but which instantly caused her to drop her own. "I was not weary; I was watching you, and thinking how—how you must be enjoying your sleep: you were so still, yet your position was not the easiest," he said, evidently checking himself in what he was about to reply. "You asked me if I would have some tea. I do not feel inclined for anything; but when you have your breakfast I will take a little. Well, John, what time is it?"

"Ten minutes to nine, Master Cyril. Now, what do you think of doing, sir?"

"In what way, John?"

"Why, sir, you see, madam" (Mrs. Treherne was always called madam) "and the admiral are sure to hear of the accident; and though the admiral will believe all's right, and that we shall turn up safe, as he thinks no sailor ever lives to be drowned, I don't think madam will be satisfied with his opinion, and she'll be nearly, if not quite, crazy till she hears you're safe; and, sir, there be others, perhaps, may hear of it, and be sending up to the Court to inquire, and—"

"Yes, John, yes, you're right; I must let my mother know I am all right. Have you seen Jim this morning?"

"I have seen no one and heard nothing since last night, sir."

"Then don't you think the first thing to do will be for you to ascertain exactly the state of things: what *has* happened, who of the poor fellows that were with us are lost? I hope to goodness Tait is not gone,—it would be awful news for his wife and children."

"Well, sir, I'm much afeard he is. The last I saw of him was when the ship struck the great rock; he shouted out to lower the boat for you and give you a chance: then came that infernal wave that swept over all, and I recollect nothing after that till I found myself, half stunned, amongst a heap of loose rock; you were beside me, and presently I heard Jim give his long clear whistle; I tried to answer it, but I couldn't hit off a silent moment as he did. He gave cries of alarm, then came help, then I thought if I did not make myself heard we should be left there to die, as every moment a huge dark wave seemed to rise up ready to swallow us up. So I shouted and bellowed, and then—but, O God, how long every second seemed!—then at last they came to us, and we found you, as we thought, dead. We managed to carry you up here. Jim's cries brought down the man from this cottage and three others, fishermen, I believe; and now, sir, you know all I do. No need to tell you what I felt on that spot where I had been dashed; it wasn't pain—I didn't feel that till afterwards; but I tried hard to say a prayer, and I wanted to say the Lord's Prayer, but I couldn't recollect the beginning of it, though from the time mother taught it me I've never missed saying it once in the day, and I couldn't bring to mind anything but the old Catechism—'What's your name?' and 'Who gave you this name?' And that seemed no manner of good under the circumstances, so I gave it up and said 'God save us!' And it was enough. Lord, how odd it is people are so fond of such long prayers when the short ones do as well, and they tire neither God nor man! Well, Master Cyril, I know no more about it."

Cyril was silent a moment; he seemed so full of thought that Cherry, thinking he might wish to send some loving message to his mother, that he did not care to give before a stranger, slipped away. But it was not that; he was thinking, had he been lost, as the poor men who were with him were, what would have been the result? Heartaches? Yes; but, after a little, perhaps forgotten : certainly the world would go on just the same. It was not a pleasant thought, and there was no need to worry himself on the subject, since he was *not* dead. Then he thought of his yacht; the wreck, if so complete as Finch described it, and the loss of life so great, his mother would be well-nigh distracted, unless he let her learn his safety before the news reached her of the catastrophe. He also wished to prevent her coming to Miles Mason's cottage for him; he was fond enough of his mother, but there was one point on which no sympathy existed between them, and that point was too often a matter of discussion at Treherne Court, and he was quite sure the present occasion would offer too good opportunity for madam to let it pass without her favourite topic being forced on him, and this he desired to escape. But time was important; ill news travels rapidly; and so Cyril determined on sending Finch first to gather all the particulars he could, and to try and find Jim, and then despatch him to his father's house.

As soon as John was off, Cherry and her father went in together to the bed-room. Cyril held out his hand to Miles Mason; he knew who he must be, and thanked him in a cordial manner for his hospitality and care. The tone was one calculated to win the heart of a man in Mason's position, and he replied as his feelings dictated, that anything he had done was amply repaid by the great pleasure he felt in having helped to save a fellow-creature's life.

"I thought it was all over with you, sir, and as I looked at you I thought of the sorrow the poor lady, your mother, would feel; for you seem young enough to have been more with than absent from her. However, you're safe, and except those few scratches on your head and face I don't think you're much the worse. Cherry, if you were to get some warm water, and take off all that blood about the gentleman's hair, it would be none the less comfortable. I must be off now for an hour or two. Is there any breakfast for me, girl?"

"Yes, father, and the gentleman will have a cup of tea also."

When Miles was gone, and Cherry had attended to her household duties, she went in to see if Cyril Treherne would get up, or if he wanted anything she could get him.

“ I think I will stay a little longer as I am,
Miss—what am I to call you ?”

“ Cherry, if you please, sir.”

“ Miss Cherry—”

“ Not Miss, if you please,—simply Cherry.”

“ Well, then, Cherry ; it is a pretty name,
and Miss before it spoils it. I think I will
wait till Finch comes back. But will you sit
by me and talk to me a little ?”

Cherry Mason fetched some needle-work, and
taking a chair sat down between the bed and the
window. Cyril was able to watch her at her
ease, and he did so till she looked up, and
seeing how earnestly those clear blue eyes were
fixed on her she coloured up and went on with
her work.

“ What are you so busily employed about ?”
he asked.

“ It is a shirt of father’s I am mending, sir.”

“ Are you an only child, Cherry ?”

“ Yes, sir.”

“ Is your mother dead ? Do you mind telling me something about yourself ? It would
amuse me if you would, and interest me too
very much ; for you must recollect that you saved
my life, and therefore as long as I live I must
think of you as a very dear friend, and we like
to know all about those we are interested in.”

Cherry looked up, her great brown eyes with a surprised but pleased expression in them ; yet she did not quite understand her companion, not his words, they were simple enough, but the tone they were spoken in made her heart beat with a strange and new joy.

"There is not much to tell you, sir. I remember very little that could amuse or interest any one. We have lived here almost as long as I can recollect ; at moments I have thought I could carry my thoughts back to the time I was alone with my mother in her native home—she was a Spanish woman, sir ; her father and mother lived in Seville, and she went at the age of sixteen into the service of an English officer's family at Gibraltar ; it was whilst there she saw my father, and married him—"

"Well, why do you stop ? Tell me all you know,—everything you can remember."

"It seems so strange, sir, you should care to know anything about me."

"Strange that I should care to know the history of one who has saved my life ! Why, do you know, Cherry,—you told me I might call you Cherry,—that I could not repay you all I owe you but by devoting my life to you ?—it is yours, is it not ?"

"No, sir: I don't know, sir, exactly how. I am sure I did nothing that deserves such—such thanks."

Cherry's face was now covered with blushes. The poor child felt shy; she had never been thrown in a gentleman's company before, and she did not understand him; she felt ashamed of her ignorance, she wished so much she knew how to answer him properly: but there was something in Mr. Treherne that frightened her; that made her heart throb so sharply that it seemed half to suffocate her. It was no doubt, she thought, because he was a gentleman, and she but a poor, uninformed girl, but it provoked her none the less. She thought him, too, so handsome; she fancied if he were only ugly she might have been able the better to hide her awkwardness and stupidity.

"Then, when your father married, what became of him?—he did not remain at Gibraltar, I suppose?" asked Cyril, not noticing the girl's confusion.

"Oh, no, sir; my father's ship was only there for a short time. I don't know where he went; but my mother remained in service till —till I was going to be born, and then she went home—"

"To Seville—and you were born there?"

"Yes; and we remained there three or four years; till father wrote to my mother one day, and told her that he had left the sea, and got put on to the Preventive Service, and that we were to take a ship at Cadiz and go to Plymouth. So we left Seville and came here, and my poor mother died in the spring that followed her first winter in England."

"Ah, this confounded climate of ours has killed more than her, Cherry. Poor little girl! you must not look sad. Such pretty eyes as yours should never glisten with anything but joy; they ought never to have tears in them."

And as he spoke Cyril held out his white, well-shaped hand towards Cherry, who was looking out of the window, far away into the past, where the history she had related had taken her back into scenes and seasons that were well-nigh obliterated from her memory. She did not see the hand held out to her; perhaps if she had she would not have understood it.

"Do you refuse to give me your hand, Cherry?" He spoke as he might have done to a child.

Cherry turned her great brown eyes on Cyril; the sight of him recalled her to herself.

"I beg your pardon, sir; I did not hear you ask me to shake hands; but—you're not—going, sir, are you?"

The girl rose as she spoke, and gave her little hand into his, a contrast in colour as well as in size, for she had inherited from her mother the beautifully shaped hand and foot that is common amongst the Andalusians.

"No, I am not going." He took her hand and held it. "If I could always have so kind and pretty a nurse it would make me satisfied to remain here for ever." He spoke without thought; he only meant to show that he appreciated her care. "Have you ever been away from here,—I mean, to London?"

"No, sir; I have never been ten miles beyond Prawle Point since I arrived here twelve years ago."

"Not even to Plymouth?"

"No, sir; never since the day we landed in England."

"Have you many friends?"

"I sometimes hear from a brother of my mother's; but I have forgotten Spanish, and so

I cannot read his letters, and I have to wait till father meets some sailor who is Spanish, and that can read it."

" I don't mean relations ; I mean friends—acquaintances ? "

" Oh, I know everybody hereabouts."

A twinge passed over Treherne's face, which made Cherry ask if he were in pain.

" No, I am in no pain—it 's nothing."

But he let the little hand drop, and Cherry went back to her chair and her needlework, and there was no more talking till John Finch returned.

He brought but scant news. Jim was there, in the next room. Two bodies had been recovered ; one was that of Tait, the skipper, the other the cook. The yacht was a perfect wreck ; it lay there on the rocks, with a tremendous hole through the side, and another through the bottom ; pieces strewn in all directions—clothes, china, glass, pens, boots, shoes, linen, pieces of stone bottles, everything that could possibly have been on board, and that could not melt, was lying far and wide over the rocky shore for more than half a mile. Nothing had been saved ; nothing but the three men escaped destruction ! The morning was calm and bright and beautiful, rendering the havoc created by the previous night's storm more sad to witness.

"Now, sir," said Finch, "I think we ought to let madam know you're safe. Shall I send Jim up to the Court, sir? You see, madam won't forgive me if I don't let her know. Or don't you think you might drive home yourself this afternoon, Master Cyril?"

"Not to-day, Finch. I will go to-morrow; but I feel very battered about, and the drive might, perhaps, force me to remain shut up for two or three days, if I were to attempt it; but to-morrow I shall be all right. You will let me remain here till to-morrow, Miss Mason?" asked Cyril, turning his face towards Cherry.

"Oh, certainly, sir: you're welcome as long as you feel unable to move or feel inclined to— to stop, sir," replied Cherry, colouring up and stumbling over her words. She was surprised at his addressing her as Miss Mason, especially after the little conversation they had had on the subject of her name.

"I would rather, then, that you went to the Court, John," said Cyril, "instead of Jim. He'll want to go home, I suppose; besides, some one must watch by the wreck, so that perhaps he had better remain. He can send a message by you to Sandcombe, and you can forward it on to his people.”

“Oh, sir, my father is sure to see to the wreck for you,” said Cherry; “he 's accustomed to wrecks.”

“That 's true enough, miss. I believe, sir, that Mason has already taken care that a proper watch is over it, but I 'll tell Jim; I doubt me but he 'll like to stop; and I 'll go off to madam at once.”

“How will you go, John?”

“On my legs, Master Cyril, to be sure. I 'll be there in a little better than two hours from this, I 'll be bound.”

“Old Simpson has a trap, if you would prefer driving over, Mr. Finch,” said Cherry; “ and he 'll be glad to let you have the loan of it, I 'm sure.”

“Thank you, miss, but I 'll like the walk.”

“Be sure and tell my mother I am quite well, and only fear a little—cold; yes, say cold, John, it will be better than talking of bruises and pains and a cracked head.”

“All right, sir; I 'll make it smooth.” And John Finch left the room to do his errand; but he had not left the room five minutes before he returned and asked, “Is the close carriage to come for you to-morrow, or—well?

I don't think there is an *or* left : you must have it."

"I suppose so, John, but empty—mind that. Don't let my mother be inside it. Ten miles in a close carriage with that dear, good madam, and just after I have escaped being sent somewhat hurriedly into the next world, is more than my nerves or my temper could bear."

"All right, sir. The close carriage—empty. It shall be so, or it won't be my fault."

"How strange," thought Cherry, "that he should not like his mother to be with him! I wonder why?"

And the young girl looked up at the man, who in a few hours had caused her to wonder more and to be more puzzled than she had ever been in all her seventeen years' experience.

Cyril Treherne was buried in momentary thought, and did not see those large, strange, startled eyes watching him. In repose his face was very handsome—a face to make any one ponder over it. The broad white forehead, with thick curly fair hair around it, the clear blue eyes, that could look so earnest and thoughtful one moment. and the next full of the mischievous merriment of a boy, the well-shaped nose, the beautiful mouth, and white, even teeth, partly hidden by a small moustache, made the sailor's simple-minded, innocent, ignorant daughter think, as he lay there and she gazed at him, she had never before believed any one could be so beautiful; and she was not the first who thought so.

Cherry's first defined feeling for Cyril Treherne was fear; a timidity arising from his being of a different class to that with which she had hitherto been accustomed to associate. She had often done for others as much as she had done for him, but never for one in his position. She had never before come in contact with a gentleman, and so she felt that shyness that amounted to fear which young girls in her station do feel for those they know to be so far above them. Then, after a little, a feeling of regret arose that after the morrow she would never see him again; he would go away, and she would know no more about him. Regret gave birth to a desire that she might be his servant, that she might wait on him, attend to all his wants and wishes, think what he required before he had time himself to do so. He looked so handsome. It was the sheer beauty of the young man's face that attracted the girl; she never once thought whether he were good or not. His face was of that type that one sometimes sees depicted in a painting; nothing remarkable as to intellect, but nevertheless strangely fascinating. The more she gazed the stronger became the charm, till, suddenly recollecting his words to John Finch, she said, making an effort to break the spell she felt gaining a mastery over her,—

" You don't feel any pain, do you, sir? You said something about making the excuse of having a cold rather than say you suffered pain."

Cyril started at her voice; his meditations had taken him home to Treherne Court, and he was picturing to himself the confusion there would arise when John Finch declared his errand. There were others besides his parents to whom the report of his death would be a terrible blow; he trusted no rumours of the wreck would be spread till all particulars were known.

" Did you ask if I suffered pain? Would you be sorry if you thought I were in pain?"

" Sorry, sir!" exclaimed the girl, the colour rising, and her red lips quivering slightly; " how can you ask such a question?"

" Why, little one, you had no need to tell me of your Spanish origin. How easily you are moved! Your Southern blood shows itself hotly enough, and does not seem to be tempered by a drop of English!"

"I like to hear that, sir," exclaimed Cherry, looking up, softened. "I love my father very dearly; but I have a sort of deep, wild love for my mother's memory—a love that makes me worship everything connected with her or her country—a sort of feeling that, I think, to visit her home, and to see her brother, I could even leave my father! But I am talking nonsense, am I not, sir?" she added, smiling, and looking very pretty from the momentary excitement. She was generally so placid and calm in outward appearance.

"No, Cherry, I do not call that talking nonsense—"

"There's my father come home," she said, interrupting him, and at the same moment she thought how quickly the morning had passed, and how idle she had been; there was the shirt very much in the same state it was when she began to mend it.

"Her mother's memory is, up to this, all that has filled the girl's heart!" thought Cyril Treherne, as he sank again into a day-dream, Cherry having gone to prepare her father's dinner.

CHAPTER III.

STANDING on an eminence, and commanding a splendid view of Sandcombe Bay and the wave-beat rocky coast of that part of South Devonshire, is the house where Admiral and Mrs. Treherne resided. Its position and the building itself were very imposing. Built of the grey stone of Cornwall in the time of the Tudors, it stood out nobly amidst grand old trees that were the pride and delight of the admiral. They were now slowly bursting into life, and a pale, fresh green tinge spread over the splendid beeches that formed the finest avenue in the county.

Spring is always too slow. We pine for the young leaves to gain strength and colour: we watch the flowers that seem so long in bud, so backward in flowering, and wonder when the cold winds will cease, and the warm sun help nature forward by making its appearance.

Treherne Court had been in the family for two hundred years, and the house dated back to 1505. Before the time of Admiral Treherne's ancestor, from whom he dated his descent, it was royal property, and was conferred on Colonel Treherne by Charles I. in 1642, as a reward for brave and valorous conduct at Edgehill in that year.

Admiral Treherne was the second son of his father, and it was not till his elder brother died in consequence of an accident while hunting that he left the navy, and, at his father's desire, settled at home, and turned his attention to wife-seeking. He was at this time about forty years of age, and held the rank of commodore. He had had his periodical attachments, having fallen in love on every occasion of his return to England, and at most stations abroad where his ship was stationed for more than a week. Going to sea invariably had the happy effect of healing all wounds caused by sweet voices or soft eyes, and so he came home heart-whole, and perfectly ready to marry; though then he, never having been in earnest, was more easily satisfied than now; or it might have been that his father, a good man, and a thorough-going English gentleman of the old-school type, wearing knee-breeches and a blue coat with brass buttons, made him feel that to fall in love was one thing and to marry another. Old Mrs. Treherne, who rarely interfered in anything outside household matters, hoped her boy— her only one now—would choose a Christian wife, and she ventured to hint that she knew one who might suit, if she but succeeded in pleasing her darling. As her darling seemed anxious to please both father and mother before any one else, he ventured to inquire who the lady might be that was considered worthy of being the future mistress of Treherne Court, and was slightly disappointed on hearing Miss Morgan, the eldest daughter of Dean Morgan, was the best selection his mother could make.

"She's so d—d righteous: mother!" exclaimed the commodore.

"Hush, hush, Thomas!" said his mother. "You must give up that shocking habit of swearing sailors are so fond of, and speak simply, letting your yea be yea, and your nay nay."

"I think then my nay will be nay, mother, in this instance. Miss Morgan goes in so preciously for tracts and prayers that I don't think I could swallow it all."

"But you won't have to swallow anything that I can see, Thomas," said the squire, "except a good fortune, which won't do poor dear Treherne any harm; there are many improvements you might make if you marry a woman with money, and you must be content to leave it as it is if you don't add to your fortune. Rebecca Morgan is a fine young woman; you might do worse, Thomas."

"Well, father, if you and my mother like it, I will see if I can get up the steam and say something decently civil to Miss Morgan when I next see her. There's no hurry, I suppose, about it; next year will be time enough? I can hardly yet realize that my life is really to go on as it does now, and that I must cruise on land for the future instead of on the sea."

However, at the end of a year Miss Rebecca Morgan became Mrs. Thomas Treherne, and her twenty thousand pounds helped but very sparingly for the needed improvements at the Court, while her tracts and prayers went very liberally to upset the daily peace and quiet contentedness of its inmates.

The old squire and his wife were compelled to knock under from sheer want of moral courage, which often, after a certain age, ceases to exist with sufficient vigour to enable the old to battle with the young. So Mrs. Treherne gradually acquiesced in the orders that were issued by Mrs. Thomas for not only cold dinners on Sundays, but early ones also. The squire cared less about it than his wife, as she cared on *his* account as well as her own, he, man-like, but for himself. As to the commodore, when he found the tone matters were about to take, he managed to have very frequent engagements on Sundays, and he was therefore often to be seen at a riotous mess on board some of H.M. ships stationed off Plymouth, instead of being at home and allowed to pass the day in comfort and respectable tranquillity.

"If Thomas won't let me save his soul alive, the sin be on his head and not on mine!" the young Mrs. Treherne was wont to exclaim, alluding to her husband.

"My dear, try a medium course," would suggest the old lady.

"There are no half measures to be taken with God," she would sternly retort. "To the devil only are they acceptable."

Upon which her mother-in-law sighed and gave up the attempted contest. Rebecca used such plain, hard-sounding expressions.

About two years after this ill-judged marriage Mrs. Thomas presented her husband with an heir. For a week or two, therefore, the old Court seemed to resume its former aspect, with good dinners on Sundays, and at an hour when people like to eat them; but this little holiday was soon brought to a close. Mrs. Thomas was not a woman to give way; she was soon in her place again, working discomfort to all around her. Not even the baby could give her sufficient occupation to stop her from reading tracts aloud till the old couple fell asleep, and she had driven her husband out of the room. There is no doubt their daughter-in-law shortened the old squire's life and his poor wife's by some years, and but for the baby boy they must have been worn out sooner still. It is a cruel thing that people, under the pretence of religion, are permitted to hunt their fellow-creatures to death; but this is not the only authentic case on record which it has actually been done.

The old squire went first. He had borne it the best in the beginning, but in the end he gave in entirely, and was crushed by the never-ceasing oppression that was brought to bear upon him. He had to listen to three chapters from the Old Testament and the Psalms of the day before he dared sip a drop of tea in the morning. He was allowed to be seated for that; but at night, before going to rest, he was obliged to go down upon his knees, and knees at seventy-six are not like knees with a lesser weight of years to bear. Tracts were found on a table beside his bed, and after his death 'The Trail that Pollutes,' 'Look Up, the Churchyard's Near,' and 'Milk and Honey for the Elect' were found under his pillow.

His death was the last blow to his poor old wife. She died a week after. There was no need to regret them. They were better off anywhere in eternity than down here to be worn and fretted day after day by frightful prognostications of unknown horrors being their dower in the other world if they did not do everything that was most repulsive to their inclinations in this, and never do anything that to an ordinary intellect seemed to be but an innocent and harmless pastime.

The coast was now cleared for the smooth sailing of all Mrs. Treherne's religious notions, and they were such as at times to baffle the ingenuity of the commodore in his endeavours to escape from some prayer-meeting or other equally obnoxious entertainment. The boy was, of course, being brought up to his mother's views. The child began the day by a chapter being read to him and then thoroughly explained; after that he said his prayers, and they were such as to puzzle the brain of a boy three times his age. Then came the family prayers; then the boy was permitted to eat his breakfast. As soon as he was old enough to offer opposition to this method of bringing him up, he was generally missing at the hours that were set apart for devotion, which for him were three times during the day,—that is, before each meal.

"I would rather go without my dinner, if I might go without my prayers," he said, one day, sitting on a chair, swinging his legs, and with a dogged expression in his face. He was always a pretty child, but his expression was becoming sour and sullen-looking.

"Better go without your dinner for ever, Cyril, than forget to pray to the good God who gives it to you."

"But I don't forget to pray, you take precious good care of that; but you make me sick of prayers, and pa too, he hates them as much as I do, and a bit more, perhaps; then, *he* can sneak off!"

"Hold your tongue, Cyril! If you show any more of such wicked feelings I will shut you up in your room for a week, and give you nothing but bread and water, and your Bible to read," said Mrs. Treherne, solemnly, " and then you will learn to love prayer, instead of talking of it as you do now."

" Shall I, though ! A nice way to make me like a thing, to shut me up with it for a week ! Why, I should hate toffee, jolly nice as it is, if I had nothing else for a week. Wait till I'm big, that 's all ! I'll go to sea and never pray at all—and it'll be your fault. Where's pa ?"

" I don't know, you bad boy ! You will break my heart, I am certain you will ! Come, Cyril, don't talk of going to sea, there's a darling child : you know I have but you, and yet you talk of leaving me."

" Then don't talk to me of prayers !"

And so it used to be till Cyril Treherne was sent to Rugby, and thus for a time escaped the tight religious rein his mother loved so dearly to hold all within that she came near. But her early training sowed the seeds of irreligion, a dread of Sunday, a horror of family prayers, and, from sheer opposition, a love of wrong instead of right ; and what, notwithstanding the strictness on the one point, helped to sow the seeds of a character not of a very desirable type was the blind indulgence with which he was treated in all other matters. Not a desire ungratified, not a wish unfulfilled. No matter what the boy did, his mother found an excuse for him, and his father was too indolent, or perhaps too indifferent, to check him. Besides the man and the child had one grievance in common, one subject on which they heartily agreed and that often drew them together, when perhaps common sense or some degree of dread of what the boy's future might be would have induced the commodore to stay him in his wilful, headstrong faults. They both hated the system Mrs. Treherne adopted wherewith to rule her household, husband and child included, for she did rule them both, after a fashion.

As time went on and Cyril was able to be more of a companion to his father, he absented himself less, especially on Sundays; this compelled him to put up with the cold one o'clock dinner. And with advancing years, so did his indolence increase; this became worse still when he awoke one morning to find a letter, with the long-expected news that he was an admiral at last; for, determined now to take life as easily as possible, he became lazier and more apathetic than ever.

Altogether, the training of Cyril during his early years was not the best fitted for any child ; and one less endowed with good natural qualities would have been irretrievably ruined. Yet much that was fine in his character was destroyed ; he could not fail to be selfish when he found that everything and everybody was made to give way to him ; when hardly big enough to stand alone he was let catch flies against the windows, pull off their wings, and then crush them to death in his small fat hand; he was never told this was cruel, was never checked in any pastime that dealt harm and pain to others, and perhaps afforded him but little pleasure in return. It was not till his mind became enlightened by growing years, that he restrained himself; and then he felt inclined to rebel against the blind indulgence that had been lavished on him.

Fortunately before the seeds sown could bear much fruit, or even have taken very deep root, he was sent to Rugby. He soon learnt that Cyril Treherne at Treherne Court and Cyril Treherne at Rugby were two very differently situated beings ; and so, as most of us do under a similar condition of affairs, finding he could not get his own way by bullying or talking big, he gave in, and kept his bad qualities well in the shade. Thus, after a little, the boy became a favourite. He had two essentially good points; he was generous and had a good temper; moreover he was very manly, very brave, and was handsome— handsomer than any other boy in the school; so recognized was the fact that he had the *sobriquet* of Beauty Treherne. He was a thorough gentleman; Cyril could do nothing mean, as understood by boys; he never told tales, and often, to save a boy from punishment, would allow himself to be considered the culprit.

His religious duties at school were so trifling compared with his home experience that the question ceased to worry him till he again came within the shadow of his mother's system. At Rugby he found he could do a lot of things whilst prayers were read, little amusements that occupied his fingers, which were hidden from the master whilst they knelt, and so prayers were over before he knew anything about them. Religion was made easy— by comparison—at school, whereas at home he looked on it as something worse than a nuisance.

When will parents learn that forcing religion down a child's throat is a terrible mistake, and is a certain way of driving them to use deceit as their sole refuge to escape what has become intolerable to them ? and the probability is, it will lead to a future that few mothers or fathers would dare to contemplate. Yet how many secure their children's temporal destruction by their terrible system, however little (fortunately for the families of those who think as did Mrs. Treherne) they may have power over their hereafter, which, according to their way of viewing it, must inevitably be all fire and brimstone!

Cyril Treherne left Rugby with tolerable honours for a boy who did not require to study for the sake of pushing his way on in the world. From Rugby he went to Oxford, where it so happened he fell in amongst a set of men whose views were so liberal that they passed the limit usually placed by broad thinkers. Thus he had but little chance of arriving at those medium opinions which on all subjects are, as a rule, the safest and surest.

When all Cyril's studying and reading days were over, and he returned to Treherne Court for good, he was of an age, and had seen enough of the world, to take a decided tone with his mother on the vexed question of his childhood and boyhood. He had a good heart; but by his mother's mismanagement it belonged more to his father than herself, and after his father in his affections came his great, big St. Bernard dog, Lion. His mother worried him; her very love for him bored him, and it was too much trouble to him to hide it. Truly she had not a happy way of saying or doing things; she generally had the ill-luck to mar most matters she attempted to interfere in. Some people have a knack of spoiling everything, even with the best intentions.

Cyril had always been in the habit of sleeping in a room exactly over Mrs. Treherne's; but one day, soon after his return home, he expressed a desire to change it, so that he might have a room communicating with another, which other he wanted for a " den," where he could smoke without annoying any one by the smell. This was not feasible in the part of the house he had hitherto occupied. Another reason for his desiring a change was that now his mother could hear him go in and out, and he had a dislike to the idea of being thus watched. Now in the west wing there were the rooms exactly suited to him, and he proposed to have them fitted up, and remove into them.

It was settled, and nearly completed, when Mrs. Treherne one morning, just after breakfast, in speaking of the smoking-room, said,—

"And it will be so nice for me, dear Cyril, because, though I can't hear you as I used, I shall be able to see you."

"Just what I would rather you couldn't do, mother; and so, if you please, I will go to the east wing, where I can neither be heard nor seen, and, moreover, I can have a key to let myself in with at any hour by passing through the tower."

"But, Cyril, my dear boy, you surely do not intend to stay out at night without my knowing it? It could only be evil that could induce you to do so, and I shall always be glad to sit up for you, my dear, and, of course, all the servants shall; so pray, dear, don't—"

"Don't bother me, mother."

"Oh, Cyril, if I could but make you see things differently! If you would but follow our Lord and Master's glorious example, and be subject to your parents!"

“ For God’s sake, madam, stop that humbug ! I can’t stand it, and won’t, that’s more. I’ll go to sea, and you shall never see me again if I am to be bullied in—”

“ Don’t, Cyril, don’t ! ” whined out his poor mother, whose religion, staunch as it was, was not proof against her son’s threats of going to sea. “ I won’t say another word, dear; go where you like, stay out as late as you like, and do what you like,—only don’t leave me ! ”

And the fond, foolish woman went up to her idol, and put her arms round him and tried to kiss him ; but Cyril was out of temper, and he turned away, then jumped up, and so prevented her. A sharp pain, like a needle piercing it, passed through her heart, and with quivering lips she went out of the room. She was already reaping pretty richly the fruits borne by her method of training her child in the way she thought he should go.

The admiral was always silent on these occasions ; but, when alone with either after, he usually said, in his bluff, straightforward way, if to his son,—“ You’re hard upon your mother, boy ”; or to his wife,—“ Can’t you leave the boy alone ! he is old enough to go out and come in when he likes, and to choose his own companions. You'll drive him away if you don't leave off that sort of canting talk. It did when he could not help listening to it, but it's different now."

This remonstrance generally brought down a wholesome reproof on the admiral, of which, however, he rarely heard a word: he went on reading his *Times*, heedless of the voice that was preaching sound doctrine with an earnestness worthy of the cause.

CHAPTER IV.

THERE was a fair proportion of society in the neighbourhood of Sandcombe,—some good old families, many of them wealthy and fond of entertaining, so there was no lack of dinners, with balls occasionally, and carpet dances frequently during the winter, whilst in the summer many pleasant hours were passed at archery meetings, croquet parties, picnics, and so on. Plymouth, too, was not at so great a distance as to prevent social communion with it. So that Mrs. Treherne had no fear of Cyril getting weary of the Court on the score of dulness, still for all that it was very evident he wanted something more than that he had. He rarely went out without coming back what his father called discontented, his mother thoughtful. One day he and his father were walking together after dinner, up and down the beautiful beech avenue, smoking their cigars, when Cyril said,—

"I wish I had gone in for a profession. I wonder, father, you never put me into something. Your father did yourself; it's horribly stupid to be doing nothing."

"You forget I was a second son; it made all the difference. The moment my poor brother died, however, I left the service and came home. You are an only son, and therefore have no need to do anything."

"Yes, I have; for the sole purpose of doing something."

"Well, begin now; it's not too late."

"What, at three-and-twenty?"

"Aye, or at three-and-thirty, if you have the inclination."

"But I am too old, sir!" said Cyril, testily.

"You're too old for the army or the navy; but there are other professions. There is the Bar and—"

"The Church! Yes, that would be a fine thing. Would not madam go crazy?" And father and son joined in a laugh at the idea of poor Mrs. Treherne's joy at such a step being contemplated. "I should have to study too long for the Bar," he continued: "and so I should for anything, indeed."

"Well, you have plenty to interest you,

surely, and to occupy you too, what with hunting, shooting, fishing, yachting, and no end of parties."

"Yachting! I have precious little of that How can I, without a yacht? I don't like always accepting a fellow's invitation and never asking him in return."

"But you can offer hospitality on shore to any extent."

"Oh, that's not the same thing."

"Then would you like a yacht of your own? If so, have one. I will give you one, and go in her with you on your first cruise."

Cyril thanked his father warmly, and they now turned their conversation to the best way of setting about the purchase of their new toy at once. It is hard to say which was most pleased, father or son, for the old Admiral seemed suddenly to have regained some of the energy of past times, at the vision he conjured up of once again being on the rolling deep.

The thought of a profession or "something to do," simply for occupation, was already forgotten by Cyril, and it was only on their nearing the house and seeing Mrs. Treherne standing at the mullioned window of the breakfast-room, a room which, being smaller than the rest, they usually sat in in the evening when alone, that they recollected she would be probably as sorry to hear of her son becoming the owner of a yacht as she would have been gladdened by the news of his becoming more orthodox—a necessary preliminary to his adopting the Church as his profession.

But, as Cyril saw no cause for his mother's oft-repeated dread of the sea, he blurted out his news at once. Poor Mrs. Treherne naturally turned round on her husband, and what Cyril termed pitched into him for having led her boy into doing what he knew she had always declared the very idea of was sufficient to nearly break her heart.

"You knew he had a fancy for the sea, you knew it as well as I did, and yet you do the only thing that is possible now to enable him to gratify it. Why, he might as well be in the navy as have a yacht!"

"How can you talk such nonsense! Don't you know I was years away, and sometimes without being heard of for months; and now the outside he will be absent will be a week or two; he has no desire to go round the world. Besides, you must not expect to keep him tied to your apron-string all his life."

"I don't want to keep him tied to anything.

But there is no use arguing with you. I only know I am a miserable woman; but 'whom the Lord loveth He chasteneth'!"

"Well, my dear, that is a very consolatory statement; but," he mumbled to himself as he left the room, "I would just as soon believe God can love me without the rest."

So the yacht was bought — the ill-fated Marguerita, as pretty a craft as ever floated, fitted up to perfection, like a lady's boudoir. A sybarite could not have desired anything better; and Cyril, all impatience to test her powers, determined to make the usual hackneyed tour that probably every yacht ever built in Great Britain has made some dozen times. His father felt as much delight on again feeling himself pitched and tossed and rolled about as any young sailor on his first voyage who was unconscious of sea-sickness. The old admiral and his son spent a very happy three weeks, and regretted much when they put into Sandcombe Bay on their return home.

During their absence, poor Mrs. Treherne puzzled her brain to conjure up some new pastime that would divert her son's thoughts from this senseless yachting, as she termed it; and finally, in utter despair that her own intellect would instigate her to discover the right thing, she resolved to consult her dear friend, Mrs. Henderson. The thought no sooner suggested itself than she determined to follow it, and, ordering her carriage she went off at once to Sandcombe House, the residence of that lady.

Mrs. Henderson was the widow of an Indian civilian, who had, as many did at that time, made a large fortune, and left it to his wife and daughter, an only child, now, at this period, about six-and-twenty. Mrs. Henderson loved money and titles and grandeur of all kinds very dearly, but Mrs. Henderson was nevertheless a very religious woman, and she and Mrs. Treherne called themselves bosom friends, though they were never heard to speak too well of each other; this is not very uncommon amongst very dear and religious people.

Sandcombe House was about three miles from Treherne Court; the drive was very pretty, through narrow lanes with banks yellow and purple with primroses and violets, till you came to a steep hill; on the top there stretched away a piece of table-land, well sheltered on all sides but the south; on it stood the house, which was large and well built, but nothing noteworthy in its architecture. Mrs. Henderson fixed on Sandcombe as a residence from its peculiarly mild climate.

When Mrs. Treherne was announced, Mrs. Henderson and her daughter were sitting in the drawing-room, which opened with French windows on to the lawn. The room, if not pretty and to every one's taste, was remarkable as being furnished and decorated with everything Chinese, even to the paper on the walls. Mrs. Henderson was a thin, wiry-looking little woman, dark, active, and sharp, always neat in her dress, and, but for the tall daughter by her side, she might have been a spiteful old maid, to judge simply by appearances; but she was not really ill-natured, though she had the misfortune to not only appear so, but for many to think her so. This prevailing opinion arose from those strange religious principles that in some unaccountable manner sour the sweetest temper and harden the gentlest heart. You cannot speak well of people of whom you think ill, and if you are Methodistic you cannot fail to think ill of every one who does not share your ideas and convictions, and as— thank God, for it—Low Church views are not universal, but are, on the contrary, confined to but a handful of people, so to speak, it stands to reason that bitter things are said and sharp arrows sent at random, but generally striking the most sensitive, by this charitable sect, that believe themselves to be the only real Christians.

Miss Henderson was a fair specimen of her kind, as Cyril Treherne was of his, of the influence such bringing up has on the heart and disposition. Being a girl Harriet Henderson could not kick, either metaphorically or in fact, against her mother's mode of educating her, as Cyril had. She, on the contrary, from her earliest childhood, took to it kindly; it seemed to suit her narrow mind—or, we may do her an injustice: her mind was narrowed, and then she rather liked the system. Her heart was never permitted to expand, except for herself, so there could be no blame fairly attached to her if she displayed a want of generosity for others. But she was a virtuous, conscientious Christian woman, as the Reverend Samuel Snape, minister-in-chief of the Methodist chapel at Sandcombe, had said; and what greater praise could a mother of the Henderson type desire?

Mrs. Treherne was greeted with a quick, sharp embrace from her dear friend, and equally affectionately by the daughter; only one might, if a mere looker-on, have fancied

Mrs. Treherne had been guilty of some misdemeanour, for which Mrs. Henderson was intending to admonish her, but that was her manner only. She began, cordially enough,—

"What a warm day; but how kind of you to drive over! I wonder, now, if you came to have a chat about this new project of dear Mr. Snape's in connexion with our branch of the missionary society?"

"No, my dear; I have not seen our dear Mr. Snape for some time; you must tell me all about it. We may feel sure that whatever Mr. Snape suggests the Lord will help in carrying out, for he is truly one of His elect, and he is so good and so humble, and sets such a blessed example to all his poor, erring flock."

"Yes, indeed he does!" chimed in Miss Henderson. "Only yesterday I heard him tell little Tommy Rose to go home and tell his mother that he must stop her allowance altogether now, as he was obliged to contribute all the money he had in hand to send out good men to teach the wicked heathens about Christ; and when Tommy cried, and said his mother would die, that kind, good Mr. Snape shook the little fellow till he nearly tumbled over, and then told him it would be a blessed privilege if the Lord allowed his mother to starve, because of the money that had hitherto kept her alive going to so great and grand a purpose. 'Better the body to perish than the soul'—so beautiful, wasn't it? and he said it in such a lovely tone. And Tommy, of course, was convinced, for I heard him afterwards telling Freddy Day that Mr. Snape 'wouldn't eat no more, nor nobody else, till everybody believed in Christ.'"

"It would be a heavenly consummation if Tommy's words were true. I suppose, then, Mr. Snape is getting up a subscription?" asked Mrs. Treherne.

"To be sure he is, my dear," replied Mrs. Henderson. "The dear, good man's wish is, to fit out and send from Sandcombe, entirely at his own expense, two missionaries; and if he do he gets a medal, or something of the sort, from the Society. I have given a hundred pounds, and Harriet fifty. I think he wants five hundred."

"Five hundred, to fit out two men only!"

"They have to live when they get there, and there is their passage, and—well, I don't know, but Mr. Snape does, and he is sure to be right. I dare say he will explain it to you if you will have any doubt as to the correctness of his estimate of the expenses, but *I* should not like to ask him."

Mrs. Henderson spoke more sharply than usual, and Mrs. Treherne, not being in a contradictory or quarrelsome mood, let the intended reproof pass, and turned the conversation to her own affairs, which for the moment, at any rate, interested her most.

" I want your advice, my dear Mrs. Henderson. I came over to-day to talk to you about my dear boy. I am very anxious about him, and I know no one whose opinion on all subjects I value more than yours."

" My dear friend," exclaimed Mrs. Henderson, enchanted, as most people are when their vanity is flattered—and nothing succeeds better than asking advice—" if in my poor way I can help you or comfort you, believe me, I will. The Lord will direct my lips aright."

" You know, my dear, my son has long shown that he has the same liking for the sea his father had as a young man ; and I have been most terribly distressed by the admiral's having encouraged him in it to the extent of his giving him a yacht. Imagine the good the money spent on that foolish vessel would have been to Mr. Snape ! I would not have cared had it been spent in a handsome drag and four fine horses; but a ship! and for what?—to take him away from home. Now, my dear, I want to find something that will wean him from this senseless and profitless manner of passing his time, and I have come to ask you what you think will be the best way of succeeding."

"Get him a wife; marry him as soon as you can," said Mrs. Henderson, sharply: "a wife of your way of thinking, one who will view the great question of faith as you do; one whom *you* can guide, and who will be amenable to your wishes; one who has been brought up to look up to parents as beings sent by a merciful Father to help and direct children, and to whom obedience is due; one who has learnt to love prayers and good works better than operas and balls; one, also, who has a fortune sufficiently ample to marry into your family, for, as you know, my opinion is that in this world money is as necessary as breath is to life."

" But where am I to meet such a paragon as you have drawn? Look around at our circle; it is truly a large one, but where is there a girl to be found such as you describe?"

Mrs. Henderson hemmed and hawed a little, and then turning to her daughter, who during this discussion had kept her eyes intently fixed on a piece of embroidery she was supposed to be working, but whose thoughts, having travelled more rapidly than her mother's words, rendered her fingers incapable, she said,—

"My dear, kindly go to my room and look over that list Mr. Snape brought me yesterday, and see if I did not promise to go and read to poor Mrs. Dawson this afternoon, and to take some tracts to Billy Brand; I think he leaves to-night. Just see, my dear; and, if I am right, will you attend to it?"

"Certainly, mamma," replied Miss Harriet, dutifully, and at once rising she left the room.

"I could not speak before that dear child so freely as I wish; but it has more than once flashed across my mind that she would make your son exactly the right sort of wife. By his marrying a true Christian his soul may be saved; for you know well, my dear friend, painful though it may be for you to dwell on it, that your son has strangely wrong views, and there is no time to be wasted if he is not to be lost eternally: Think of the everlasting torments he is storing up for himself in the next world if he do not see Christ in this; if he do not let himself be washed in His precious, cleansing blood!"

Mrs. Treherne, with all her deep-rooted Low

Church views, did not care to hear of her son's short-comings and probable sufferings in the next world if he did not mend in this, so she interrupted her dear friend, and said, somewhat snappishly,—

"Well, young men will be young men, and I do not think my son is worse than any other. I know he is hot tempered and obstinate in his opinions at times; but, no doubt, when a man ceases to be a boy he will form his own theories and have his own convictions."

"Dear Mrs. Treherne," now broke in Mrs. Henderson, thinking she had gone a little too far, and would lose her prize before she had fairly won it, "it is because I have such a deep affection for dear Cyril—as I must still call him—that I spoke as I did. You must feel that I could not possibly have entertained the thought of my Harriet ever becoming his wife if I did not think he had the germ of good in him, and that it only wants a gentle, tender, womanly hand to lead him into that narrow but blessed path that will conduct him to glory. But, come, tell me what you think of my suggestion."

"I think well of it, my dear friend, if we can bring it about. I know how good dear Harriet is, and I am sure she would make Cyril more what I wish him to be if she once gained influence over him; but there is the difficulty. However, we can but try, and it will be a good work, so we may hope the blessing of the Lord may rest upon our poor endeavours. We are but helpless, short-sighted children; we must pray, my dear; we must humble ourselves before the throne of Christ and implore His help and guidance."

" My own feelings, exactly ! " whined Mrs. Henderson; and then, recollecting she had a large stake in the balance, she bethought herself to suggest that the young people should be brought together as soon as possible. She did not, with all her faith, entirely cast aside material aid in the shape of human contrivances for advancing her desires.

" Come and stay with us, my dear Mrs. Treherne, and perhaps the peacefulness of our daily life, our simple habits and early hours, may draw the wandering sheep again into the fold. Oh, how blessed will be the day when we can exclaim, ' Now is there joy in heaven for the sinner that has repented ' ! "

Mrs. Treherne could not be outspoken, or she might have said one or two unpleasant truths to her dear friend. It is not agreeable to hear your own child—and an only one—called a sinner and a wandering sheep. And as to

Cyril going to stay at Sandcombe House, he would as soon pass a week or ten days inside the county gaol. So Mrs. Treherne answered, in a mild tone,—

" It is very kind of you, very kind indeed ; but for dear Harriet's sake it might be better if you came to Treherne ; besides, we should put you out of your usual quiet ways : men in a house make such a difference."

" Oh, it would not in the least disturb us, I assure you," replied Mrs. Henderson, never for a moment intending to be put out of her ordinary ways for any one, " not in the least ! Still, if you would like us to go to Treherne, I will, of course."

And so it was agreed that as soon as the Marguerita returned to port Mrs. and Miss Henderson were to go to Treherne. Whilst driving home, though tolerably satisfied with the result of her visit, some conflicting thoughts arose which slightly upset the equanimity of Mrs. Treherne's mood. In the first place she liked neither Mrs. nor Miss Henderson in her heart. She thought the mother took too much on herself, gave forth her opinions in a set-me-down sort of manner that was most offensive ; gave advice when it was neither asked nor wanted—though in this instance she did her the justice to admit she had sought it; and, lastly, she thought far too well of herself to be attractive to others. As to the daughter, she was precisely what her mother had made her: prim in manner and appearance, thinking that every one, saving her mother and herself, ran fearful odds of being damned, that talking good was quite as advantageous to her own soul as doing good, and that wholesome advice went, in the sight of God, as far as wholesome food—what it went for in the sight of the hungry recipient was not worth considering. And this was the girl Mrs. Treherne was consenting to accept as her son's wife!

At any rate, she would give him other chances, she thought, as she drove in at the beautiful old ivy-clad archway that led through the beech avenue up to the house. And then, after all—she went on to think—Cyril could choose for himself. She had not compromised him in any way; he need not marry Harriet Henderson if he did not like, and something assured her—and it was not an uncomforting assurance—that he would not like.

Mrs. Treherne ended by being vexed with herself for confiding in Mrs. Henderson, and fidgeted and worried till she had arranged in her mind to invite the Howards and Thorpes and St. Aubyns, and one or two of Cyril's favourite friends, and so have the house full for a week.

"Surely," thought the poor perplexed mother, "he will take a fancy to some one; and if all are not such perfect beings as Miss Harriet is, they are most of them certainly more attractive," and perhaps, she continued to argue, under her care and direction the one chosen may turn out as pious and good as she could desire.

The next day Mrs. Treherne received a letter from the admiral telling her that she might expect them home on the following Saturday; so without delay she sent off her invitations for the Monday succeeding.

"If Cyril would only marry one of these Howards, I think I should be happy," thought his mother, as she sealed the letter that asked all the family to come. "Or Miss Thorpe," she continued, as she concluded her letter to that young lady's father.

Any one, in short, but Harriet Henderson!

CHAPTER V.

As Mrs. Treherne did not like to choose the Sabbath day for the discussion of the following week's entertainment, she kept her husband and son up till the hand of the clock pointed to within a minute or two of midnight on the Saturday of their return home, to confer with them as to how their expected guests were to be entertained.

"Why, mother, what put it into your head to ask all the county in this way? If you had only waited till we returned home and consulted us about it! It's a horrible bore! I'll go off on Tuesday in the Marguerita," said Cyril, leaning back in his chair and tilting it backwards and forwards on its hind legs.

"Well, well, boy," remarked his father, "you need not be put out; as your mother has asked all these people, we must not desert her; we must try and help her through with it; always stick to your colours, you know." And the admiral laughed a good-natured, forced laugh, for he saw nothing funny; but he loved peace, and would buy it at any price.

"And they are all such nice people," chimed in Mrs. Treherne.

"As to that," mumbled her husband, "it's a matter of opinion."

"Why, admiral," cried Mrs. Treherne, who could always settle her husband, however difficult she found it to deal with her son, "you know you think the Howards charming girls, and every one thinks Miss Thorpe so pretty that, of course, you must do the same, and the St. Aubyns, one of our oldest families; really, admiral, I am astonished you should attempt to say it is a matter of opinion."

"Well, I am astonished myself, my dear; but still, is it not a matter of opinion? However, you have asked them all, and so we must do our best to make their visit agreeable."

"And—the—the Hendersons are coming too," said Mrs. Treherne, very hesitatingly, and looking sideways at her son.

"Those d—d Methodists! Why, mother—"

"Hush, Cyril! How shocking to hear you swear in that dreadful manner! Don't do it,

Cyril; it makes my blood run cold, and I feel afraid of going to bed."

"My swearing cannot possibly hurt you, mother," said Cyril, unable to refrain from laughing; "but I won't do it," he added, "so don't look so d—so awfully frightened. And, as I am not afraid of going to bed, I am off, for I am horribly tired, and so must you be," he continued, turning to his father.

Cyril thus, so far as he was concerned, put an end to any further discussion by leaving the room; but the husband and wife arranged as best they could to give their guests a fitting welcome, and to have two or three large dinners during the week they were to be at the Court.

Mrs. Henderson and her daughter were the earliest arrivals on the Monday. They were evidently very confident and perfectly satisfied with the plan they had drawn out for the assault on Cyril Treherne's heart and fortune.

"Remember, Harriet," were Mrs. Henderson's instructions to her daughter as they neared the house, "remember, you are not to heed his irreligious talk, and even hide your own feelings: to save his soul you must risk something; so appear to agree with him; if he scoff at our dear Mr. Snape, laugh a little too; you must wait till you are his wife to let him become acquainted with all your great and good qualities; and the Lord will reward your obedience to my word. Avoid as much as you can all talk of prayers or prayer-meetings, or any of those subjects we know he hates; and—here we are, my dear. How my heart beats! May the Lord hear my prayers, and may you leave this house but to return as its mistress!"

Miss Harriet listened; but on the whole she did not feel quite comfortable; the advice her saintly parent had tendered her seemed, to say the least of it, questionable. She was too simple-minded, or perhaps not yet Snape-ridden enough, to accept it as she ought: however, she bore it in mind, and had she had the chance, or it had signified, she probably would have followed it, for the best of us are always more apt at wrong than right. There is an indescribable charm in doing what one feels one ought not to do, in seeing what is forbidden, in going where none are permitted to tread, in hearing what none are allowed to know; the very prohibition suffices to create desire. But Miss Henderson had no chance; her tall, thin, prim person was only noticed as a kind of set-off to others more favoured in appearance and manner. She was wanting in *savoir dire* and *savoir faire*. It must be admitted she had to contend with formidable rivals. The two Howard girls were handsome, dashing—a little fast—London bred beauties, not over amiable, thinking a great deal of themselves and very little of others. Miss Thorpe—Willie Thorpe—was altogether a different style; she was a thorough type of a well educated, well brought-up English girl. Gentle, loving, unselfish, sweet-tempered, with a Hebe face, her red, full lips when parted showing her fine, even, pearly teeth, and her joyous, merry girlish laugh, were worth a fortune to see and hear.

What a lovable face it was! Her dark blue eyes, her clear complexion, neither fair nor dark, her soft brown hair, which she wore in a thick roll coiled round her small, well-shaped head, her face rather round than oval, her pretty nose, the least degree *retroussé*, her little hands and feet, her slight, graceful figure—she was not tall—the whole formed a picture such as the severest critic would delight to look on. An only child, the idol of her father, who was a widower, she had never been left to be ruined by either servants or governesses, for she was with them only when necessity required it, and never during her leisure moments.

Mr. Thorpe was a Devonshire squire with a tolerable fortune and a very pretty place a few miles from Treherne Court. He had lived almost entirely abroad during his daughter's childhood. He could not bear the thought of having a resident governess; he had tried it when first her education was beginning, and found his home ceased to be one but in name, his child was so rarely with him; so he shut up Yardley Wood and taking Willie and the servant who had been with her from her birth, he resolved to remain on the Continent till such time as his daughter could return and head his table and keep his house without other superintendence. So between Paris, Dresden, and Florence, which they made respectively their headquarters for educational purposes, they remained abroad till Willie had completed her seventeenth year. Then Mr. Thorpe resolved to return once more to his home, and there remain till death put an end to any further questions on the subject. But *l'homme propose et Dieu dispose*, and events occurred which overturned Mr. Thorpe's proposed plans for peace and repose.

Sir Gilbert and Lady St. Aubyn, with their only son, Charles, an old college chum of Cyril Treherne's, were in no case likely to cause any rivalry amongst the assembled guests at the Court, as Lady St. Aubyn, though she had been a beauty, was one no longer, and only attempted to claim attention when dowagers were at a premium. She was the daughter of a man who was supposed to have a large fortune, and was sought after accordingly, but when it came to the closer question of £. *s. d.* the aspirants for some reason withdrew; yet for all that she married very well in the end, and money was forthcoming,—in a smaller degree, it is true, than was expected, still she had not so bad a fortune for a girl who had, moreover, two sad defects—her hands were large and red and bony, and her voice unmusical. But Sir Gilbert, an ordinary kind of man, yet rather conceited, thought her perfection, and only saw her pretty face; one eye was shot away, that might account for his defective sight, though both his ears were in order. However, they got on very well, and were very proud of their only son, a good-natured fellow, with no great amount of brain to boast of, and with a difficulty in pronouncing the letter *s*, which generally he turned into *th*; but he was an eligible, being heir to a good old baronetcy and a fine estate, Stanmore Park, about six or seven miles from Treherne.

There were, in addition to those already named, two or three men, Major Kingsford,

Captain Mayne, and Captain Thurston, pleasant, agreeable fellows for filling up odd corners and to talk nonsense, dance, sing, or at any rate turn over the music, play round games. and ready to be useful as well as ornamental. They came over from Devonport, where they were stationed.

Though all the guests knew each other more or less intimately, the first evening passed off rather heavily. They had been unfortunately placed at dinner, and they seemed obstinately to adhere to each other afterwards in the same ill-matched couples. The admiral, Sir Gilbert St. Aubyn, and Mr. Thorpe were standing on the rug discussing the weather and the effect of it on the crops; Cyril entertained his listeners about his yacht and her matchless beauty; the Miss Howards sang and played duets; Captain Mayne succeeded in getting Miss Thorpe to look over a sketch-book with him; and Charles St. Aubyn talked unintelligible rubbish to Miss Henderson. The three matrons were discussing dress. a subject Mrs. Henderson thought frivolous. and almost injurious to the Christian mind. She never wore flowers—imitation flowers; she thought it wicked. She always dressed very plainly on principle, and of course Harriet did the same.

"I think it very shocking," she said, looking at the grand display of flowers and laces on the dashing Miss Howards, "for girls to dress in that manner. Look at their hair, too—why, it is quite dreadful! Where is the simple braiding of the hair, the modest apparel, the shame-facedness and sobriety that St. Paul tells us is necessary in a woman professing godliness?"

"My dear Mrs. Henderson," replied Lady St. Aubyn, who did not quite like a reproof to others that struck home to herself, for she was a handsome dresser, "depend on it St. Paul never saw a decently dressed woman in his life, and so did not the least understand what he was talking about."

Now Lady St. Aubyn was a very good woman, but not one of the elect according to the ideas of her two listeners, and both these ladies put their hands up to their ears as they heard her daring to speak of St. Paul in so monstrous a manner. To them it sounded almost blasphemous, and, after a "hush" from both, Mrs. Henderson went on to say,—

"St. Paul is the greatest master after *his* Master that we have; all he says is inspired; all he teaches beautiful in the extreme. Oh, dear Lady St. Aubyn, do not speak flippantly on such mighty subjects!"

"What, dress? Dear me, I would not speak flippantly about it. Look, Mrs. Treherne, at that pretty Willie Thorpe. What a lovely face she has!" said Lady St. Aubyn, determined to close the discussion on St. Paul.

"She has, indeed," replied Mrs. Treherne; " but she is too foreign in her manners to please me: and she is not the least shy. I like to see young girls shy."

"So do I," joined in Mrs. Henderson, "modest and silent. Why do they call her Willie? it's so like a boy!"

" Her poor mother's name was Wilhelmina, and she was always called Willie, and when she died Mr. Thorpe resolved the child should be named after her. Willie Thorpe is **not** shy nor is she silent: but she is modest and gentle, and though educated abroad is as free from all that could be thought forward or unmaidenly as any girl I ever met with in all my life. She has all the prettiness and fascination of foreign manner without any of its drawbacks. And surely her dress is simple enough to please you, Mrs. Henderson, or even St. Paul himself."

Mrs. Henderson, however, did not hear the latter part of what Lady St. Aubyn had said, for her eye caught sight of Cyril Treherne standing by her daughter and talking to her;

he had not done that with either Miss Thorpe or the Miss Howards, and her heart beat with pleasurable hopes. She looked at Mrs. Treherne, but she was talking to Lady St. Aubyn. Presently the music ceased, and the clock struck eleven, and then there was a general move, candles were lighted, and the ladies ascended the broad, old oak staircase, and when they were quite out of sight the gentlemen went off in another direction to the billiard-room.

Mrs. Henderson was very furious at the interruption. She questioned her daughter ve y closely as to what Mr. Treherne had said to her, and she did not feel more amiable on learning that he was merely extolling the beauty of that detestable little thing Willie Thorpe.

A day or two after, when all had shaken down into an easy friendly footing, and Cyril seemed quite to have recovered his annoyance at his mother having invited people to the house without consulting him, she was standing in the dining-room looking over the hatches, matches, and despatches column in the *Times*, waiting for her son to come and arrange with her what was to be the order of the day; as on the previous evening a picnic to the High Rocks had been suggested, but he had begged her to say no more about it till he had talked to her himself. So when breakfast was over she waited for his coming, which he did at last, full of spirits and looking so joyous that his mother wondered what had occurred to give rise to so much pleasure.

"It's all right, mother, we are going to the High Rocks; so please have some hampers prepared," he said. "We had better start about eleven or a little after, we shall arrive about half-past one, and with a couple or three hours there we can be back at six."

"Who is going?" asked Mrs. Treherne.

"Oh, all, I suppose; but I really don't know; you can see about that. I will drive Miss Thorpe in the pony-carriage, and I think it would be a good plan to order the barouche, it will take four, and one on the box, and then the saddle-horses; and let those who can't find room stay at home."

"But Cyril, my dear, do you think Miss Thorpe will like going with you in the pony-carriage? You know you cannot take any one else, it will only hold two."

"That's just the reason: yes, she will go with me—she has just promised."

"Oh, very well."

Mrs. Treherne made her answer in rather an

absent tone. She was wondering, as she spoke, whether that bright, laughter-loving girl would be a suitable wife for her boy.

She wondered. Parents are always wondering and hoping, wishing and praying, and all to no purpose; young people follow their own bent, be it for apparent good or palpable evil, and none can stop them. Cyril Treherne thought he had never seen anything more fascinating than the lovely, lovable face of Willie Thorpe. Her piquant winning manner, her utter disregard of what are termed the rules of society, when they in any way clashed with her childlike yet gentle, pretty ways, made every one like and admire her. There was not a man at Treherne who did not think her the most attractive and charming girl he had ever met, but it was so evident after the first evening that the young squire intended to try his best to win her, that out of pure courtesy they resolved, at any rate whilst they were his father's guests, not to run in the same race with him.

And Willie herself was ready to receive all his devotion; frank, free, warm-hearted, and impetuous, she let a liking for Cyril take root, without casting one thought as to the wisdom of doing so or not; and had she possessed the experience of years, which will sometimes make a woman pause on the threshold before opening her heart to love, she could but have admitted Cyril Treherne to have been a very eligible young man—a good match for any girl. But had he been in a different position, had he been poor and a nobody—a thorough detrimental—she would not have cared, she would have given him her little hand, and her large, true heart, with perhaps a greater feeling of satisfaction, if possible, than now. But beyond a little quickening of the pulse and a brighter hue on the cheek, Willie Thorpe knew nothing as yet of what love meant. She thought Cyril very handsome; she thought his voice soft and musical when he spoke to her, and his blue eyes full of expression; and she liked him to be with her; in short, there was nothing about him that she did not like, and the future never troubled her.

Cyril could be very fascinating; he knew it, and he exerted himself to be so to the utmost now; so no wonder the drive to the High Rocks was very delightful, and whenever Mr. Thorpe caught sight of his darling's face, as occurred once or twice, he following with Sir Gilbert St. Aubyn and Major Kingsford in the dog-cart, he thought how radiantly happy she looked, and perhaps a hope crossed his fond heart that his treasure might pass through the stormy era of a woman's existence without those sorrows or regrets that most of them are called on to endure. He wondered, as Cyril's mother had done a few hours before, if he would be a suitable husband for his only one—his sole earthly treasure. He knew in a worldly sense he was all a father could desire, but was he a man likely to secure her happiness, not for a week or a day, but for life? and then he resolved to watch him carefully, and to learn all he could concerning him, especially his character as a son.

So on they drove, and at last they reached that grand piece of wild rocky coast near to Bolt Gaol, that artists have made familiar to us all. It was a beautiful day; the sea was calmer and bluer than its wont, its ripples sparkled in the bright sunshine, the white clouds studded in patches over the blue sky, like pearls of all shapes in enamel, and just enough of them to make the heavens seem of a deeper hue. The High Rocks stood out dark and majestically, for the tide was low, and being so calm the water scarcely touched them.

The carriages and horses were left in charge of the servants just beyond where the sand begins; deep, soft sand, so unpleasant to walk on, but which must be tramped through before the hard pleasant ground is reached, which was a mass of firm, even ridges, telling of the soft rippling waves that had washed over it, for a rough, boisterous sea leaves smooth sands. They walked down all together to the water's edge. It took time for the party to separate in twos and threes, besides, luncheon had to be gone through.

"Stupid work, eating; isn't it, Miss Thorpe?" remarked Captain Mayne, a handsome young man with black hair, fair skin, and pink cheeks—something like the wax heads in a hairdresser's shop.

" I don't think so," replied that young lady, whose drive had given her an appetite; " that is, if you are hungry."

"I thought young ladies were never hungry."

" Oh, indeed! Of course I can only answer for myself: but I am hungry three times a day. What a stupid man!" thought Willie, walking away, and stooping to pick up a shell.

" How excessively matter of fact she is!" thought the captain.

Then there followed another remark: it came from the eldest Miss Howard.

" What a terrible flirt Miss Thorpe is! I

wonder if it arises from her foreign education."

"It arises from the want of a mother's care," said Mrs. Henderson.

"Well, certainly," remarked Miss Mary Howard, turning to Lady St. Aubyn, who was chaperoning the two sisters, their mother not caring to join the party, "a mother's care has pretty well crushed out any flirting propensity, that is proverbially inherent in woman, in Miss Henderson, has it not?"

Lady St. Aubyn smiled. Then, turning to Mrs. Henderson, she said,—

"You are rather hard on Willie Thorpe. She is as little given to flirting as any girl I ever saw. She is natural, if you like."

"Well, then, flirting is natural, that is all!" said Miss Howard.

"What are you ladies talking about?" said Cyril, coming from behind the largest of the High Rocks, where he and Miss Thorpe had been superintending the spreading of the luncheon; and not waiting for a reply, he continued, "If you are so disposed, will you come and take something to eat?"

In a few minutes all, even Captain Mayne, were doing full justice to the contents of the well-filled hampers, though one or two were not sorry when luncheon was over, and they were able to stroll about and enjoy the wild and grand scenery around them.

"Let us agree to meet here at four o'clock," said Cyril, "in case we get parted. It is now a quarter to three, and I have ordered the carriages to be ready by four."

All assented, and in a few minutes they were on the move in fours and sixes. It required a little time to wander away in couples; it was accomplished very rapidly, however. When both are willing it is easy to separate from the rest, so Cyril and Willie soon found themselves alone, scrambling up the sides of rocks that at a little distance seemed almost impossible.

"Give me your hand, Miss Thorpe," said Cyril, being a little in advance of his companion.

And the girl gave her hand, which was held in a firm grasp, till they both reached the summit, and then, looking down into her blooming face, he asked her if she felt tired.

"Not in the least. I am so fond of this sort of excursion and I so enjoy rambling about that if even I were tired I should not feel it; besides, I am accustomed to climbing, though I do not think I displayed any wonderful capacity for it just now!"

There was silence between them now for a few minutes; a busy silence, though, for the mind was so active that they hardly knew themselves whither their thoughts were leading them. A silence more dangerous than any spoken words. At last it was broken by the girl, who, looking up, with a merry laugh in her deep-blue eyes and on her lips, said,—

"Really, Mr. Treherne, you are so quiet that I am afraid I am boring you to death. And do you see where we have placed ourselves?—look at the sea! The tide is rising, is it not?"

"It is indeed. But we have plenty of time. Let us sit here a few minutes longer, and enjoy this peace and calm. You were not boring me, Miss Thorpe," continued Cyril, as she, complying with his request, sat down again, whilst he half sat, half lay at her feet. "You were not boring me. and you know it. I was thinking of you."

Willie coloured up, and her eyes fell, more at the tone than the words. She made no answer; for once the tongue that always had a ready reply found none now. She played with the tassel attached to her parasol, twisting it round her little gloved hand till the glove looked as if both it and the finger must get cut. Cyril took it gently from her, and, moving a little nearer, he held her hand for one moment in his. Then he said,—

"Miss Thorpe, tell me your thoughts now. What are they at this moment?"

"I cannot tell you. They are stupid thoughts—not worth repeating. Something about the sea, and about the weather, and—about papa, and—I don't quite know what else."

"You were not thinking of me, then? I thought you were."

"And so I was!" broke out poor Willie, touched by the humble tone and downcast look. "I was, and it was very mean of me not to say so at once, and very stupid, too. But—oh, Mr. Treherne, look at the sea! Look where we are! What shall we do?"

And as Willie spoke she sprang to her feet, and stood up on the rock, looking round with a blanched cheek and a beating heart. Cyril was by her side in a moment, and as quickly saw their position. The sea had advanced rapidly, and they were surrounded by it.

"Good God! what madness made me forget as to where I had brought you! Never mind,

Miss Thorpe, trust to me. Do not be alarmed, there is no danger, only inconvenience."

"I am not afraid," said Willie, putting her hand on his arm in her terror, for her words were belied by her looks.

CHAPTER VI.

"No danger." said Cyril Treherne to his companion, yet his heart misgave him as he looked around and saw how they were situated. Perched on a rock which, at high tide, was a hundred and fifty yards out at sea, with several feet of water over it ; the waves. which a slight breeze caused to roll in with more than their usual vigour. were now rapidly nearing it on all sides. At best they must walk through enough of water to take them in ankle deep, and amongst rocks which they must at almost every step come in contact with. And there was no time to be lost ; every moment rendered their position more perilous, to say the least of it.

"You must trust yourself to me, Miss Thorpe, and I will get you safe out of this dilemma, but we must move at once."

"Why, of course we must. But can't you get a boat? Is there no one near who could hear you if you called? Try—do. Why did you come here? You must have known the tide would soon be up and surround the place, rendering it unsafe._ Why, my boots will be wet through!"

"Your boots! Yes, they will, indeed, unless—you will let me carry you. Let me carry you, Miss Thorpe!"

"I shall not! I am much too heavy; but you said there was no time to be lost, yet you stand there talking."

Poor Willie, both frightened and cross—cross because she was frightened—jumped off the rock, held up her dress, looked at her pretty little French kid boots with regret, and bravely started to walk right into the sea.

"Take your boots off, Miss Thorpe. I'll put them in my pocket."

"No; they are not valuable enough for that," she answered, laughing, her courage beginning to rise a little.

"Give me your hand; or take my arm, that will be better. The tide is strong, and it is not easy to walk through deep water."

So she took his arm, and together they waded through the water, which was deeper than they had anticipated, the roughened waves bringing up the sea very rapidly. Every now and then they had to stand steady and firm to do battle with the receding water which threatened to take them back as fast as they advanced. They still had some distance to go, and Miss Thorpe already began to show symptoms of fatigue. Cyril saw it, but hardly knew what to do. He silently reproached himself for his stupid folly, and began to feel anxious as to how it would end. She looked a strong, healthy girl, but she was but slight and fragile for all that.

"Could I rest a moment?" she asked, presently, feeling her strength failing, and a strange singing in the ears.

"A little further on—yes. Between those two pointed rocks, which are one at the base, there is a seat, and once we are there we shall be tolerably safe, as at high tide the water is not more than a few inches deep there. You look pale. You are not feeling ill, are you?"

"No," she replied, faintly, and leaning heavily on Cyril's arm; "and yet I feel anything but comfortable. Those two tall rocks in front, do you mean? What a distance to go! And my dress is so heavy with the water."

Poor little Willie, she was in a piteous condition; but she struggled on courageously till within a step or two of the rocks, and then her strength gave way, and she fell senseless into Cyril's arms. He was strong and powerful, fortunately, and he took her up, carrying her to the rocks, and then he placed her on them in a lying position. A pleasant state of affairs, truly! Not a soul within hail to help him. He took the little hands in his and chafed them; he removed her hat and pushed back her hair, smoothing it gently; he called her by her name; he put his hand to her side to feel if her heart still beat; he was beginning to be desperately frightened, and very much in love. Supposing anything happened to her! and a pang shot through him at the bare idea. How pretty she looked, he thought, even with the rosy lips and cheeks blanched, and the laughing blue eyes closed, though that but served to show the long, sweeping eyelashes. Yet he could not stand there watching the beauties of the unconscious girl. He must do something, and the only thing that suggested itself was to take her in his arms and carry her as best he could to dry land. He succeeded in raising her, and, with her head leaning against his shoulder, he took her on through more water, till at last **they** reached a spot where the tide ceased to rise.

And now that he felt she was safe, so far as being drowned went, he became doubly anxious to obtain help when he found she still remained unconscious; yet he could not leave her, so he sat by her with his arm supporting her, till at length she began to show symptoms of returning life. Her lips parted and she said something, but Cyril could not tell what. He bent down his head to listen, and, as he did so, an irresistible temptation took possession of him to kiss that pretty mouth. And why should he not? he asked himself; it could hurt no one, for no one, not even herself, would know it; and so his head went down a little lower, and he pressed his lips to hers, slowly, gently, almost timidly, as if he feared to rouse her from her state of insensibility. But the temptation was too great; for a moment he gave way, for a moment human passion was stronger than reason, and Cyril Treherne had never attempted, in great things or small, to curb his inclination: and he took the half-conscious girl in his arms, held her to him, and kissed her lips, her cheeks, her eyes, her hair, till, struggling to life and to free herself, she brought him back to his senses.

Willie Thorpe was too bewildered at first to

understand clearly what had happened; and when she, by his own words, began to understand it, she was too confused and ashamed and angry to know what to say.

"Miss Thorpe, forgive me! Willie, forgive me! I was half mad with fear and love. You are angry—what can I say? I was wrong; I know it; but—forgive me—"

Willie looked up. Cyril looked so penitent and so in earnest that the girl could not bear him ill-will very long; besides, she liked him; she had liked him, independently of this day's work, and her liking took another form during the drive in the pony-carriage: her heart, for the first time, beat with a feeling very near akin to love, therefore she was not disposed to feel hostile very long: moreover, she remembered he had saved her life, without one thought arising as to his having first placed it in jeopardy; so she muttered something; the words were not very distinct, nor was she very sure herself that she answered, but the tone and manner were more intelligible, and Cyril was satisfied; and then, with a little more tenderness on one side, and a little more shyness on the other, they appeared in view to the assembled party as wretched a looking couple as it was possible to picture.

Mr. Thorpe was terribly distressed, and was extremely anxious to get his child quickly back to Treherne Court.

"It will be a marvel if it do not kill her; she is very delicate—never had wet feet in her life. No! no! not in the pony-carriage," he said, as Cyril was putting her in; "let her go in the barouche. I dare say one of you ladies will kindly change places with her?"

"My daughter will, with pleasure," quickly answered Mrs. Henderson. "Harriet dear, go with Mr. Treherne in the pony-carriage."

"And, Thurston, do you take the reins: I'll go on the box of the barouche," said Cyril, instantly.

"How dreadfully wet you are, Miss Thorpe! Why, you must be wet up to your knees," said Mrs. Henderson, who was very cross at the failure of her daughter's *tête-à-tête* with Cyril, and doubly so at having such a dripping mass against her silk dress.

"I will put this shawl round me." said Willie, seeing the distress pictured on Mrs. Henderson's face, "and then I shall not touch you. Don't look so gloomy, papa," she continued, turning to her father, who was standing at the carriage-door, seeing her safely packed in. "You know sea-water does not give cold; I shall be all right to-morrow."

And they drove off, Willie Thorpe leaning back and closing her eyes. She thinks over Cyril's kisses and Cyril's words; then, opening them for a moment, she looks up at him, and closes them again, thinking how handsome he is, and what beautiful curly hair he has; and, after all, she need not have been so angry with him; and then she hopes her father likes him, and will receive her news with pleasure: and so the drive was not so long, and they arrived at Treherne Court, and Cyril was by her side helping her out of the carriage and whispering something as she passed, of which she only caught the word "darling," before she thought they were more than half-way home.

A slight cold, a spoilt dress, ruined boots, and a heart lost and won, were the results of the picnic to the High Rocks, so far as Willie Thorpe was concerned. Hopes frustrated, dreams rudely shaken into reality, was Mrs. Henderson's portion. As to her daughter, she was one of those blest mortals who thought, with Pope, that "whatever is, is right," therefore she did not really understand what disappointment meant; and then there are people —and she was one of them—who are positively incapable of feeling anything more than the little palpitation of the heart produced by a sudden fright ; susceptibility is utterly unknown to them ; they even sneer at it in others, being thoroughly devoid of even a reflection of it themselves. So Harriet Henderson heard of the engagement between Miss Thorpe and Cyril Treherne with the same stoicism she would a proposal from him to marry herself. Not so the Miss Howards: they tossed their heads and declared poor Willie to be a wretched little flirt, and that Mr. Treherne would soon be sorry for having made choice of such a childish, silly, empty-headed thing.

It was two days after the picnic that Mrs. Treherne summed up courage to confide the news to Mrs. Henderson ; and Mrs. Henderson, in rage and vexation, told dear Mrs. Howard, making her own comments at the same time on the unfortunate choice Cyril Treherne had been fool enough to make; and so it was that, within an hour after Mrs. Treherne first spoke, every one in the house knew the important fact. Cyril had told his father the same evening, when smoking their last pipe together, all the others having gone to bed.

"Well, my boy, she is as pretty as the first flower in spring, and her father is one of my oldest friends, so, as far as I am concerned, I can say, God bless you both, and the sooner you are married the better. I don't suppose she is sufficiently 'goody' to please your mother, but if she please you, that is the main point."

Mrs. Treherne was and was not satisfied. "It would be better if she loved the Lord a little more, and dress and the world a little less," she said to her husband. "Of course, as far as family and fortune go, we may be satisfied."

"Ugh! and in everything else," muttered the admiral. "She is good and gentle; and let us hope she is a long way off from the next world; there's plenty of time to mend if anything is amiss with her."

"Ah, but we must not leave till the eleventh hour what we—"

"No, no,—that is, yes, yes,—I know all about it, my dear," and the admiral slipped out of the room.

When Willie, stammering and blushing, told her father Mr. Treherne had asked her to become his wife, she explained, in a manner, that he did not actually say those words, but she knew that was what he meant; and that she thought she should be very happy always to be with Cyril, and that she hoped her father would like it, and that she thought he had better speak to Mr. Treherne; and she went on with a few more remarks, with pauses in between, till, finding her father remain silent, and that she could not go on talking any longer without the help of a rejoinder, she began to twist her breloques about, and in her nervousness she broke off the forefinger of her little coral hand, a charm against the evil eye, which, in her girlish folly, she thought was a bad omen, and she looked up quickly at her father to see whether she read aught in his countenance to bear out her fears. It was a sad-looking face, but she met such an expression of deep love that she instantly, following the promptings of her heart, went up to him and, twining her arms round his neck and kissing him with the old fondness of her childhood, said,—

"Dearest papa, if you don't like him, if you are not happy about it, never mind; I'll give it up, and we will go home, and we will forget all about it, and Treherne Court, and—and everything and everybody but each other!"

Bravely spoken; but just at the last there seemed a difficulty in getting out the words; as Cyril's face rose before her, her courage failed, but for all that she spoke distinctly; and then she buried her head on her father's shoulder and tightened her arms round him, as if by so doing she could keep back the tears she felt were welling up.

"My own dear child!" murmured her father, "your happiness is my only anxiety; to secure it I would give my life, as I would to save you from a heartache. But, Willie, marriage is a serious thing; it is the most important step taken in a woman's life; by it you alter the whole tenour of your existence. Your duties, your hopes, your fears, your affections, all—all become changed. You leave your father's home for ever, or, at any rate, it is with that hope, as it is, generally speaking, but sorrow that brings a child back—the sorrow of death, or—worse still, the sorrow of disgrace. Then, again, your first thought, your first care is, and ought to be, your husband: therefore, my precious child, it is necessary you should love that husband with all the depth and intensity of which you are capable; and though I dare say nine out of every ten girls that marry think they love, it is very rare but that eight out of those nine discover, when too late, that there was more imagination than affection guiding them. Moreover, love alone is not sufficient for a wife's happiness; to be secure she must respect, honour, and look up to the man to whom she resigns life. Now, Willie, before you decide on becoming Cyril Treherne's wife, will you **wait a year?** Will you, by so doing, test not only **your own** feelings, but his also? You know, my dear one, I never left a wish you ever **expressed** ungratified, and therefore, if you tell me now—after thinking over what I have said, badly said, poorly expressed, but my heart is too full, too anxious, for me to talk to you as I could to another—after pondering over our conversation you still prefer engaging yourself to him,—I will not oppose it ; only you must not think of marrying till you have completed your eighteenth year. I promised your mother, Willie, if you were spared to me, I would **fulfil her wish** in that ; it was one of her dying requests to me, child, one that you will, I am sure, put no obstacle to my fulfilling."

"Dearest papa ! you may depend on me. I will never do anything without your consent, still less go counter to your wishes. I won't engage myself for a year, and I will tell Mr. Treherne—or perhaps you had better."

Mr. Thorpe stooped down and kissed his daughter. Something like a pang passed through him as he thought that other lips than his would touch that pretty mouth; the fresh girlish bloom must soon be brushed off those cherry lips. But if Cyril proved worthy of so great a prize he would not grudge her, and living at Treherne Court she would, at any rate, be near: better far than for her to marry a man with a profession that might remove her from him altogether. These ideas flitted through his mind as he looked at the blooming face of this, his earthly idol.

"Another reason, my Willie, why delay is advisable, independently of your age: you know very little of Treherne."

"Oh, yes, papa, I know him better than any-one else you can name. Look at the numbers of times we have met, and how he always danced with me whenever we met at balls."

"My child, you have been home scarcely a year, and you have not been to more than two balls."

"Well, is not that enough; and is not a year a tremendous time? I think so. Not that I want to make you change about waiting, only don't say, papa, that I do not know him. And don't you like the old admiral, papa?"

"Yes, dear, I do: and I think him as honest and upright and honourable a gentleman as I ever knew. But the father is not the son."

"No, of course not: but he may be just as good."

"Let us hope so. I not only hope it, but I have no reason for thinking otherwise. But, Willie, those are not points you can quite understand how to judge. Leave all to me. And now I am going to ask you to give me a promise—only one, and not a difficult one; at least, hitherto you have not found it so."

"What is it, papa? of course I will promise you anything."

It is never to have a secret from me till you are a wife, no matter with whom or under what circumstances. Will you promise me?"

"I will; but I am not likely to have secrets."

"You do not know; we none of us can tell what may arise; often the most improbable, unforeseen events take place, those we least anticipate, and are least prepared to meet. However, I am satisfied. And now, my dearest child, I will see Treherne and his father, and hear what they have to say. I may tell them you have acceded to my wish, and no engagement is to take place for another year?

"Yes, papa."

And Willie ran off to her room, her heart brimful of happiness and hope. There was none of the overpowering joy that to be felt must have had doubts and fears, uncertainties and suspense, to contend against, where love has seemed hopeless, where jealousies have been roused and nurtured. Desolation, misery, despondency, almost to desperation, must have been endured first, if that overwhelming, stirring, thrilling joy is to be felt; but Willie's was a quiet, girlish happiness that dimpled her face with smiles, and made her eyes beam and sparkle.

After looking out of her window, and twisting and pulling some flowers to pieces that lay on her table, then tumbling over her dresses, and upsetting everything that before had been in perfect order, she thought her father must have had his talk out, and that she might go down. Why she should stay in her bed-room because her father was probably in the library, was a question that never occurred to her. But when she determined on going down, her courage failed he. Where should she go? She might see Cyril, and that would be awkward, she would not know what to say to him; and —she might not see him, and that would be worse. She would be horribly bored if she had to talk on common topics, or about Mr. Snape and the missionaries, to the ladies.

Better stay where she was than that: so she recommenced the turning over of her drawers, and then looked to see what she should wear that night. For the first time in her life she felt anxious about her appearance : yet there was no need to fear on that score : her bright, beautiful face required little to set it off ; the quantity of rich brown hair she had was sufficient ornament for the head, and her pretty girlish figure looked graceful in anything ; she was like a flower, and one perfect of its kind.

Presently there was a knock at her door, and her maid brought in a note, that is, a wisp of paper tightly screwed up. It was not from her father, she knew, so she felt it must be from Cyril. What a thing for a first love-letter! And the contents were in keeping with its outward appearance :—

"I have been waiting in the conservatory two whole hours. You promised to come here directly after breakfast. I am sick of the flowers. If you don't come directly I shall send Jackson with a verbal message."

Miss Thorpe coloured up, and told her maid there was no answer; but on being pressed, and learning that Mr. Treherne was waiting for one, she said she would be there presently.

" Be where, miss ? "

" The conservatory," said Willie, a little shortly. " How stupid of him to send up to me like that, and then to say if I did not go he would send Jackson with a message ! " thought Willie, as she stood before the glass, putting on her prettiest and most becoming hat. She was glad, for all her seeming crossness, that Cyril had sent for her; but if he had been in the conservatory ever since breakfast how was it possible he had seen her father? and if he had not, she would have to tell him all. Altogether it was very provoking. By the time she arrived at that conclusion she also reached the conservatory. It was built away from the house, but a long glazed-in passage led to it, which was rarely used but in bad weather. Willie therefore crossed the soft green grass, and stood for a moment to pick a wild flower, partly because it was pretty, partly as an excuse for Cyril to come out and meet her, but he did not; he advanced to the door and looked rather gloomy.

" You don't care a straw for me ; you don't love me," were his greeting words.

She looked up and held out her hand, slightly hurt at his reception, and sorry he had mis-understood her.

"What ought I to have done?" she asked, in a penitent tone.

"Darling," he said, fondly, disarmed in a moment, "come in and sit down." She was still standing on the conservatory steps. "I have so much to say to you, so much to ask you." And he led her in, and made her sit on a low wicker seat, something in the form of a sofa. He sat down beside her, and, putting his arm round her, drew her head towards him, and gave her one of those long, loving kisses that remain in the memory as a landmark of time in after years. "My own darling," he murmured, as he released her, her face suffused with blushes and her eyes on the ground, "look up at me; let me read in those dark blue eyes that you do really love me."

But she dared not raise them even when he turned her face gently upwards. She moved hastily away with "Don't tease me," uttered rather indistinctly.

"Well, I won't tease you: but tell me, then, you love me; let me hear you say, 'Cyril, I love you.'"

"Cyril, I love you." Very softly but very sweetly were the words uttered.

"'And will always do everything you wish

and ask me to do.' Well, say that also. You are silent."

After a little pause, " I cannot say that." Then she raised those truthful, honest eyes, no longer kept down by modest girlish shame.

" Not promise to do all I wish, and yet you tell me you love me! Why, the one is impossible without the other."

" You might ask me to do something that would be wrong, or that papa might not wish me to do.   I will do all I can, Cyril," said the girl, hastily, seeing a cloud gathering on his brow, " but papa made me promise just now that till I was a—wife," her voice fell as she spoke the word so full of mysterious meaning to her, " I would never have a secret from him."

" That could not be a reason for refusing me a promise."

" But supposing you asked me to do something you did not wish papa to know?   I must break the promise to one or the other."

Cyril walked up and down the conservatory once or twice, and then, his handsome face free from all traces of vexation and anger, he sat down by her side, well content to feel that the girl who would be truthful and faithful as a daughter would be equally so as a wife. They talked then of the future till the great house-bell rang the summons to luncheon.

Cyril was vexed and annoyed at Mr. Thorpe's determination both as to the engagement and the time the marriage was to take place. He was so unaccustomed to be thwarted that the least disappointment irritated him. From his babyhood up to the present time he had had every wish gratified, and now to be opposed, and on so important a matter, taxed his patience and his temper.

His cup of annoyance was not either yet full, for he had still to learn that the Thorpes were to return to Yardley Wood on the following day but one.

" Then I shall be off in the Marguerita," said Cyril. " But I can go and see you as usual, Mr. Thorpe ; that is a matter of course?"

" Certainly, as usual, but not oftener."

" That was about once a week, sir, was it not?" Cyril spoke doubtfully.

" No, nor once a month; once in two, per-haps," replied Mr. Thorpe. " But let it be once a month, if you like."

CHAPTER VII.

So it came about that Cyril Treherne started off in the Marguerita with the intention of cruising about for a week or ten days, and that on the third day he came to grief at Prawle Point, as we have seen.

Mrs. Treherne's sensations as she walked from the breakfast-room to the large low dark groined-roofed hall, where the servant told her John Finch was waiting to speak to her, were such as to call forth sympathy, even by her sincerest ill-wisher. Everything as she passed seemed to be swimming before her eyes; she trembled in every limb; a cold shivering feeling came over her, her breath seemed suddenly tightened; she knew she was to hear something horrible; she knew John Finch had gone with his master in the Marguerita, and now he came back to tell her—what?

She was there before him now, his great
burly form swinging from side to side, with his
head—and hat in hand—all bowing together.
She could not see distinctly, so she did not
remark that his face bore rather a pleased
expression than the stamp of ill-tidings.

"Quick! Tell me at once, Finch—what has
happened? All, the worst at once—quick,
man!"

But poor Finch was too surprised to be
quick. He had never seen Mrs. Treherne so
strange looking before; it was a mystery to
him what was wrong with her; it never
occurred to his thick head that his mere appearance there omened evil.

"The worst, madam," began Finch, "is
that the beautifullest little craft in the world is
gone to pieces—right to smashes, and—"

"And—well, quick!—and what?"

If Mrs. Treherne could have sworn at John
Finch, she certainly would, and it would have
done her good. What was the craft to her?
she always hated it, and was indifferent to its
fate.

"And the young master is down at a cottage yonder; he's all right, but shook a bit."

"There—that will do for a moment. Stop
a minute, Finch; don't speak—thank God

thank God!" And, putting her hands to her face to hide the tears of grateful joy that would force themselves up, she sat down and waited a moment to recover herself before she could command her voice sufficiently to speak.

"Where did you say he is, Finch, and where did it happen?"

Finch now gave a succinct account of the whole matter; and, just as he had concluded, in came the admiral from smoking his first pipe.

"God bless my soul, what has brought you here?" he asked. "Did you not go with Mr. Treherne after all?"

"That is *so* like you, admiral!" exclaimed his wife, irritated at his not being alarmed as she had been, and glad of any one to quarrel with; for after a great fright no one is amiably inclined. "First to take the Lord's name in vain, and then to take it for granted, because you see Finch here, that he did not go with Cyril. He *did* go, and a fearful accident has befallen them. I told you yesterday when the wind was howling so awfully that I was afraid some evil would happen, but you pooh-poohed all I said; I am never right—of course I am not—never!"

And Mrs. Treherne's tears again rose to the surface, but this time with vexation. She was

not a woman given to cry, but she had received
a terrible shock, and it certainly had upset her.
For a moment the admiral looked anxious, but
the next he was reassured; nothing could have
happened to the boy, or his mother would not
be blowing *him* up.

"Well, John, what is it? You don't seem
the worse, at any rate, whatever may have
occurred."

"How cool he is!" thought John, "a regular
one to put people in their right senses when
they go wrong. I thought he wouldn't care
like madam."

And so the admiral was misunderstood, as
most people are who are unselfish enough to
smother their feelings in order to save others
unnecessary pain; and though in this instance
he was the only sufferer, his wife knowing all,
he had through life made it a rule to hide any
emotion that by indulging would cause anxiety
or fear, so it had become to him almost natural.
John Finch soon told him all he had related to
Mrs. Treherne. For a minute or so the three
remained silent, then Mrs. Treherne said,—

"I will go over and see him. I must go,
and at once, admiral. How far is it, Finch?"

"Well, madam, across the fields and over
hedges I was a good hour and three-quarters.

I don't think round by the road it can be less than twelve good miles; and it's late now, madam, and the roads are right bad about there, and with all this rain they be like a bog. Better wait to see the young master to-morrow; he is all right, and got a sweet pretty nurse to look after him. He begged me to tell you he had nothing but a slight cold, and if you would send the close carriage for him to-morrow em—empty, madam—he doesn't like close carriages, you see."

Mrs. Treherne fortunately did not hear or heed the latter part of the request. She was hesitating about herself: twelve miles in a bad road, and with horses that were well fed and little worked; night too would come on before she could get back—and he was safe.

"You are sure he is not hurt? You are certain no bones were broken when he was thrown on the rocks?"

"Bless you, no, madam. The waves played at ball with him, but he isn't the worse for it this morning."

"I will ride over, Rebecca," said the admiral, in a kind tone, "and I will report to you by dinner-time."

He thought if he should like to see his boy his mother might well be excused for a similar weakness; at the same time he saw the impossibility for her to go now; the day was too far advanced, and the roads were not fit for their carriage, if it were to go at any other than a foot-pace.

"Take the dog-cart, sir: you'll go faster, I think," said Finch.

"Very well; go round and order it for me: tell them to make haste. You return with me, I suppose?"

"Oh yes, sir, I am going back, of course."

"Now you see, admiral, what mischief you have brought about by encouraging Cyril in his taste for such senseless and dangerous amusement. Oh, how I wish Mr. Thorpe would let Willie marry at once! and then he would stay at home and give up such reckless folly."

"I don't believe he would!" muttered the admiral. He had a peculiar way of muttering whenever he spoke, as if he had his mouth too full of words—an easy, good-natured sort of indistinct mumbling; and yet one generally understood him. "I don't believe any number of wives would keep a man on land if he have a liking for the sea."

"You gave it up, Thomas."

"But I had had some five-and-twenty years

of it.—I had had quite enough of it; still I enjoyed my trip the other day with the boy immensely."

"Oh, men are all alike!" sighed Mrs. Treherne: "self first, and then whatever comes best next; it may be shooting, it may be hunting, or it *may* be the wife, but she rarely comes in second!"

"Well, well, you have nothing to complain of, at any rate. Here is the cart, so I'll be off. It is past two now, so do not look for me before six or half past. Good-bye, old lady; don't fidget; the boy is all right, depend on it."

It was a rare occurrence for the admiral to speak affectionately to his wife—people do not as a rule after a quarter of a century of matrimony: but their child's escape was a common joy to them; and joy, like sorrow, will draw hearts together. So he left Treherne with a warmer feeling at his heart for his wife than he had felt for many long years.

The drive was not an easy one; more than once the wheels of the light dog-cart got into ruts, and threatened to jolt Finch off: he sat behind—a perilous seat for any one not accustomed to it, especially with such roads to go over. But sailors have a peculiar knack of holding on to anything; though they are wretched horsemen, they are rarely thrown; so Finch sat there as if he were screwed on.

"There's the cottage, sir," said John, as they reached the high ground where stands the little village of Shelton, and from whence you can see far across the broad open sea. with the picturesque coast. The village is wild, straggling, and uncultivated, with nothing of interest about it but the little piece of ground, where, as I have already told you. lie so many of those who have met their death amongst the rocks below.

"How can we reach it? There seems no road," said the admiral.

"Yes, sir, there is. You must drive between those two cromlechs; and then we must go over that turnip field, which will take us on to a kind of road that leads up to the cottage."

"Ugh!—a nice drive this, for a carriage and pair!"

They had now to proceed at a foot-pace, for the mare was over her fetlocks in mud. It was rough driving till they came to within a few yards of the cottage; but they reached it without any accident.

"I had better go in and tell the young master you are here, sir," said Finch.

"Why he's not ill, man, is he?" asked the admiral, quickly.

"No, sir, not that! I only thought—"

"Nonsense! His nerves will stand his seeing his old father, I'll be sworn. Here, hold the mare's head, and see and get some of the mud out of her shoes. I ought to have brought Tom with me. I forgot you were not coming back; however, I shall manage."

Admiral Treherne knocked gently at Miles Mason's cottage, and in a moment the door was opened by Cherry, who, curtseying, asked what the gentleman wanted. She began to think some charm had fallen on their house, for such a thing as a gentleman had not been seen there to her knowledge till Cyril Treherne was brought in as one dead.

"There is a gentleman here, my pretty girl," said the admiral, looking with a pleased expression at Cherry's blushing face, "a gentleman you have been kind enough to give shelter to; he is my son. Can I see him?"

"Oh, pray walk in, sir. He is in the next room: he's not ill, sir," said Cherry, looking up suddenly, as if it suddenly occurred to her the stranger might be anxious about his son.

"No no," answered the admiral, smiling, "thank you for your thoughtfulness in telling me. I have heard all about the accident: a very shocking one, but it might have been worse."

"Will you follow me in here, sir, if you please?"

And Cherry led the admiral into the little room where Cyril was lying, though he was dressed now, on the outside of the bed. Then she left them, and went herself about her household duties, which had been seriously neglected that day.

"Well, my boy, this is a terrible business, but thank God you are safe. You seem to have had a narrow escape," said the admiral, grasping his son's hand. "Your mother wanted to come over, but I prevented her—the roads are in a shocking state; so I came to reassure her and please myself. Now, tell me how it all happened, for, though Finch has given me one version, I should like to have yours."

Cyril related all he knew, but he had so soon lost consciousness that he had not much to tell. He regretted the loss of his beautiful yacht, and the death of the three men.

"As to the yacht, my boy, she can be replaced, and we must do something for poor Tait's widow. I don't think the other men were married."

"I believe not, but Finch will know. We must do something too, father, for these people here."

"Yes, yes, to be sure. Give the man a present, and do something for the girl—anything you like, boy, anything you like."

So they chatted on a little; but the admiral recollected his wife, and how anxiously she would be looking out for his return, so he reluctantly bade his son good-bye till the morrow, when he had arranged to send over for him.

"But it must be the dog-cart, Cyril; nothing else would live in such roads: and I don't think your cold seems very bad; it is those scratches on your face that make you look so pale, I suppose."

"All right: the dog-cart will do famously."

Just as the admiral was leaving, and about to close the room-door, Cyril called out to him to come back for a moment.

"Shut the door, father, and come here a minute. Willie may hear of this, so will you send a line over to Yardley Wood to-night? If you send it by post she will not get it till to-morrow morning; so I would rather it went by hand. Tell her I am quite well, and that I will ride over and see them the next day, if she will let me know her father will make me welcome."

"All right, my boy, I will send Jackson over to-night. God bless you."

Admiral Treherne found Cherry endeavouring to mould some flour and water into some kind of shape or other in a less time than is usually allotted for such work. She wanted clearly either to make up for lost time, or to leave herself as much as was yet left of the day free from culinary employment. If the mixture were intended for pie-crust it did not promise well even before the admiral interrupted her. But it certainly gained nothing by the way it was hammered down afterwards in a thick layer at the bottom of a dish, and a lot of things, bits of meat, potato, bread, onion, and carrot thrown on it, and then another thick plaster of the flour and water covering it over. It did not look as if it could possibly turn out a savoury dish—hardly eatable, one would think. But how was it possible for Cherry to make a pie with a real admiral in the house, and he the father of the handsome stranger who, by a few words, said in a way Cherry had never yet heard them spoken, had already gained the first blossom of her young love?

When the admiral asked her to tell her father that he should call again to see him and thank him, and that he must always remember she

whom the neighbours called the little foreigner
—meaning the appellation to be contemptuous,
for she was too pretty not to create envy,
hatred, and other uncharitable feelings in the
breasts of those young girls who lived near—
had rendered him, Admiral Treherne, and Mrs.
Treherne, of Treherne Court, a service that
they could never repay, that they owed her a
debt of gratitude that words could not express,
poor little Cherry coloured up, and looked up and
then down with those large, wondering eyes,
and seemed as uncomfortable as she well could
be. No wonder the pie was uneatable, for she
vented her feelings on the paste that ought to
have turned into crust—feelings that angered her
excessively, for she had felt stupid, and could not
answer a word to that kind, good-natured looking old gentleman—an admiral, too, the first she
had ever seen; heard of them she had often,
but always mentioned with a kind of awe, as
though they were kings in their way. Then
her heart beat with a little innocent pride that
this great man had talked to her, and even
seemed, as far as she could recollect, to be
coming again, and that he had felt obliged to
her for taking care of his son; and then of a
sudden the fair, handsome face of Cyril rose
before her, and she wondered how long she had

been sitting there with her floury hands wrapped round in her apron and the pie scarcely finished before her. She looked up at the old Dutch clock; it was a quarter to five, and her father came in at seven, and supper was at eight. Two hours, then, she had before her—two hours to sit and look at that face which was promising fair to haunt her through life. A few minutes she must devote to her toilet; sailor's daughter as she was, poor and humble, she loved dress and finery, like all the rest of her more favoured sisters. A piece of new ribbon, red or yellow—those colours suited her dark complexion and black hair the best—had hitherto sufficed to make the girl's heart beat with pleasure. She would want more than that for the future, if one were to judge by the feeling that prompted her to run upstairs and twist amidst her thick, dark tresses a bit of red ribbon, and put on her best clean print frock. There was no looking at the ribbon first, no admiring of the dress itself; the effect was what she seemed anxious about.

"It looks quite dirty," she thought, as the faded colour of the ribbon for the first time fully developed itself. "And the frock all washed out! I wish father could give me a new one."

Yet, for all the grumbling and dissatisfaction at her appearance, Cyril thought she looked very beautiful when she went into the room a little while after.

"Why, Cherry, I verily believe you left me here all by myself in order to go and make yourself grand. Are you expecting visitors?"

"No, sir," replied Cherry, confused at her manœuvres being so easily seen through. "I only changed my frock; I do generally in the afternoon."

Half a lie this was to begin with: if she did change it, it was not to put on her best frock.

"And this smart ribbon, Cherry; do you put this on too every afternoon? Come closer to me, and let me look at you."

"Sometimes, sir," replied Cherry, at the same time obeying Cyril's command.

"Well, it is very pretty, and suits you admirably. Look up at me,—I want to see what colour your eyes are; brown, I declare, and I thought they were black; what big frightened-looking eyes they are! Look up, child! you are not afraid to look up at me, are you?"

"No, sir," stammered out Cherry, trying to

withdraw the hand Cyril had taken, and was holding very fast.

"To-morrow I am going away; and though I have not known you many hours, little Cherry, I feel as if I had known you for months; and I shall be sorry not to see those great startled eyes again, so don't turn away from me."

Cyril spoke to and treated her as if she were a mere child; and there arose the great danger, for though Cherry looked childish from her timid manner, her feelings were even more advanced than her years,—she already had the feelings of a woman. She tried to look up, but her eyes were more under the dominion of susceptibility than will, and they no sooner met the half-affectionate, half-admiring expression in Cyril's than they fell instantly.

"Shall I never see you again, sir?" she stammered out at last.

"Would you like to do so?"

"Oh, yes, sir!" Her voice was hardly above a whisper.

"Then you shall, Cherry. I will come and see you next week."

"Miss Cherry, aren't you at home?"

"Who is that, Cherry?" asked Cyril,

releasing her hand, as a stranger's voice was heard asking the question in a loud, noisy tone.

"It must be some of our neighbours, I suppose. I will go and see."

"Send them off soon, and come back to me, little one; for I am dull lying here by myself."

"Yes, sir," said Cherry, who would have turned away the most favoured of her father's guests at that moment in obedience to Cyril Treherne's request.

In the parlour—Miles and Cherry too preferred calling the front room the parlour and not the kitchen — waiting to see Cherry Mason was George Cooper. He was the son of Henry Cooper, a fisherman who had been one of those that had gone to the help of the Marguerita the previous night. George was about two-and-twenty, a tall, gawky, boorish lad, but honest, true, and hard working. He worked in the quarries near, not caring to follow his father's business. George was a steady young man, attended church regularly on Sundays, was never drunk, never even went to the public-house, as he might have done, for an hour's amusement, to read the papers or play at skittles, for there was a good skittle-ground at the Coventry Arms at Shelton; but George

spent his evenings at home, or, when Miles
Mason was not out on duty, and would ask him,
he was content to sit and smoke his pipe there,
and look at Miles's daughter, and occasionally
speak to her, which he did only when he
thought he should not disturb her, as, oddly
enough, whenever George Cooper was there
Cherry would read,—not that she was given to
study, but the fit came on on these occasions.
The truth was that George Cooper was in
love with Cherry Mason, and Cherry did not return the sentiment. She liked him well enough,
she could not do otherwise,—he was too honest
and good for any one to dislike; but the fact
of his showing he cared for her more than
any other girl in or near Shelton made her
care less for him than she might otherwise have
done. And yet it was by mere instinct Cherry
knew this, for no word had ever passed
George's lips that could make her imagine he
loved her; but he never found any strange
pebble or a piece of marble but that she became
the owner of it. If he happened to have a
bird given to him in the shooting-season, or a
hare or a rabbit, it was sure the next day to be
seen on Miles Mason's table, and George, of
course, an invited guest to partake of it. There
was always something George was giving—it

was the silent language in which he expressed his love. And Cherry was always kind and gentle in her manner, and seemed to welcome him, so he never broached the subject; there was time enough, he thought, when he got a rise in his wages, which he should do soon: and, besides, there was a quiet evenness in Cherry's bearing towards him that made him perhaps fear to touch on the question just yet.

"I called to inquire for the young gentleman, Miss Cherry. Father says it was a near thing with him; and to think of those other poor fellows being lost!—oh, it 's a horrible life is that seafaring!"

"He is getting on pretty well, George, thank you. He is still in bed, but he will go back to-morrow."

"Why, where does he come from?"

"Treherne Court—close to Sandcombe."

"Law, yes! I mind me—across through Thurl fields and over the Downs, and so on to Oswald. I 've seen the old Court! Law, bless you, Miss Cherry, you never could believe there was such a fine grand place to be found out of a story-book. And so he lives there, do he?"

"Why, when were you there, George?"

"Oh, I went over for the master once, to see

about carting of stone there for some building or other—I think to make bigger stables."

"And is it very big, George? and are the gardens very beautiful?"

"I believe you! Beautiful and big are not the words; it's all splendid! and—and—well, I can't tell you more. Perhaps you'll see it yourself some day, as you have been so kind to the young gentleman, and then you can tell me the right words to use about it; for you read so much, Miss Cherry, that you must be a deal cleverer than I."

"Yes, George, perhaps so," said Cherry, absently. Then, recollecting that she had been talking there too long, she said, intending to be as polite as possible, "If you please, George, will you go now? Mr. Treherne may want something, and I do not like leaving him long."

George did not look pleased, but he prepared to do as he was bid.

"You're Sunday dressed to-day; what's that for, Miss Cherry?"

"Am I?" said Cherry, looking disconcerted. "I was in a hurry, and put on the first frock that I could find."

George now wished her good-bye.

"She was not too hurried to put that red

ribbon round her hair," he thought, as he took, in his great, big, bony, rough hand, hers, which was small and soft, though she, too, did some hard work now and then.

"How different to *his!*" thought Cherry, as she returned to Cyril's bedside. A pity she ever had the chance of judging.

"What a time you have been, Cherry!" said Cyril. "Who was your visitor?"

"George Cooper, sir; the son of one of the men that helped to bring you in last night. He came to ask how you were."

"What did he say besides asking for me? for I heard you both chattering away the whole time."

"He was telling me about Treherne Court, sir."

"Why, what does he know about it?"

"He says he was there once, about some work to be done at the stables."

"Oh!" Then, after a pause, "I wish this little cottage stood amongst the rocks near Sand-combe Bay instead of here. I wonder if I could not get your father moved up to our part of the coast. I think there is a station at Sandcombe for the coast-guards."

"Oh, father would not like to leave this cot-tage, sir. Mother died here."

" But you would, Cherry ? "

" No, sir : I like this house, too, for the same reason."

" Then you do not care to see me again ? If you were nearer to Treherne I could see you constantly ; and now, if I see you once a month, it will be the outside."

" I never thought of that, sir," and Cherry's heart beat with a sensation unknown to her before ; " but I 'm sure nothing would induce father to change, so don't ask him. sir, please."

" I will not ask him, child ; do not fear."

Then there was no more talking for a while ; but Cyril became restless, and tossed about on his bed till, at last, he resolved to get up for an hour or two. Though free. as he had felt all day, from actual pain, when he attempted to rise he found himself terribly stiff, and it fatigued him to sit long ; at the end of half an hour only he was glad to return to the bed.

" I wonder," was his last thought that night, " if I shall be able to get home to-morrow. I must, if possible, for my Willie's sake " ; and then he fell asleep. His night was restless, dreams of dark blue loving eyes and large brown wondering eyes being mingled confusingly.

THE next morning when Cyril awoke he found himself so much better there seemed no doubt but that he would be able to return home. The assurance brought him great relief; with health he had the power of going wheresoever he pleased. Had he been detained another day in Miles Mason's cottage it is probable he would have fretted at his imprisonment, and consequently been irritated at the sight of those to whom he felt now both gratefully and kindly; as it was, mingled with gladness at his being well, there was a feeling of regret at leaving the care of the sailor's daughter, whose simple talk amused him.

Love grows apace, and, like a weed, the wilder and more uncultivated the soil, the quicker it seems in flourishing; hence Cherry Mason awoke on the morning of the day on which **Cyril Treherne** was to leave her to the full consciousness that she loved him with a love of the existence and power of which she had never even dreamt. She lay in her bed in a dreamy state, thinking simply of the fact: as to what could or might arise through such a state of things she never gave it a thought, nor if she had would she have cared; for though young enough not to think of the future beyond that of the coming day, she was yet old enough, and with her Spanish blood impassioned enough, to let her feelings have full play. The old Dutch clock from downstairs now struck six; every stroke seemed to jar upon her; at last, when the hour was struck, she jumped out of bed, but only, it appeared, to recommence the same unprofitable employment as before.

Could **Cyril** have seen her now, he might have been **pardoned** had she for a few minutes driven the memory of **Willie Thorpe** from him. She was sitting on the edge of her bed—a wretched old four-post, without any top, but each post having a spike sticking out of it; her naked feet did not touch the ground—they were crossed, as were her hands, her long, black hair falling like a mantle over her night-dress, her large brown eyes gazing out of the window; but she saw nothing of the great blue sea, the giant rocks, the vessels moving now so smoothly over those silent waters that seemed as if nothing could stir them into life, and which yet, like her feelings, would soon be raging and surging with the violence of a storm.

The passions of the heart are as varied amongst mankind as peculiarities of complexion and expression; hardly two beings in life are like in any of them, and what may stir one up into wild frenzy may leave another unmoved. Cherry Mason was one of those girls who, with a calm exterior, was yet endowed with deep-rooted passions, though as yet they had never been called forth, and she was ignorant of their existence. She had never loved before, so she knew none of the workings of love; jealousy, hatred, revenge, envy, had never been known to her otherwise than by name, yet they were there—it only required circumstances to call them to the surface. George Cooper's quiet, silently proffered affection was all which as yet Cherry had knowledge of in the form of love, and that had never made her heart beat one pulse the quicker. Now it was different: she had already felt the influence of the real feeling; her colour came and went, her heart throbbed with the first breath of a new-born love, tender, delicate, and fragile in its first hours of life, but so soon to gain strength and force with the nursing it but too surely ever receives when it were better it should be stifled in its birth.

"Cherry, what are you after this morning, girl? It's just upon seven, and you are not down!"

Her father's voice roused her to herself, awoke her from her day-dream to the solid household cares which are rarely very palatable when the heart becomes occupied with less material matters.

"I'm coming, father, directly!" she replied, and then, performing her toilet as quickly as possible, she again entered on the every-day cares that hitherto had afforded her a not unpleasing occupation.

When Miles Mason was about to go off on his usual duty he went in to his guest to bid him good-bye.

"Well, sir, I'm right glad to see you about to leave our little place; for I needn't mind telling you now that I never expected you would go out of it alive."

"Thanks to you, Mason, first, and your daughter's care afterwards, I am all right; but I suppose it was a near thing."

"Indeed it was, sir! Well, good-bye, sir."

"Good-bye, Mason. Give me your hand. You will let me come over and see you sometimes?"

"We shall be honoured, sir. But what's this?" And Mason looked at a piece of paper Treherne had left in his hand. "It's not money, sir, is it?"

"Simply a little present, Mason. I have been a great trouble to you, and—"

"No, sir, not money. I can't take money, thank you." And Mason laid the bank-note down on the table.

"You are not annoyed, I hope?" said Cyril, to whom it was difficult to understand a sailor having feelings sensitive enough to be hurt by being offered money as a reward for a good action.

"No, sir; I won't exactly call it annoyance, but I am sorry you thought it necessary to offer me payment."

Mason's tone of voice, however, told very plainly how much he was hurt.

"Well, then, forget I did so," said Cyril, thinking the man was a great fool, and did not know what he had refused, for ten-pound notes do not find their way every day into the pockets of such men as himself.

Cyril stood at the cottage-door, watching Mason walk down the grassy, sloping road towards the sea, till, the man taking a short turn, he lost sight of him. Cyril was leaning against the door, and seemed buried in thought. He stood so for some time; when, suddenly turning round, he saw Cherry gazing at him with pensive, dreamy eyes. She was not startled when he spoke and asked her of what she was thinking; it seemed a continuation of her reflections that he should speak and ask her her thoughts. She answered, simply,—

"I was thinking of you, sir."

"Of me, Cherry? Why, I thought by your eyes your mind must have been far, far away, in your own sunny land, thinking of beautiful Seville."

"Ah, sir, I cannot think of Seville so as to dwell on it, for I cannot recollect it."

"Then, what about me were you thinking?"

Cherry was silent. Her thoughts had been on the probability of her again seeing Mr. Treherne; and whether, if he never came to Shelton, could she go to Treherne Court to see him. She could not tell him this.

"You won't tell me. I suppose it is that you are glad I am going away. You will not have all your time taken up by waiting on me, and you will be able to see that—what's his name?—George something, without being troubled by my presence in the next room; and he will make love to you, and—"

"Stop, sir, oh, pray stop! I *hate* George Cooper! I never cared for him, and *now* I hate him!"

Cherry spoke with flashing eyes and heightened colour, and with a ring of truthfulness in her voice that augured ill for poor George Cooper's hopes on the day that, with raised wages, he offered her his name and hand.

"Well, never mind George Cooper," said Cyril, coming towards her, and amused at the vehement tone in which she proclaimed her worse than indifference to the quarryman. "But tell me, Cherry, are you sorry I am going, or glad?"

"You know I am sorry, sir," replied the girl, with quivering lips. "And you said yesterday you would come and see us once a week; will you, sir?"

"I will. What are you doing?" he asked, after a pause, and lifting her hand from her work; "cannot you leave that for a little and take a walk with me? I should like to go down to those rocks before I leave, and see where it was I so nearly lost my life, and what remains of the poor Marguerita, if it be not too far."

Of course Cherry could leave her work, and did so but too gladly. In a few minutes she was ready, and together they strolled down to the shore almost in silence, for Cyril did not any longer feel so strong when once he began to walk, and Cherry did not like to disturb her companion. Now and then he said a word about the weather or the wild scenery, and then relapsed into silence. At last they reached the huge sharp-pointed rocks, and then the spot where the Marguerita and three of her crew came to their ill-timed end.

"Let us sit here," said Cyril, as they came to a smooth, small bed of rocks, and away from the *débris* that strewed the greater part of the coast where the rocks were higher. The tide was low, and the sands hard and dry.

"You are tired, sir, I am afraid?"

"A little; a few minutes' rest will put me right. Do you often come and walk about here, Cherry?"

"No, sir; I don't like these great black giants,—they almost frighten me. I like the green fields and meadows best, where the flowers grow, and the birds sing."

"There is not much of that sort of thing

about here, I should think. The birds seem all sea-gulls, and the only flowers sea-weeds. I wonder you have not grown to like all this."

" The storms are too frequent, and the danger to the ships too great, even when the weather is calm, for me ever to like it."

They were silent again. Cyril thought of the last time he sat on a rock as he was now doing, and how, with pretty, Hebe-faced Willie Thorpe, he sat talking till the waves surrounded them, and the result of that misadventure was his becoming her affianced husband; at any rate, though not allowed to be called so, he was tacitly acknowledged as such. And, thinking of her, he longed to see her, and to hasten home and find some word from her with the permission to do so. It was a pleasant reflection, that of having gained the love of this bright, pretty girl—one that any man might be proud to call his own; but it made Cyril exclaim, in a tone of impatience almost amounting to irritability,—

" How long the morning is!"

For the first time in her life Cherry felt one of those passions so strongly rooted in her Southern nature rise into life; but as yet she knew not the meaning of jealousy, though she was feeling its effect. There was a gnawing sensation at her heart, a sinking weight that seemed to draw her voice downwards, and deprive her of giving utterance to the words that were on the edge of her lips.

"My father said the dog-cart would be over by two; it is nearly one; we can walk back, and perhaps it may, after all, come a little sooner."

"Yes, sir," said Cherry, her voice hardly above her breath.

Cyril did not perceive anything; he was too occupied with himself and his own thoughts to heed the lowering countenance of the usually cheerful, happy-looking girl; and in complete silence they returned to the cottage. The whole time Cherry was puzzling her poor head to know what could possibly have made Mr. Treherne so suddenly anxious to get away. Not his mother, she felt sure; she remembered well his injunctions to John Finch not to let her fetch him. Not his father, for he had seen him yesterday. Perhaps a sister, it might possibly be a sister; and she resolved to ask if he had one.

The dog-cart had not yet arrived, and they were sitting with the cottage-door open, so that when it approached he could see it instantly. Cherry was seemingly busy with her needle, though few were the stitches she made; and Cyril was twirling the key of his watch about, and looking out over the open sea, wandering in thoughts—pleasant, happy thoughts—of the future, in which Willie formed the principal feature. He was interrupted at last by his companion.

"Have you a sister, sir?"

"A sister, Cherry! No. What made you think I had?"

"I don't know, sir; I fancied you had."

"I am an only child; I never had either sister or brother."

Then Cherry began again to worry her brains as to why he seemed so anxious to leave, when the looked-for dog-cart drove up to the door. John Finch, who had remained at Shelton with his master, now suddenly appeared: clearly, he too had been, though invisible, on the look-out.

"When will you be ready to start, sir?" asked John, coming forward. "The mare ought to have a feed and half an hour's rest, the groom says."

"Very well, then, in half an hour's time I shall be ready to go. Don't be later."

"All right, sir."

And away went the cart and men to the

Coventry Arms, and once more left Cherry and
Cyril to themselves.

"You seem very anxious to go, sir," Cherry
ventured to say at last.

"Well, it's natural, Cherry, is it not? After
such a misfortune, and yet to have come out of
it without harm, it is natural I should wish to
see my—mother; and she, of course, is fidget-
ing to see me. Had I the sister you fancied I
had, then, perhaps, she would not care so
much for me; but as it is I am her spoilt
child."

"And yet, sir," said Cherry, with a mixture
of determination and hesitation, "you were
not so anxious yesterday; you rather dreaded
having to pass two hours alone in your mother's
society."

"Ah, that is quite a different thing. I hate
shut-up carriages, and still more if a lady be
with me, for they all seem to have the most
unaccountable love of chattering in carriages;
and the greater the rumble, the more they
seem to like talking. I suppose it makes a
pleasant accompaniment, but to me it is very
disagreeable." Then, presently, as the time
was passing and Cherry made no rejoinder,
but with her heightened colour and full pouting
lips, the mouth slightly falling at the corners,

was looking wondrously pretty, he said, "Yet, though I shall be glad to get home, little one, I shall be sorry to leave you. I do not like saying 'good-bye' at any time, and very often escape without it; but I cannot do that with you; I must say good-bye, and we part as friends, Cherry, do we not?"

"A gentleman like you, sir, can't think of a poor girl like me as a friend."

"And yet you say that in a tone, Cherry, that would lead any one to think your ideas were very different. I want to be your friend —if you will let me. I want you to feel and believe that anything I can do for you at any time will be as much gratification to myself as benefit to you."

Cyril spoke earnestly and kindly, yet the tone displeased the girl.

"You are very kind, sir, especially as I have no claim on you."

"But you have; and I told you so before. Now, will you believe me, Cherry—will you trust to me, and if ever you have a wish I can gratify, will you let me know it?"

He was standing close to her now; she was still sitting with her work, her head so bent he could not see her face; but she had given up pretending to use the needle, she was simply pinching up into tiny plaits the calico she was manufacturing into some useful garment.

"Yes, sir," she said, at last.

"I do not think you would say 'Yes' if you meant 'No,' though your answer is rather concise—but I think I hear the trot of the mare's feet," he added, hurriedly, "so say good-bye to me, Cherry; you know we are friends, and friends always part—so."

And he raised her from her chair, and, lifting up her head, which reluctantly she let him do, and looking into her great brown eyes, that now seemed more abashed than wondering, he kissed her half-parted red lips three or four times, rapidly, impetuously, as if to gratify her, yet get it over, more than from any tender feeling he himself experienced; then, before she had recovered herself, before she had time to follow him to the door, he had sprung into the dog-cart and was gone.

When Cherry regained her senses sufficiently to think at all, she found as it were another being in her place; her home was unchanged, her dress was the same, all surrounding her unaltered, but herself, the self of old, was no more there; she could no longer recognize in the thoughts and hopes and fears and undefined sensations that kept her heart and pulse beating in an uncontrollable manner, the Cherry Mason of even twenty-four hours ago. She sat down again on the chair from which he had raised her, and, closing her eyes, went over and over and over again the scene of the last quarter of an hour, and with each repetition her blood warmed and her breathing became short and quick; every nerve in her body vibrated with the passionate feelings that foolish, thoughtless embrace had roused within her. It was time for something to happen to divert her mind, and prevent her dwelling longer on such a shallow, superficial cause for happiness, and it came in a form that, if not welcome, was at any rate, under the circumstances, very wholesome for her, for it brought her back, though somewhat rudely, to herself. It was the tall, bony figure of George Cooper that appeared on the threshold of the cottage, and thus broke on the wild and dangerous dreams poor Cherry was recklessly indulging in.

"Law, Miss Cherry, how flustered you do look! Have I startled you?"

"No—yes, I think—I was so busy with my work."

"Well, I won't hinder of you; but I just called in to tell you that this very morning I have heard that in a few weeks I shall get a rise in my wages, and you know, Miss Cherry, I always wanted to wait—for that time—time to—to—just before—you see, before I—"

"Before you gave your mother that new dress you told me you wanted me to choose for you," interrupted Cherry, perfectly restored now, and, with a lively perception, quite understanding what poor George was trying to say.

"Well, no, not exactly that, Miss Cherry. I find it difficult—"

"Never mind, George, I will choose it for you whenever you like; I think it was to be green, wasn't it?"

"I'm sure I don't know; I don't recollect. I seem as how I had most forgotten everything." And then to himself he said, "I had arranged all so well to speak it, and she's drove it all right away out of my head. I must leave it now for another time." Then again, aloud, "Mother bid me tell you she'd be glad if you'd go over and see her soon: she's a bad walker, even for so short a distance, and it pleasures her to see you."

"Yes, I will go and see her, George; but you may tell her I seldom leave home but for marketing; I don't seem to care for going out like other girls."

"No, you're not a bit like other girls, Miss

Cherry, and, though they call you the little foreigner, they'd all of them jump out of their skins if they could be like you."

Cherry smiled. "I know few like me. I dare say it's my own fault, but I can't help it. Are you going by the Rectory, George?"

"I wasn't; but if I can do anything there for you, it won't take me a hundred yards out of my way. I am going to the quarries; I have just come from having my dinner."

"Your dinner! Is it dinner-time? Three o'clock; good gracious me! I had no idea of the time."

"And haven't you had no dinner?"

"No."

"Well, if that isn't a rum go! Why, whoever would believe any one could forget their dinner!"

And George laughed heartily—a laugh that was coarse and loud, and grated on Cherry, whose ears had learnt very quickly to like the soft, musical laugh of refinement and good breeding.

"You will be late at the quarries," she said, after he had done, and was silently watching her.

"Yes; I must be off, or I shall be fined. What is it you want done at the Rectory, Miss Cherry?"

"Just to leave that parcel for me. I promised it to Mrs. Jackson in the beginning of the week, but I could not get it done sooner."

"Perhaps she knows you've been occupied. She must have heard of the wreck, of course."

"I don't know. Maybe she has; but she does not often know what goes on. It is not as if she could walk about like other people, poor lady."

"The young gentleman's gone, Miss Cherry, ain't he?"

"Yes."

"Well, good-bye, miss. I'll leave your parcel; and you'll come and see mother soon?"

"Yes. Good-bye."

"And then," he thought, as he walked away, "will be my time, if I'm at home, to tell her what stuck so in my throat just now. What an ass I am, to be sure! Any other fellow would have fired away, and not been scared by the mention of a green dress. Law, bless me! what will the old woman think when I tell her she's the cause of my failure to-day? But, at any rate, there's not another Miss Cherry likes, I think, if—ah, that's a horrid thought! Yet I couldn't help fancying yesterday something was up; and then to-day she—she was odd, and forgot her dinner. O Lord, O Lord! if that fair-haired gentleman were to wrong her, I could tear him to pieces with my own two hands!"

And George Cooper ground his teeth and clenched his hands with rage at the bare thought of such a consummation being possible.

When George left her, Cherry congratulated herself on the escape she had had. At any rate for the present, she had put a stop to his offering her his big heart and big hand; then she took a piece of dry bread, and drank off a large tumblerful of cold water, and considered her dinner done. She had no appetite, yet she feared to go without food entirely, in case her father asked her, as he often did when he was absent during the mid-day meal, whether she had made a good one. Then, again, she began that sorry, profitless work of thinking, and she sat thinking on till her father's return. Then her duty and affection for him gave her the power to rouse herself from her reverie and exert herself to see to his requirements and comforts.

CHAPTER IX.

YARDLEY WOOD was a very pretty place. The house was built in the Italian style, and looked as if it had dropped down into Devonshire from the banks of the Thames, where, between Kingston and Hampton Court, there stands, on the Surrey side of the river, a house very similar to it.

White, low, and spreading, a centre with two wings, it stood on table-land, with a beautifully mown, velvety lawn sloping down to the narrow, winding river Yardley, little more than a rapid stream where it passed through Mr. Thorpe's property, but very beautiful as you saw the glistening waters shimmering in the bright sunlight through the trees. It made the place always appear gay ; there was a joyous sound in the echo of the waters rushing and leaping over big pieces of rock that most unaccountably found themselves in the most eccentric positions, rendering it impossible, however, to use a boat of any kind whatever. Indeed, it looked an unlikely river altogether for anything but fishing; and the reputation of its trout was such that Mr. Thorpe had to keep a sharp look-out to prevent poaching in the portion to which he laid claim.

The old house that formerly stood there was destroyed by fire some thirty years ago; and, as the home of his childhood was gone, Mr. Thorpe determined to build a house entirely different; and certainly, however beautiful of its kind, it was utterly unsuited to the country and position it was in. However, there it was; and, during the years he passed abroad for his child's sake, he never lost an opportunity of purchasing works of art which, independently of gratifying his own taste, he knew would precisely suit his English home.

Though Willie Thorpe hardly recollected Yardley Wood, she yet loved it with a strangely clinging affection. Till the time of their last visit to Treherne Court, when she had learnt another sort of love, she had never, from the day she had returned to her native land, desired to leave it: all she cared for on earth was there. Friends she had few—at any rate, in her own country; relations she had still fewer; and all that the most indulgent of fathers could do to gratify her every fancy or desire was done. so it is not to be wondered at that hitherto she had found Yardley Wood perfect.

In a long narrow room. stretching from one end of the centre part of the house to the other, and called the gallery. were some fine paintings and some beautiful pieces of modern sculpture. Lombardi's celebrated 'Susannah' was among them, Willie's favourite statue, and one she never tired of looking at. The indignant, proud gaze of the beautiful face, with its exquisitely formed features, the graceful bending figure, the fine, delicately shaped limbs, all combined to create a subject which the least artistic in their taste must have liked to dwell on. The room was hung with rich crimson silk, and luxurious seats *dos-à-dos* down the centre, covered with the same, throwing a warm colouring over the pure Carrara marble. The drawing-rooms, two long rooms taking up the entire depth of the house in the east wing, were all a mass of white and gold, with Dresden china mouldings framing the looking-glasses, the furniture satin-wood with purple velvet. Ornaments of all kinds were studded about, with several gilt cabinets full of shelves covered with the rarest and most valuable specimens of old china, the whole striking one on first entering as more like a fairy palace than an English home. At the opposite end of the gallery, the west wing, was the dining-room, where Willie's pet picture, and the most valuable in the collection, hung,—a Madonna and lamb, by Murillo. The library, Mr. Thorpe's "den," led out of this. Here he generally sat all the morning alone, and all the evening, when the weather was the least chilly, with his daughter; for it was an excessively warm, cosy room, and in summer too much so.

Willie's own sanctum was upstairs, and there, when indoors, she passed her morning, reading, writing, or playing with her pets,—a little dog, a blue Skye terrier, called "Dust," and an owl, a white serio-comic owl, taken from the nest out of a tree in Yardley Wood, and called "Snow." He had been taught to change his ordinary habits, from at any rate screeching at night to screeching in the evening; he was allowed to remain up till the last in the house, and then he was consigned to the servants' hall, where he was supposed to sleep—at any rate, he could if he chose; he had no cage, but a pole like a parrot's, with bars across. He knew Willie so well that he always endeavoured to get close up to her, and, if allowed his freedom, used it only to sit close by her, or perched on her shoulder, if she would let him.

Snow and Dust were happy specimens of pets. Dust, the gentlest, most intelligent of little dogs, with but one palpable sensation at the heart, and that was pure, unadulterated devotion to his mistress, led a life of unmingled pleasure, and the two favourites were no bad friends. They had their little squabbles, but they learnt to cede certain points one to the other; for instance, when Willie, as she sometimes would, went out on an expedition to the Yardley with her two pets, Snow was bound to remain, with his strange, almost sightless eyes, quiet and resigned, whilst Dust indulged in what Snow doubtless thought most insane gambols in the water. Dust, on the other hand, had to stand at a respectful distance on the lawn when Snow was searching for some rare *bonnes bouches* in the shape of worms, and to remove very far from that round beak if he desired to make use of the grass as a towel to get rid of some of the water which his long thick matted hair sopped in and retained like a sponge.

Of late—that is to say quite recently—Willie Thorpe had somewhat neglected her pets; they ceased to fill the important offices they had hitherto done; they no longer ministered to her amusement as before. Her Hebe face was not sad, but it no longer wore the bright, joyous look it was wont to do when Dust bounded into the water, or when Snow, if angered by his companion, perched himself on his back, refusing to move for all the barks to which Dust in his indignation gave vent, till Willie went to his rescue. There was a more sober expression, a more thoughtful look, that made her seem none the less lovely, but that destroyed for ever the last remnant of child-hood.

"I sometimes think, Willie," said Mr. Thorpe, when they were sitting together in the library on the afternoon of the day on which Cyril Treherne was expected, after his escape in the Marguerita. "I sometimes think you regret the promise I asked you to give me."

"About what, papa?"

"Not marrying for a year. It may seem selfish to you, child, and as if I had stipulated for another twelve months for my own sake; yet it was not so, my child, but my own solemn promise to your mother, Willie: I never thought of self in the matter."

"Indeed, dear papa, I am sure you did not; you have no need to tell me so. And I do not regret it; I don't indeed, papa." Willie coloured up as if her conscience accused her of not speaking with her usual strictness to truth. "And I am sure you are right," she continued. "Time goes so quickly, too. At any rate, do not think, dearest papa, I am wanting to leave you."

"No, my own child, I am sure of that!"

Still there was an inward warning that made Mr. Thorpe aware his time for being first in Willie's heart was nearly, if not already, over. She loved him no doubt as dearly as ever, only she had now learnt that love which is stronger than any felt by a child for a parent: it passes all other affections; it stands alone, powerful to crush every other feeling but itself. It makes the weak woman strong, and the strong it will make weak. There is no describing it; it is like a second soul to the human body, giving life to many, yet ofttimes destroying it. When first it bursts forth, a new existence at once seems to open before one, full of hope and joy; how often those hopes are marred, how often fulfilled, daily life around us tells.

Willie Thorpe's face was one that somewhat falsified her nature; to look at it, you would think nothing could gloom over that brightness, or, if it did, it could but resemble a cloud in the summer sky—a few heavy tears and then all sunshine again. To look at her face you would never dream that she could love with a deep, intense, passionate love. The merry ringing laugh, the trifles that had hitherto sufficed to amuse her, the light-hearted voice that was so constantly carolling through the house, told nothing of the warmth and force and power of her nature. Though not quite of the opinion ot those who consider first love idle nonsense, second love something to believe in, and third love the only one really to be relied on, I still think as a rule first love is empty, vapid, and meaningless; also, as a rule, at sixteen the heart may receive its first lesson, but the fancy is generally conceived for some stupid boy, just gone into stand-up collars and tail coats. In Willie's case her first love was of a different type, and was the exception that forms the rule. Though she had known Cyril Treherne only since her return to England, she had seen a great deal of him, and her love had grown imperceptibly. She knew little about it till he spoke to her, perched as she was, half in her senses, half out of them, on those wild, wicked rocks. Then it at once burst into full bloom, the blossom had grown strong in its hidden state, and only required the word to bring it to perfection; and Mr. Thorpe's questionable plan of keeping the two as much apart as possible, and not permitting of an acknowledged engagement, but tended to increase the girl's love. The very fact of having her liberty made her long for the bondage that, for all she said, yet seemed such a long way off. Then she felt a great fear come upon her when she heard of the narrow escape Cyril had had; it made her face the possibility of death coming in between them and dividing them for ever. But, for all that, she found the courage to speak the words she had to her father, his remarks and questions being prompted by the first shadow he had ever noticed on his child's countenance—a shadow that, when once it hovers over a woman's face, rarely leaves it, but settles down on it for ever.

Willie was sitting near the window; she could see every arrival from where she was, the library being what is termed on the front side of the house, that is the entrance side. She pushed the heavy, hot velvet curtains aside and placed her chair in the furthermost corner; she was enabled now by her position to see some little distance down the drive.

"Is that three striking, papa?"

" No—yes; I think it must be. No, half-past two."

Mr. Thorpe was reading his paper and was indifferent to the hour. He removed his glasses in a moment, looked at his daughter, then put them on again, and continued his occupation.

"That must be three, papa; I hear the stable clock striking, I am sure," said Willie, a few seconds after.

" Well, I dare say it is. Where is your own watch, Willie ?"

" I forgot to wind it up last night."

" Very careless of you; I advise your winding it up now."

Willie seemed not to heed this piece of advice ; but she took out a crumpled letter from her pocket—an oft-read letter apparently —and she glanced over it again, till she satisfied herself as to the hour of Cyril's arrival. She was sure enough before looking that he had said three, but there was a pleasure in being doubly assured. It was the first time in her life that Willie felt nervous or anxious, and now she was both. A few minutes of this novel kind of discomfort, and she heard the distant rumbling of wheels, then the squeaky, scraping noise of the carriage coming up the gravelled road, with the clatter of the horses' feet.

"Oh, papa, I hope to goodness Mrs. Treherne has not come," exclaimed Willie, as she saw the great lumbering family coach coming along.

"Well, my dear, if she has, you surely will be glad to see her. I hope you have ordered a proper dinner?"

"I have done nothing of the kind. I only said Mr. Treherne was coming over and would probably stay to dinner. It is not the dinner I care about."

"Admiral Treherne; Mr. Treherne."

A relief to poor Willie when she heard this announcement. The admiral she did not mind, on the contrary she was pleased to think that if she went for a stroll with Cyril her father would have a companion; but the idea of being compelled to entertain Mrs. Treherne, to be obliged to play the hostess to her, when she would be wanting to listen to Cyril's account of his accident, and to do so by herself, would have been more than she could patiently have borne.

A silent pressure of the hand, a faltering attempt a minute after to say how anxious she had been and how glad she was to see him, and poor little Willie rushed out of the room, up to her own, where, with none but Dust and sleepy Snow to see her, she threw herself on the sofa, and, burying her head in the soft embroidered cushion, let the tears fall fast and thick—tears of joy and gladness, tears of relief and gratitude; and then, ashamed of her weakness, she brushed all traces of them hastily away and quickly returned to him in whose keeping she had placed all her earthly hopes.

"Well, Willie," said the admiral, "a pretty business this would-be sailor has made of it, hasn't he? A narrow escape, Thorpe, a very narrow escape! But, now it's over, it is a grand thing to have witnessed such a wreck as that; if poor Tait and those other fellows had not been lost, I believe I would not have grudged the money gone in the craft, for a shipwreck is a splendid sight; a thing you can't imagine: no use reading about them; no one can describe them."

"Really, sir, you ought never to have given up the service," said Cyril, who with Willie by his side was so standing that he managed to gain possession of the willing little hand unseen.

"And so give you a chance the sooner to step

into my shoes," he replied, laughing. " But it is
a glorious profession, and I never should have
given it up unless I had been forced."

" Willie thought Mrs. Treherne had accompanied you," said Mr. Thorpe, " when she saw
the close carriage. You could not persuade her,
I suppose ? it is a long drive."

" We never asked her," said Cyril, with a
smile ; " but to please her we came in the old
lumbering coach ; she was so afraid of our
taking cold driving back."

" Put out the ' our,' boy," said the admiral,
" She was afraid you might. I believe she
thinks me cold proof."

" What are your plans, then ? Must you
return to-night ?" asked Mr. Thorpe.

" Certainly, certainly ! If we were not back
before midnight the whole household would be
sent after us. We must leave this at ten by
the very latest."

" Then we need not alter our dinner-hour.
What are you inclined to do, take a turn in the
gardens, or sit still ?"

" Let the young people go out ; we can stay
quiet for a while, at any rate. Do you smoke
in this room, Thorpe ?"

" No, not here ; but come away to the
smoking-room. And, Willie, if you are going

out, do not stay too long: remember Cyril had a fatiguing bath the other day."

" Very well, papa."

" Oh, sir, I am as strong as a horse; it is only my mother who imagines I was half killed."

" You are looking pale, Cyril," said Willie, as they walked out by the gallery window on to the lawn. " You must tell me all about this horrible accident, every little detail you can remember. Shall we go and sit by the river?"

" Wherever you like, my darling; I do not care where, so that I have you beside me."

So they walked on slowly till they came to the stump of an old tree, that was in a slight hollow near the water's edge, and which proved a very comfortable seat. Here they sat down, and then Cyril did as he was bid, and told Willie, to the best of his power, all he knew. She listened in silence; every now and then she pressed his hand, which held hers, with a kind of convulsive grasp, and her breath came quick and short as she listened to him repeating what John Finch had told him of his being dashed on the rocks.

" And were you terribly frightened when you heard about it?" asked Cyril. " Did you wish to come to me at once and nurse me?"

Willie looked up; her deep blue eyes seemed

to take in at a glance the jealous exaction
which prompted the question.

"I only knew of the danger you had escaped
when it was past."

"And so—you did not care who it might be
that looked after me and to the little necessities
of my state?"

"I could do nothing, Cyril, but wish you
safe at home. Are you vexed that I could not
do the impossible?"

"Not vexed—no, darling. Forgive me, but I
love you so dearly that I do not wish aught in
life to come between me and you."

"And what or who ever can?" asked Willie,
with a startled expression. "I don't understand
you, Cyril; you do not fancy that my father
or I for a moment ever thought you were in
need of any care, or that both of us would not
have been with you instantly? You forget you
were to be home within a few hours of our
hearing of the horrid accident."

"No, my darling, I did not; I am sure your
father would have done anything required
under such circumstances. Only, Willie, listen
to me; do not trifle with my love, do not play
fast and loose with my heart. I love you very
dearly, as dearly as man ever loved woman,
and—" Cyril's foolish words, and still more

foolish kisses lavished on Cherry rose up before him, and the thought flashed through his mind that were Willie to act by him as he had done by her, what would be his feelings? "I wish your father had not insisted on our waiting a year before we are to be openly engaged," he said, suddenly, with a gloomy look overspreading his face, which he turned away, knowing full well she would notice what he could not conceal.

"I am so young, Cyril; papa says it is better for both of us to wait a year."

"And you are satisfied to do so?"

"If you—if I feel certain—if—"

"Well, Willie?" and Cyril turned round and gently put his arm round the trembling figure of the young girl, drawing her nearer and nearer to himself; "if—?"

She looked up, her honest, truthful eyes telling what her tongue refused to utter; but as they met his they fell suddenly, and a deep blush spread over her face—that bright, beautiful joyous face, always a gladdening sight to every one. He drew it near his own, and pressed his lips to hers; then he started from her suddenly. Again rose the recollection that, though in the sight of God his promised wife, hers were not the last lips his had touched;

he started with a feeling of remorse and regret; he could not recall his folly towards Cherry Mason, which now for the first time appeared to him in its real colours, without feeling for a moment the sharp sting of an accusing conscience, for he loved Willie Thorpe with a deep and sincere love; but it was for a moment only; after all, he had done no great harm, for he had meant none; he had felt towards Cherry as he might towards a pretty child who had amused him for a moment; moreover, he owed her kindness, for had she not, in all probability, saved his life? so he comforted himself and quieted his conscience.

Willie, however, noticed Cyril's manner instantly. We are all terribly alive to the least change in those we love. She looked round, her first thought being that he had heard footsteps or seen some one approaching; but all was still, and no sound to be heard but the rushing of the stream, nothing visible but little Dust, enjoying himself doubly, from being with his mistress unaccompanied by Snow—a rare treat to him, but one he had the chance of enjoying more frequently now than heretofore, as Cyril had once remarked that owls were birds of ill omen, and Willie recollected this when, sitting by herself, she endeavoured to recall everything her lover had ever said before he stood to her in the light he now did.

"There is no one near us, Willie," said Cyril, as if in reply to her glance, and smiling slightly at her idea of that being the cause of his movement.

"What made you start so?"

"Oh, a mere nothing—a thought—a recollection."

"Won't you tell it to me?"

"No, I think not, Willie." Cyril spoke half seriously, half smilingly.

"And yet, when you bade me good-bye the other day, you asked me to give you the same promise I gave papa—to have no secrets from you."

"I did; but what has that to do with it?"

"Why, everything! You have a secret from me if you will not tell me what you thought of at that moment."

"I, a secret from you? Yes; that is different to your having one from me. There are many things it might be necessary for me to keep from you, many things that would only cause you useless worry were you to know them. Now, listen, darling—don't look cross, or if you do I must kiss you till I make those red ips cease to pout, and part again in smiles."

"I shall retract my promise," said Willie, looking still cross, for all the threats held over her, and, turning her face away, she made a sign to Dust, which brought him to her side. "If you don't tell me what you were thinking about, I shall never tell you anything at all, not even if—I thought it would make you happy to know it!" And the dog now came in for a share of petting he had not been indulged in of late.

"Then I will tell you, Willie, since you are so determined. I was thinking—and the thought, I suppose, made me half mad—that if any man ever kissed your lips as I have done, I could take his life and—yours too!"

Cyril Treherne meant what he said, so perhaps he may be excused for the want of thorough truthfulness in the explanation he gave; the thought had but then occurred to him. Yet, angry with himself for having to speak a falsehood, his countenance showed his vexation. Willie turned round, and, with love beaming over her face, she mistook the cause of his expression; she fancied it to be the effect of his own words—a feeling of jealousy roused within him.

"Dearest Cyril!" she murmured, and put her head down on his shoulder, "you need have no fear, and—I will always tell you everything," she added, in a humbled, submissive tone.

And Cyril stroked the little head that rested so lovingly and confidingly on him, and then, looking fondly into her blue eyes, he held her in his arms for a moment and pressed her to his heart, and whispered loving words in her ear; and then, after a while, when the beating hearts were stilled, they walked slowly back to the house, Willie with her love for Cyril stronger and intenser than before his arrival that afternoon.

CHAPTER X.

The days passed, not quickly, like pleasant days, but slowly and heavily for Cyril Treherne and—one other.

After his last visit to Yardley Wood, Cyril took himself to task, and resolved for the future that he would be content with the treasure he had won, and give up all his old, careless, thoughtless ways. There was no harm in him; he was neither better nor worse than other men; he had sown his wild oats, and reaped little harm as yet: but, were he now to continue the planting of these ungovernable seeds, Heaven only knew what they might not bring forth! He did not feel sure whether Willie Thorpe's nature was not too gentle and trusting to bear with deception. A woman with a more fiery disposition, who would love passionately, but perhaps less deeply, would go into a fit of jealous rage, and then forgive rather than lose the man she loved; but the enduring, confiding love would be more likely to give up, and the cold weight of faithlessness crush the heart till it ceased to beat. Cyril determined never again to give rise to the necessity of telling a falsehood, and he resisted the temptation of riding over to Shelton to see Cherry Mason; and yet he had promised to go and see her, and this promise rose up to his recollection at moments when he felt bored and knew not how to kill time.

The Thorpes drove over one day, and relieved the monotony of his life at home for a few hours; then Cyril told Willie he thought of hiring a yacht and going for a few weeks' cruise, in order to pass the time between then and their next meeting; but she pleaded so hard that he would not, that he could not refuse her; so he was forced to fall back on something else for amusement. Better had she let him go; better for her, and better for him, and better for all, but it was not to be.

It was full three weeks after the wreck of the Marguerita that Cyril was riding over the sand-hills near to Shelton, with no thought of going to Miles Mason's cottage; he had fought successfully hitherto against his desire, but now fate seemed leading him on. He did not know that when he once gained the summit of the hill before him he would be at the little village itself, but so it was; and as he pulled up his horse by the side of the pretty church, he looked down the sloping land far away to the water's edge, where he so nearly lost his life; then, turning his head slightly westwards, he saw the roof of Cherry's home: there was no harm in looking at it from a nearer point of view. Moreover, thoughts of his promise to go and see her rose up in a reproachful form, and he argued that he was wanting in common gratitude in not having fulfilled it: there could be no possible harm in his seeing her; so little, indeed, that he saw the whole matter in another light; and he persuaded himself that were Willie to know how much he owed to Mason and his daughter she would be the first to urge him to pay a visit to his humble friends. So, without further consideration, he walked his horse down till he could see the cottage distinctly. The door, as usual during fine weather, was ajar, but he could not see inside without going quite close up to it; so he dismounted, and, putting his arm through the bridle, he led his horse up to the very window, and he stood so that he could see without being seen.

The scene within, to judge by his countenance, did not please him; and yet it was a very simple, homely one—nothing that ought to have roused an angry feeling in his breast. Cherry Mason was standing in front of George Cooper; he was seated, and she was doing something to his left hand, apparently sewing a button on to his shirt-sleeve. After looking for a few seconds, Cyril's first impulse was to get on his horse and ride home again; his second was to go in and—he fortunately stopped at his third, which was, to kick that big, burly young quarryman out of the cottage. He a moment after smiled at the absurdity of his entertaining such a notion, yet he entered the cottage with anything but an amiable feeling towards the young man and the girl. He knew he was wrong; he knew the best thing Cherry could do would be to marry George Cooper; and yet his vanity was hurt; he fancied she cared for him, and he did not stop to consider the misery such a feeling, if encouraged, would bring about.

Hearing a footstep, Cherry looked round and gave a sudden start and a little scream, which was followed by another, much more violent, from George, the cause being Cherry having stuck the needle somewhat firmly into his wrist in her surprise and pleasure at seeing who it was, and there leaving it.

"Oh, sir, I am glad! I thought you had forgotten me. Are you quite well, sir? You are tired, I am sure. Shall George take your horse, sir?" said Cherry. all in a breath.

"Miss Cherry—if you please, look here; the needle, miss! I beg your pardon, sir," and George touched his hair by way of bow. "If you please, Miss Cherry."

"Gracious! George, why did you stick the needle there? You had better pull it out, I think."

"I never stuck it there, miss; you stuck it in!"

And George, finding it best to pull the needle out, as desired, did so, and broke the thread off, seeing there was little chance of his button being made any tighter.

"Yes; if that young fellow will take my horse and lead him up and down for a few minutes, I shall be much obliged to him," said Cyril, thinking it would be a very good way of disposing of the man.

"Oh, George will be delighted; won't you?" said Cherry. "Just lead him about a little."

Reluctantly, as Cyril saw, did George take the reins from his hand and lead the horse away, then he went into the cottage and closed the door.

"I very nearly went away, Cherry, without coming in," said Cyril, in a tone that marked a certain degree of vexation.

"Why, sir?" asked Cherry, her manner now becoming shy, and her big, brown eyes no longer able to look up bravely, as they could do whilst George Cooper was present. "It would have been breaking your promise. You have been, as it is, a long time in coming to see—us."

"Who do you mean by 'us'?—you and that great hulking fellow?"

"No, sir; father and me. Of course I never thought of your coming to see—George; he's only a neighbour, sir."

"Neighbour or not, I do not like him. What were you doing for him just now?"

Cyril felt, as he spoke, that he did so in a tone he had no right to assume, and that his common sense told him was most injudicious and unwise; but for the moment he allowed his temper to get the better of his reason. Cherry, on the other hand, felt frightened. She thought Mr. Treherne looked handsomer than ever, but changed.

"I was sewing on a button," she answered, in a confused sort of way.

"And has he no one but you to do those kind of things for him?" Then, not waiting for an answer, he continued, with a softened expression in his voice, "Were you expecting me, little one?"

"I hoped, sir, you were coming; yes, every day, every day for a long time, I have looked for you. I have never been out in the day-time since you left us, fearing you would come and I should miss you."

"And are you glad to see me?"

"Very, sir; oh, very, very glad!"

And Cherry's great, wondering eyes softened down to an expression that well bore out the truth of her words.

"I wish you had not such big eyes, Cherry, or such a pretty, bewitching face. You are too pretty, child, to throw yourself away on that awkward lout out there."

"What do you mean, sir?"

"Why, I suppose you are going to marry that fellow."

"I, sir; never! Why do you say so?"

"Because young girls don't have men always going after them if they do not care for them."

"But I don't care for him," said Cherry, her lips quivering with vexation. "I never did care for him; I told you so before!"

" Then why is he always here ?"

" Father likes him, and—he likes father."

" But he is not here now on your father's account."

" No, sir." And Cherry crimsoned to the roots of her hair with anger at the undeniable fact. " He's here, I suppose, to—to please himself."

" And—you."

"No, sir; it's not true ! it isn't, indeed, true !"

Cherry could bear it no longer, and burst into tears. Tears are never becoming to the prettiest face ; they are the ugliest possible expression of feeling, and Cherry knew this well enough, and hastened bravely to wipe them away, and then, with a smile, that looked all the more sunny because of the bygone April storm, she said, in perfect innocence and simplicity,—

" If I liked George well enough to care about his coming here, I should not like you." Then, seeing an amused and pleased expression on Treherne's face, she feared she had said something silly, or perhaps unbecoming her position, and hastened to remedy the mistake by adding, " I feel as if I could work for you, be your servant—I mean—do anything, anything that you wanted."

"Even to sewing on my buttons and making a needle-case of my wrist. No, no, Cherry, when I want a proof of your affection, it will not be in the shape of work I shall ask it. But never mind George; we will not talk of him any more. I have not long to stop, and I would rather talk of yourself. Tell me whether—"

A thumping at the door interrupted Cyril, and Cherry went to see what could have made so extraordinary a noise.

"Look here, Miss Cherry," said George, for it was he, as the girl opened the door, "I can't tramp up and down here any longer, for no gentleman. I'm now past my hour for work, and I shall be fined threepence; but it's not the fine, and it's not—not the threepence, but it's him being along with you all this time. What's he got to say, I should like to know? Better come and take his horse, or—or I'll let him go loose, as sure as my name's George Cooper!"

The young man spoke so rapidly, Cherry could not manage to interrupt him. Cyril had heard every word, and before Cherry could answer he was by her side, and spoke himself.

"Here, fellow, give me the reins, and be off! Here is sixpence for you—threepence to pay your fine and threepence for drink." And as

Cyril spoke, he pitched a sixpence across to him.

"I'm no more a fellow than you are!" muttered George, in a surly, portentous tone, and, flinging the reins out of his hand, he walked slowly away, leaving the sixpence untouched on the ground.

Cyril was almost more angry with himself than with George Cooper, as he watched his tall, powerful figure turn the corner of the road. He felt he had been himself in the wrong, that he had no business where he was, and that he would not again place himself in so false a position. He attached his horse for a few moments to the latch of the door, and fixed it open, so that he could do no mischief, and was also visible.

"That fellow was born to annoy me, I think," said Cyril. "It is now nearly four o'clock. I have lost all my time here talking of, or to, that stupid donkey, and I must now be off. I dare say I shall not find my way back so easily as I came."

"Which road did you take, sir?" asked Cherry.

"I cannot tell you. Shall I tell you the truth, Cherry? I did not intend coming to see you at all. I have been resisting the desire to do so ever since I left you; and yet, with all my endeavours to avoid coming here to-day, I found myself at Shelton without knowing it; then I could not withstand the pleasure of seeing you for a moment, and so I rode down quite close to the house, and, looking in at the window, saw that charming picture of you and —well, I won't speak of him! What's the use, child, of my coming here?"

"It's a great pleasure, sir, to see you."

"But the pleasure is soon over, and then comes the pain."

"Not to you, sir."

"Not to me; and why not? If I come and see you often, Cherry, I shall have your father looking after me, and perhaps telling me to keep away."

Cherry thought it very probable, but she did not say so. She was young, very young, but girls in her grade of life know much more than those more carefully educated. She knew perfectly well that gentlemen did not marry girls in her position, but she also knew they sought them none the less, and that the end of that seeking was generally sorrow, disgrace, shame, and, perhaps, complete and crushing ruin. Yet Cherry had allowed her feelings to open the gate through which, if she once passed, she could never again return; once in, the door is irrevocably closed. She was still on the threshold, and if Cyril Treherne never more rode over to Shelton the door would of necessity shut itself; but if he returned, he knew, and she felt, that escape would be next to impossible; and feeling it, she yet asked him to do so.

"Come again, sir; only once! It seems so hard to think one is to part and never meet again, and without knowing it is the last time beforehand. I can think of it now, and will try then, never to think of—of that dreadful stormy night again."

"This day week, then—is it to be so, Cherry?" his good resolutions once again shaken.

"Yes, sir; or—this day fortnight will be better still."

"You are a strange girl, Cherry," said Cyril, looking at her. "Why do you wish it to be a fortnight, instead of a week hence?"

"It is a week more to think about it."

Cherry had a conviction there was no use in not speaking out the truth, as he read her every thought. There was a pause for a moment. Cherry was looking on the ground, Cyril watching her; presently he said,—

"Come here, Cherry, close to me—closer

still; there, now give me both your hands, and now—kiss me: now again—once more; there, child, that will do!"

Cyril put the girl from him, and, without another word, without even another look, he unfastened his horse, mounted, and rode away at a quick trot. As soon as he got on to the sand-hills he gave his horse his head, and let him go off at his own pace. The rapid motion through the fresh air cooled his heated brain, and brought him back to himself. It was time. He felt how near he had been to the edge of the precipice, and, becoming calmer, he once more resolved he would not again return to Shelton; he would not put Cherry's large wondering eyes in the way of his happiness, happen what might; his continuing to see her could but end in regret and trouble. And so, by the time he reached the old gates of Treherne Court, he was in as reasonable and sensible a state of mind as when he started.

With Cherry it was otherwise. Her Southern blood had been stirred up past stilling; it surged around her brain till wild, frantic passion took firm hold of her, and kept her chained in his unmanageable arms. Then she gave herself up to it, revelled in all the mad pleasure that she experienced in giving those kisses. Cyril was miles on his way home before Cherry began to think even of his absence. She was in a dream, a dangerous but enchanting dream. Love had taken strong, deep hold of her, and had received for the moment the uttermost gratification. She knew nothing of the danger of thus leaving all these distracting feelings uncurbed; with her heart beating so that she heard no other sound, her brain in a whirl, she sat, unconscious of aught else than the memory of those impassioned kisses, till, worn out by the tumult working in her whole frame, reaction slowly commenced.

My reader, did *you* ever wake from one of those day-dreams where neither hopes nor fears nor wishes had ever stepped in to mar its happiness, which from its sheer intensity was unalloyed? If not, you can hardly realize the ardent pleasure or the wild grief experienced in a few short hours by Cherry Mason. She had forgotten in her joy all but Cyril's impetuous, passionate farewell. It was only when she gathered her dazed senses together that she recollected one more interview was to end this brief period of a new existence; then as passion had roused her nearly to frenzy, so did sorrow take her down to the lowest depths of despair.

"I *will* see him again and again!" she exclaimed aloud, as with her hands holding her head she leaned her arms on the little table where already her father's evening meal should have been prepared. "If he will not come here I will go and see him—I will and must see him, on and on till my eyes have lost their sight! A fortnight to wait; two whole weeks before I see him again! O God, I cannot live without him! Will he kiss me again, I wonder, as he did to-day?"

And the girl shivered through every fibre as she recalled that embrace. Then tears, large, heavy drops, coursed each other down her smooth cheeks, till at last she gave way entirely, and cried long and bitterly; and then, her strength all spent, she gradually calmed down and became tranquillized. After a while she remembered her father, and she hastened to remedy her forgetfulness by quickly preparing his supper, and getting ready for him what she knew he most liked. It was barely prepared when Mason came in.

"Why, girl, I am half an hour later than usual, and yet supper does not seem ready. What have you been about?"

Cherry, utterly worn out, and too confused to

have a ready answer, muttered something about a headache.

"Headache! Headaches are for ladies, Cherry, not for girls like you. If you attend to your duties, and then when your work is done take a proper walk, you'll have none of those headaches. You've not been like yourself lately, I don't know what has come over you, girl; but, whatever it is, the sooner you shake it off the better."

Miles spoke a little gruffly; he thought it his duty, for he was too keen sighted by his very love for his daughter not to have noticed that a change had come over her since the night of the wreck. And one great indication to him was the way he constantly came in and found her sitting unemployed, her hands before her, or else standing at the door gazing out apparently at nothing, for there was little to see from Mason's cottage but the huge black rocks and the roaring, tossing sea.

Cherry's conscience smote her when she heard her father's admonition, and for the first time in her life a fear of him crept over her as the events of the day rose up before her. She could not tell him of Mr. Treherne's visit at that moment, and yet, if she delayed, the probability was he would never hear of it. Her first secret weighed more heavily on her than she expected. Her father's silence during his supper repelled any confidence, and so the evening passed; and, as was his wont when he had not any night duty, he went to bed early. As he wished his child good-night, he said, in a more softened tone and in a kindlier manner, "No one is happy, girl, if he fails in his duty, no matter what it may be, and yours is not difficult; but keep true to yourself, Cherry. Be assured of this—if your poor mother was living you would not break her heart sooner than you will mine if you don't turn out worthy of being her child. God bless you!"

And Miles Mason kissed his daughter's forehead; she bent her head low, a double feeling struggling within her. She could not bear so soon for other lips—even her father's—to wipe away the freshness of those intoxicating kisses, and she did not wish him to see the conscious blush that overspread her face. She was young at deceiving; she could not, with the lie she felt herself already to be acting, look her father in the face—that good, kind father who had ever been so careful and fond.

Miles Mason went to sleep with a shadow on the wall for the first time since his wife left him and her child alone in the world. He felt

certain this night that all was not right with
Cherry; the clear perception of a father's love
made him at once see a change in her. There
was a nervous haste in her movements, a quick
and more than ordinarily startled look in her
eyes, a forgetfulness of the veriest trifles;
and as he tossed on his bed, restless and wake-
ful with this new care, he determined, if a rapid
change to the old state of things did not soon
take place, to send her away for a time; or if,
as he suspected, George Cooper was mindful to
make her his wife, then to marry her to him at
once, young though she was. This last idea
seemed to quiet him a little, and as daylight
began dimly and slowly to define the objects
around him he once more fell asleep; but this
time it was a heavy slumber that lasted some
time over his usual hour for rising.

A few days after Cyril Treherne's visit
Cherry was endeavouring, for two reasons, to
get back into the old groove and fulfil her daily
duties as was her wont before Cyril had crossed
her path: the one was that her love for her
father was strong enough to induce her to make
the exertion, and the other—and the stronger
of the two—that time passed more rapidly
when she had any occupation on hand, and her
great longing was to drive on time as quickly

as possible, to bring round the day—though she had herself put it off a week—when Cyril would once more, and for the last time, be with her.

Mrs. Jackson had sent her some more needle-work, requesting her to complete it as soon as possible, as she had herself undertaken to send it back to her sister, who lived in London, in a fortnight at latest. Cherry knew this, and determined to oblige Mrs. Jackson, if feasible; and, after getting through her trifling household matters, bravely set to work, resolved not to let her thoughts interrupt her. Yet, unfortunately for Cherry, her brain was able to be as busy as her fingers, and it went on in a riotous manner back to the old story, thinking of the last visit and counting the hours till the next, wearing and tearing herself to pieces with the wildest conjectures as to the hour of his coming, and whether he really meant never to see her again, and, if he did mean it, whether life would be bearable to her. The head and hands were thus both employed, when a knock at the half-open door made her start from imaginary to real life. Her heart gave a great bound as she for one second thought it might be Cyril; but the next a feeling of anger took possession of her, as George Cooper asked if he might come in.

" I won't disturb you, Miss Cherry," he said, meekly, "so you can go on with that bit of work "—George thought he could even say what he had to say better with those great brown eyes looking away from him—" but I just wanted to tell you—I've wanted to tell you for a long time, but—"

" If it is anything I can do for you," said Cherry, as he hesitated, " I shall be glad to do it."

" It is, miss; it's a great deal you can do for me." And George now felt he could speak out; he had gained the courage he had again lost, as on the previous occasion, and so he resolved at all hazards to go on this time to the end, and say what he wished. " I told you, not very long ago, that in a few weeks my wages would be raised: well, I have been informed now the rise will begin on the first of the month; and I am here this morning, Cherry" (he ventured to drop the " Miss "). " to ask you if you will become my wife." George stood near the window when he began to speak; but he came nearer to her now, and, bending slightly over her, he pleaded his cause in an earnest tone. " I can give you a home, Cherry, as comfortable as you are in now, and soon it shall be better, for with you to work for no work will seem hard, and I will strive to make you happy. You don't know the strength and capabilities your love will give me. Tell me. Cherry, you will accept me; give me your hand, darling, and let me feel sure it is to be mine."

George's voice was not so firm at last. Cherry's head remained down, and her fingers worked on nervously and rapidly; she never ceased a moment, and never moved. The time had come at last that she so dreaded; she had felt sure it would not be long delayed—more sure than ever after George had had to play the groom for Cyril Treherne. She knew she must speak in the end, she knew her answer—her refusal—must be given, yet she went on working as if he had not even been present. He stood there with his hand held out, waiting, expecting, hoping; yet, knowing his hopes were vain, he had hardly dared to indulge them since that dark day to him—that dark day to her—that Cyril wound the circlet of love so tightly around Cherry's heart that the mere loosening it would prove a wounding process, done ever so gently.

"I can't, George," she whispered out, at last.

A feeling of something clutching his heart

a swelling in his throat, stopped his replying
for a moment. But men know better than
women how to master their emotions, and the
young quarryman was not long before he
gained sufficient control over himself to speak;
though any other than she to whom he addressed himself would have noticed the hesitation every now and then, the sudden pauses he
was forced to make, if he would not that she
should hear his voice falter.

"Is that the only answer you can give me,
Cherry? Will you not tell me the reason?
You do not—love another, do you? Oh, tell
me—tell me if it be so! Tell me, and then I
must never more hope to win you. But if it
be only that you do not love me, don't you
think, Cherry, you might some day? I will
wait, wait even patiently, if you but give me
a little hope—ever so little will give me courage.
Speak to me, oh, speak to me, and tell me that
in a few months, a year, even two, you will,
perhaps, be my wife!"

Cherry's hands fell; her fingers refused to
hold the needle: and, looking up for one moment at George's face, almost handsome with
its mournful, earnest, pleading expression, she
remembered Cyril's words,—" I don't like him;
you are too pretty to throw yourself away on

that awkward lout," and she regained the indifference that for a moment had been replaced by regret at the thought of giving pain.

" I shall never marry," she said : her voice sounded harsh, even to herself, and she endeavoured to soften it—to speak with more feeling, more gentleness. " Do not hope, George, for I feel sure time will not alter me; and it is better, you know, not to hope at all than be disappointed in the end. I am very sorry," she continued, presently, as he remained silent. " for you have always been kind to me, and father likes you. It is a pity you ever thought of me, for I am afraid it will make all uncomfortable."

" Not you. Cherry, I hope," said George, mournfully ; " not you. I may not, then, even hope that time will make a change ? "

He went on, in his despair, making one more attempt to soften her, never thinking—as at the moment none ever do—how utterly vain it always is seeking to change the heart's feeling through compassion. If love does not exist, commiseration will not give birth to it. Love alone never begets love : it is some sympathetic feeling calls it into existence ; you cannot force its growth or retard it.

"No use," replied Cherry, shaking her head slowly.

So George Cooper left her. This first blow in his life fell heavily on him; he seemed stunned by it. The world seemed suddenly to be a thing apart from him; he walked on with a weary burden, a weight to carry on his heart for many a long day. On and on he went, without thinking of turning towards his home, but always onwards till he found himself amidst the gaunt-looking rocks with sea-gulls hovering round him, and then he threw himself down close to the pale green sea, and, with no human eye to pry into his grief-laden heart, he gave way as men do give way once in their lives, and the strong, square-built form of the young man shook beneath the convulsions of his sorrow.

The sun was fast sinking into the outstretched arms of the broad Atlantic when George Cooper rose up and shook off, with a sullen, determined will, the paroxysm of agonizing grief he had endured—shook it off with a manly resolve to conquer his misplaced love, and not, like a weak woman, allow it to crush all his future.

It was a good resolution, at any rate, whether he were able or not to carry it out, for it helped him through with the first weary days and weeks of his disappointment. The only change those about him remarked was that he had grown somewhat taciturn, and preferred being alone to joining his friends in a walk, as had been his habit during the summer evenings, after his work was over.

CHAPTER XI.

"My dear Cyril," said Mrs. Treherne, one morning, "will you not go to London for a few days, or do something to cheer you up? You seem so dull that I think perhaps you want a little change."

Madam was anxious about her son, for, notwithstanding his occasional outbreaks with her on the one subject, which, now that he was of a more reasonable age, were half in joke, he was decidedly of a cheerful and good temper, but lately he had become irritable and gloomy. Mrs. Treherne had spoken to the admiral, but the dear, good man never saw anything wrong in any one. Cyril, no doubt, and very naturally, was worrying at old Thorpe's persistency in permitting no engagement, which virtually closed the doors of Yardley Wood to him as a lover, and admitted him only as an acquaintance. "Or," mumbled out

the admiral, "he was perhaps bemoaning the
loss of his yacht; and, if so, that evil was easily
remedied, if madam would not make a row
about it." But she seemed on the instant to
give strong evidence of intending to do so if
the idea were mooted. So then the admiral
muttered something about women's folly, and
offered no further suggestion. It was then
Mrs. Treherne proposed Cyril's going to
London, which, however, he somewhat indignantly declined, reminding his mother that
August was not the time of year for London.

"Can't you ask the St. Aubyns over? and
then the Thorpes will perhaps come," said
Cyril. "Ask them for the first of September,
It will get through a week or ten days, at any
rate. I must travel either by land or sea this
winter: I cannot go on with this idle life."

"I don't know what sort of life you would
lead, Cyril," said his mother. "You are rarely
at home more than two or three days together.
You only yesterday returned from Plympton:
before that you were with Major Kingsford:
and you can, if you choose, be visiting from
month's end to month's end, or invite any
one you choose here. If you want to travel,
you surely can be satisfied with Great Britain;
you need not cross the sea."

"There is nothing to do in England. The seaside places are crammed with snobs and children. You would not recommend my making a tour of the principal towns of England, mother, would you?" asked Cyril, with a smile.

"You might do worse. You know nothing of your own country, and there are some beautiful spots in it. At any rate, I should have thought you had had enough of the sea with your last attempt. By the way, that reminds me of those people who took you in. I saw John Finch the other day, and was asking him about them. I have always been wishing to go and see them, and take the girl a present of some sort."

"Oh, there's no need, madam; and it's a devil of a way from here," said Cyril, carelessly.

"Hush, Cyril! Do not use such shocking expressions! I have almost given up talking to you about religion, for you are so hasty, and try to stop me in so—so sharp a manner that it is very painful to me; but I cannot hear you say such wicked words and not tell you of it."

"The devil may be wicked, if there be one, but I can't see that the word is. However, never mind him, mother; you know neither I nor my father can please you on that one knotty point, so I 'll go, as I don't feel in the humour for discussing such nonsense."

"No, dear, don't go! You know I am never so happy as when I get a little chat with you, and it is so seldom I do. I won't talk any more on that subject, only if you can manage not to use those words it—well, well I won't; there, sit down, I won't say another word. I should like to go over and see those good people, Cyril; will you come with me?"

"I don't think I need go," he said, hesitatingly. "I will if you particularly wish it—it is something to do. after all," he added, getting up and pushing his fair curly hair off his broad forehead; and then, putting his hands in his pockets, he went out of the room, whistling.

Again then, with all the best intentions not to see Cherry any more. was Cyril almost driven to do so. He liked to think it was but right he should accompany his mother; it would seem strange and even ungrateful, after all their kind care of him. if he refused to go with her and jointly give them the thanks that were so thoroughly due. So it was settled that the first fine afternoon they were to start early and drive over.

The next morning Cyril Treherne rode into

Kingsbridge, the largest town within ten miles of Treherne Court, with the object of getting some little gift for Cherry. If his mother gave her a present, he ought not to go empty-handed. He made for the jewellers—no Storr & Mortimer or London & Ryder, yet a very decent shop for all that, and with a very fair choice, so he was sure of finding something quite pretty enough for what he required. After the whole contents of the shop had been displayed to the best advantage, Cyril picked out a plain gold locket, with a pearl horse-shoe on it, and a chain. First wrapped in white silver paper, and then put into a nest of pink wool, and finally into a white cardboard box with gilt edges, with B. Baker, jeweller, Kingsbridge, in gold letters on it, Cyril placed it in his waistcoat-pocket, and rode back to Treherne thinking of Cherry's large eyes, and wondering if that strange startled expression in them would give place to one of pleasure when he gave her the locket, or if he should again see that look of deep love, the same as when he last bade her farewell. Poor Cherry! Her love was deep—a hungry, craving love, and she had tasted its sweets, and now would never rest till she drank down to the bitter dregs.

When Cyril reached home he found Lady St.

Aubyn and her son with his mother; they had driven over to see if Mrs. Treherne would consent to go over to the annual school feast which was generally given at Stanmore during the month of August. Mrs. Treherne was excessively fond of school feasts, and rarely refused; but she was just telling Lady St. Aubyn as Cyril entered that she was on the point of writing to her to ask her to spend a few days at Treherne, taking in the last day or two of August and the first week of September, and she feared that the feast might clash with the arrangement, as the month was already nearing its close.

"Why so, madam?" asked Cyril. "The school feast is next week, you say; what day, Lady St. Aubyn?"

"Wednesday."

"Well, then, surely you can go over to Stanmore on Wednesday, mother, and you can all come to us the next day, Lady St. Aubyn, can't you?"

"No, Cyril, I am afraid not, for the house will be full. The Delafields and Dawsons and my sister and her husband and the Thorpes are coming."

Cyril bit his lips with vexation. The Thorpes were to be at Stanmore instead of Treherne, and that owing to his mother's tardiness in asking them; and the pleasant days he had anticipated during the September shooting were slipping away from him. It was very provoking, especially to Cyril, for no man hated being thwarted more than he did.

"But, Thyril," said Charles St. Aubyn, " you can come and stay with uth. It would be precious hard lineths if you could not when Willie Thorpe ith to be there."

" Well, Charles, I am afraid—vexing as it is to me—I dare not second your invitation. Mr. Thorpe begged me not to ask Cyril whilst Willie was with us."

" What a jolly old papa!" exclaimed Charles. " Were I you, Treherne, I'd come in thpite of him. Milady may keep to her promith, if she gave one; but I may athk a friend if I like, I thuppose, and if you don't come, old fellow, it'll be your own look-out."

" Well, Cyril," said Lady St. Aubyn, "come with your mother at any rate on Wednesday, and then we will try and get Mr. Thorpe to ask you himself."

" Much obliged, Lady St. Aubyn, but I would rather accept Charles's invitation than Mr. Thorpe's," replied Cyril, annoyed at Mr. Thorpe's precautionary measures. " However,

I will be with you on Wednesday, when your company is expected, I suppose, to distribute tea and buns till the other company bursts: then we may begin to think of amusing ourselves."

"Really, Cyril," said Mrs. Treherne, "Lady St. Aubyn must think you have very little feeling for your fellow-creatures; for we are all one, remember, in the sight of God, the rich and the poor, the high and the low; and to talk of feeding them till they burst!—not a pretty word in any case; and it is very uncharitable, very un-Christianlike. I think our dear Mr. Snape would feel ill were you to speak so in his presence."

"That is what I am never likely to do. Your dear Mr. Snape and I will never hit it off, you may be very certain. But, Lady St. Aubyn, when does the cramming begin?"

"The children are to come at two," replied Lady St. Aubyn, smiling, "and they are to have fruit to begin with; then follow all sorts of games, which will last till five; then will commence what you term the cramming, which, I imagine, will last fully an hour; then from six to eight they may amuse themselves in the gardens; and at eight there will be sandwiches and negus; then all go home; so that I hope by nine the grounds will be cleared and the gates closed. There is the programme."

"And if they can't go home? It is very possible, after all that eating and drinking, that they will not be able."

"Then they muth be carried," said Charles, "and you and I will help, Thyril; we'll thee to that!"

"So then I may reckon on you all?" said Lady St. Aubyn—"the admiral as well?"

"Here he is to answer for himself," said Mrs. Treherne, as at that minute her husband entered. "My dear, you will go with us to the school feast at Stanmore next Wednesday?"

"Of course, of course. It's all so much in my line, you know; and I enjoy the sight of a herd of uncouth boys and girls eating to suffocation. If I went it would be to go round afterwards and distribute a glass of senna tea to each gorged child. No, it's a horrible sight! Leave me at home to myself. I will go some other day. I should only be in the way of every one, and every one in mine. How is Sir Gilbert, Lady St. Aubyn?"

"Quite well. You are just like him, admiral. He would run out of the place if I did not make it a serious point with him to stay. It *is* a bore, I really begin to think my-self; still one must do these things, and do them so that the poor people should imagine it to be a pleasure to us as well as themselves. Then our rector would be hurt if he fancied we were really put out by giving it. So I put the best face on the matter I can, and try to induce as many of our neighbours to come as possible, to give an appearance of united enjoyment. I need not tell you, however, I shall wake up this day week relieved to feel Wednesday is over."

" Then how have you the conscience to ask me?" said the admiral.

" Ladies have elastic consciences, have they not, Mrs. Treherne? Besides, we are old friends, and I thought I might ask you to come when I should *not* have had the conscience to ask one I did not know or like as I do yourself."

" There's a cunning woman! After that, how do you suppose even a rough old sailor like myself can refuse you? Why, not alone must I go, but I must work too, I suppose."

" I shall be satisfied with your coming," said Lady St. Aubyn, rising and preparing to leave. " I have indeed gained a victory," she added, smiling; " so now I had better go with triumph in my train, and not stay longer, for fear of giving you time to change your mind."

"Why, do you think we sailors resemble our favourite element? Do you think we are tossed from resolution to indecision as the billowy sea is changed with every wind?"

"I do not know that instability belongs to sailors more than others; but I think that once you have succeeded in getting a man to arrive at a happy determination it is as well to leave him, and not tempt Fate by opening a possible way for change: and one never knows where conversation may lead us, or what lightly falling word may arrest him in his good intentions. If I stayed on much longer chatting with you, how do I know what horrible bugbear I might give rise to in your mind that would effectually keep you away from Stanmore on Wednesday next? No, no: I am one of those people who like to leave well alone. So good-bye, my dear Mrs. Treherne, till Wednesday."

"Well, Thyril, old fellow, don't you let yourself be that upon by Papa Thorpe. He'th a good thort of man, no doubt, ath a whole parent, but ath a half one he muth be horrible. Take my advithe and come over nexth week and stop with uth, regardleth of the old gentleman."

"Thanks, Charley, we'll see when I am there. I will come over with my father and mother on Wednesday, at any rate. When do the Thorpes go to you, Lady St. Aubyn?"

"Not till Tuesday. There are more visitors for you, Mrs. Treherne. We really must go, Charley, or we shall not be home in time for dinner."

As Lady St. Aubyn and her son were leaving, Mrs. and Miss Henderson walked in. They exchanged a few hasty words of greeting in the old oak hall, and then each went their way. Mrs. Henderson wondering whether, Cyril Treherne having slipped through her fingers, Charles St. Aubyn would not be an equally good *parti* for her Harriet; and a sudden thought that he would made her turn round to say something more, which something was intended to bring about a more friendly feeling between them. But it was too late: Lady St. Aubyn was just stepping into her carriage, helped by Cyril, who, the instant the carriage drove off, passed round by the stables to the little private entrance leading to his own rooms, thus escaping Mrs. Henderson and her daughter altogether. The admiral was equally alert. He passed out through the drawing-room into the library, going out from there by the window, and then he joined his son in his sanctum. So Mrs. Treherne had to entertain the two ladies by herself; but it was not a difficult task. She liked the conversation in which Mrs. Henderson invariably indulged, and though there was a certain amount of jealousy between them, especially when they differed in opinion, still they could easily manage to pass an hour together without the aid of others to help them through the time.

"I wanted to ask you, my dear friend, if you would join me in undertaking the district of West Sandcombe?" said Mrs. Henderson, after having discussed the weather and Lady St. Aubyn's dress till both would have been threadbare, could words wear anything but the human mind. "I mean, of course, Mr. Snape's district. He came to me yesterday, and asked me if I could help him. There are, it seems, fifty families, and all starving, soul and body; and our dear Mr. Snape says he will look after their souls if we will attend to their bodies."

"You mean, I suppose, if we feed and clothe them, he will preach to them and give them tracts to study?" said Mrs. Treherne.

"Yes, exactly; that is it," replied Miss Henderson. "So good of him, you know, to

give his time up to such people; and they are
such a miserable, wicked set.   Just think, only
yesterday afternoon that little good-for-
nothing Tommy Rose stole a loaf of bread from
Hook the baker, and, when he was caught, he
cried out that he stole the bread because his
mother was starving, and she would die if she
had not even a bit of bread. So Hook, on
hearing that, refused to give the boy in charge.
You see Hook does not attend chapel, and is a
worldly, godless man; but Mr. Snape had Tommy
shut up in the school-room coal-cupboard for
twelve hours, and only gave him one piece of
dry bread and a little water; and when he was
let out this morning it was horrible to hear all
he said,—it made poor dear Mr. Snape shudder,
and to silence him he told him if he did not
hold his tongue the devil would come in the
night and carry him off when no one would be
near to save him, and that he would burn and
burn everlastingly. Then he said if his mother
died, he, Mr. Snape, was the murderer: that
he had robbed his mother of her allowance to
send out a couple of pick-pockets to steal from
the heathens all they had; but he did not seem
quite to know what that was, for when asked
he said, ' Their ignorance, to be sure; what's
the use of upsetting their contentment ?' Then

he went on to say he had heard Mr. Parker say nothing was more cruel than to let a person see a little light, and leave them ever after in their former darkness, and that ' that was what Snape did ' ! "

" And can you imagine, my dear Mrs. Treherne, the insolence of that boy, speaking to that good, holy man, and to his very face, as Snape ! " said Mrs. Henderson, interrupting her daughter, who, she thought, had been talking quite as much as she had any right to do, and even more than her rightful share. " It was excessively ill bred and unbecoming in Mr. Parker to speak of him as ' Snape '; but, for that Tommy Rose, he ought to be beaten into better behaviour."

" That is just what Mr. Snape said," put in Miss Harriet.

" So you see," proceeded her mother, " the set we should have to look after. Tommy is only a type of the rest; not a very promising lot, I fear. Harriet and I have just been to see if the Howards would like to join us; but they are not a serious or righteous family, I am afraid, and the girls not well brought up. Miss Howard has a dashing, showy figure and an off-hand manner that may be taking with wild, fashionable men: but it is not that which attracts a sober, steady, religious young man; it would frighten him. And so, when they declined, saying they thought they were not fitted for it, I was very much inclined to agree with them; and that Mr. Snape would be driven out of his senses if he saw a mass of bright colours and clouds of tulle and muslin filling up one of our modest little cottages. Miss Mary said poor people always had catching diseases, and she should be afraid; besides, she hated dirt, and they were always dirty. I tried to talk to her of the dirt of our own evil natures, of our duty to our fellow-creatures, of the sweet example of the best of Christians, our dear Mr. Snape, who never allows distress or disease in any form to stay him in his work; and I pointed out the infinite pleasure of trying to make others do right. But I do not think they heeded me much; I fear, at least, they did not."

" I am sure they did not, mamma: for Miss Howard was counting the money she had in her purse, and then said something about ' that horrid dressmaker's bill,' and that her father was very mean and would not help her: and Miss Mary was making most extraordinary faces at some one,—I could not see whom, for it was only her face reflected in the glass that I saw. Perhaps the faces were at the thoughts of the poor."

" Ah, they will come to some shocking end, if they do not alter! I wish Mr. Snape would try to take them in hand."

" I heard he was going to buy, or had done so, a pony and carriage; is it true?" asked Mrs. Treherne.

" Yes, I believe it is," said Mrs. Henderson, rather shortly.

" But how can he possibly afford it on his 'no income,' as he always calls what he has to live on?"

" I do not know," was the curt reply. " People know each their own affairs and means. I suppose he has come into a little money."

" Very probably."

And Mrs. Treherne recollected that five hundred pounds had been collected some little time back for sending two missionaries out to China, and perhaps it did not take the five hundred quite, and perhaps— And here a wicked thought suggested itself, as wicked thoughts will suggest themselves to the best of us; but it was instantly crushed, and the poor old admiral came in for abuse in consequence, for she invariably argued, " I never should have thought such wickedness possible had the admiral not so often dinned into my ears that people did do those sort of things; truly 'evil communications corrupt good manners'!"

After a little more conversation, in which Mrs. Treherne consented to help Mrs. Henderson in visiting this Snape district as far as it lay in her power, for she was not, as she reminded her friend, a free agent like herself, the Hendersons left. As they drove away, the mother remarked to the daughter,—

"How thankful we ought to be, Harriet, that we are as we are, and have remained pure and unspotted from the world! I fear poor Mrs. Treherne is falling into the ways of the devil, like all the rest of them!"

"Yes, mamma, I think you are right. She is less anxious about the precious doctrines of our good Mr. Snape, and I did not see a single Bible on the table,—not even a tract was there lying about. She still keeps to the cold dinners on Sundays, though; and you know, mamma, we have given that up, unless there is any one with us to see it."

"Yes, dear; example is better than precept. Eating cold dinners with no one to see you practising self-denial is no better than precept but doing so when you have visitors staying with you is example.”

“ Oh ! ”

And mother and daughter relapsed into silence.

CHAPTER XII.

FIVE days more before Cyril Treherne could hope to see Willie. A long time when the heart is anxious; then the hours seem longer than their rightful sixty minutes, and the days seem to have eight-and-forty hours in them at the very least; still, for all that, the sun goes to rest at the usual time, and rises to bring in another day to the world not one second later than he should; he goes on his even, steady course, regardless of human passions and human desires.

"Will you drive over to Shelton to-day, madam?" asked Cyril on the Saturday morning, Friday having proved doubtful as regarded the weather, and it was too long a distance to go with a showery sky, threatening rain every half-hour.

"I can't to-day, Cyril. I am so sorry, dear, but Mrs. Henderson sent up a note to me this morning, begging me to be with her by three, and I sent back word I would.”

“ What is that canting old humbug wanting with you ? ”

“ Do not call her such horrid names, Cyril. She is a good woman, a holy, Christian woman, devoting her time and means to good works; and she wants nothing with me, it is only that I undertook to help her with some poor people in the neighbourhood, and it is but right I should. We ought to help our poorer brethren more than we do. I sometimes think I am growing a very wicked woman, I do so little for others.”

“ I only hope you are not going to let yourself be led by that Methodist and her grenadier daughter! ”

“ Do you not admire Harriet Henderson, Cyril ? ” asked his mother, in simple surprise.

“ Admire her ! ” and he laughed at the bare idea—a natural, joyous laugh, for it was genuine. “ Can I, mother, possibly admire a gawky, hard creature like that?—a female, if you like, but hardly a woman ! ”

“ I do not know what you mean,” retorted Mrs. Treherne, in an offended tone. “ I thought a woman was a female.”

“ Yes, generally they are; but a female need

not of necessity be a woman. But never mind those two. So you cannot go with me to Shelton; it is a fine day for a ride, so I will ask my father to go with me to Dartmouth."

" Dartmouth is a long way, Cyril. If Monday be fine, I will go with you to see these people, if that will do."

" Oh, perfectly !"

Cyril went out of the room whistling, to seek his father. But the admiral could not go with him to-day either; he had some people coming from Exeter touching the sale of a farm, and he must be at home when they arrived. So Cyril, thrown back on himself, ordered his horse to be saddled and determined to ride over alone to Shelton ; it would, at any rate, occupy the remainder of the day, and bring him one nearer to the wished-for Wednesday. He remembered, also, that the fortnight elapsed that very day ; and he had promised poor little Cherry to see her once more at the end of that time—once more, and no more ! And now, how delighted she would be to hear that on Monday she would see him again ! though he would not tell her that till after a while ; she should imagine his mother only was to go. Then his little gift ; he felt glad he should be able to give her that when alone with her; if any one were present he would not be able to see and enjoy her pleasure. So all things combined to make him think it would be advisable for him to go over to Shelton that Saturday afternoon.

It was a pleasant ride for a bright August day over the wild sandhills, and then down into the narrow lanes, where the banks on either side were laden with summer flowers; then up again on to the heights looking down on the broad blue sea, and watching the white-sailed ships skimming over its shimmering waters. Cyril Treherne never saw the sea without longing to be on it. It was a pity he was not a sailor by profession; he would have made a good one. As it was he never grumbled at any roughing when afloat, however he grumbled at the least want in his daily comforts ashore. He would throw himself down in his berth, and with a rug over him sleep as soundly as a child; yet at home if there happened to be a fold in the sheet his mother was sure to hear of it at the first meeting the following morning.

He walked his horse along the edge of Oswald Hill, which rose up perpendicularly from the great extent of sand that about a mile further on joined the Shelton sands, whither he was bound. It was a dangerous path in winter—indeed at any season when the wind blew off the land. But all was calm now, even the fine grains of sand lay still amidst the hard, harsh grass growing out of it here and there, giving a verdant hue over the hill when seen from a distance.

"Why should I not go somewhere for a month or two?" thought Cyril, as he sauntered along, his eyes fixed on a little ship, not unlike his own ill-fated Marguerita. "It is true, Willie has asked me not, but that is all folly; if I could always be with her, or even see her when I liked, it would be another matter. Why, I am not even allowed to be invited to the St. Aubyns' because she is to be there: it's simply absurd! I really will have it out with old Thorpe on Wednesday, and either he shall give in a bit or I'll be off to the Mediterranean."

Cyril, having come to this determination, turned his horse off from the brow of the hill; and, touching him lightly with his spurs, rode quickly on till he came in sight of the little cottage, then he reined in, and walked slowly up to within a few yards of the door. As on his last visit, he dismounted before getting to the window, so that he saw before he was seen. There was no George this time, but Miles Mason was at home; however, Cyril went up and knocked with the head of his whip against the door. The coastguardsman looked round; for a moment a dark expression crossed his face, but it was soon swept away by a look of welcome.

"I'm glad to see you, sir; it's very kind of you to think of coming all this distance; or perhaps, sir, it's something I can do for you. Come in, sir; come in."

Miles had stood filling up the doorway at first, as much as to say he had no intention of admitting his guest.

"I merely came to shake hands with you, Mason, and to see how you and your daughter are. I can't forget, you know, that I owe my life, perhaps, to you. How is Miss Cherry?"

Miles turned round. "Cherry, where are you, girl? She was there this moment, sir; I didn't notice her leaving the room. She's well, I thank you." Then, in a louder and, to ears familiar with the man's usual voice, an angry tone, he called to his daughter, "Cherry, come here; you're wanted."

A moment after Cherry opened the door—the one that led into the room Cyril had occupied. Her face was flushed, but her hair had evidently just been smoothed, and her dress was perfectly fresh, clearly just put on. Her father looked at her with an expression that boded nothing pleasant.

"What have you been about? What's this for? Do you mistake Saturday afternoon with all your work on hand, for Sunday? Go and put on the frock you had on just now, and take off this red piece of finery," he continued, with a pull at the little ribbon poor Cherry had hurriedly twined round her hair, and which seemed to have as enraging an effect on Mason as a red rag has on a bull.

All this while Cyril, who was standing inside the cottage, but holding his horse's reins over his arm, felt extremely annoyed. He pitied poor little Cherry with all his heart, and longed to comfort her; but even by a look he could not do so, for her great brown eyes were fixed on her father, and she never removed them till he finished speaking. Then, with an effort suppressing the angry feelings his words had aroused, she spoke very calmly,—

"I thought Mr. Jackson was coming, and I was not fit to be seen."

"You 're lying, girl!" shouted Mason; and he neared his daughter in a menacing manner.

The girl never stirred; but Cyril quickly fastened his horse to the handle of the door, and came inside.

"Don't be angry with her, Mason," he said. "After all it is no great crime to like a little dress, and all girls are the same; and if she expected Mr.—Mr. Somebody, why, it was but natural she should try to look as well as she could."

"But it's a lie, sir! She knows as well as I do that Mr. Jackson is busy writing his sermon on Saturday afternoons, and that he never comes at this hour on any day."

"Because he never has is no reason why he never should," replied Cherry, crossly; "and if it isn't Mr. Jackson it is Mr. Treherne, and I suppose I am best tidy, am I not, whoever it is?"

"If you put it on that, why, it's another thing," said her father, his passion moderating, meeting with a spirit in his child he had never seen before astonishing him. Had she appeared frightened, he would have waged war still further, but finding opposition and a defiant manner rather cowed him; besides, he recollected he was perhaps making a great fool of himself before this gentleman, as, if there were no reasons for the suspicions that had for some time been taking root in his breast, he was creating a cause for them really to exist. "This is not a very agreeable welcome to you, sir," said Mason, presently; "but you see I must look after her; she has no mother, no female relation, to take care of her, and she's no longer a child. Won't you take some refreshment, sir?"

"I am very thirsty; if you will give me a glass of water—"

"You can manage that, Cherry, I think," said her father.

Without a word, the girl went and fetched it and brought it to Treherne—the tumbler, a show glass, with little balls of crystal studded over it, and the water looking so clear it was hardly visible. As Cyril took it from Cherry's hand, he managed to touch hers without her father noticing it, though he saw the look the girl gave as he did so—a look, rough sailor though he was, he understood but too well. He read it as correctly as did Cyril, and the father's heart sank within him. It was no longer anger he felt, it was fear, and the worst form of fear, for he feared for the loss to his child of that which is dearer far than life, the loss of peace of mind, and—virtue. He sat a few minutes without speaking, his hands clasped between his knees and his head sunk.

"Are you ill, father?" asked Cherry, as her eyes rested on his pale face. She spoke kindly; she had softened, and was again her own self; the mere touch of Cyril's hand sufficed for that.

"No, child! oh, no, I'm not ill! What made you think of such a thing?"

He tried to laugh, but it was useless; it was a miserable attempt only. Cyril understood it all, and was pained at the poor man's but too evident distress, and repented, as he had done once before when Willie was by his side, of his folly. He was vexed, too, at the father's clear-sightedness; better far had he been blind, especially in his position. But fathers and mothers, too, are apt at times to be blessed with understandings and eyesight utterly out of keeping with their positions. It may have been very annoying for a coast-guardsman to see the love that was growing up in his daughter's heart past her management, whatever a Mr. Thorpe might do, nor need he have read the expression of those wondering eyes which, with all the years Miles Mason had watched over his child, he had never seen in them before, and it was that which struck such cold terror in his breast, and which made him curse the storm that led to his sheltering Cyril Treherne in his humble, honest home.

The hour for his returning to his duty was come and past; still he could not go and leave Cherry by herself with that man, who must know what the girl could not, and seemingly did not, attempt to hide from him. Now how he longed for a wife or a sister to look after her; he felt so helpless.

"Do you go back by Oswald Hill, sir, or by the lower road?" asked Mason, looking up at the big Dutch clock.

"I came by the hill," replied Cyril, "but I thought of returning by the other way; it is quite chilly upon those downs after five o'clock."

"I am going that way, sir, and could walk a bit with you, if you would allow me."

"By all means," said Cyril, wishing at the same time some blessed chance would take him off, for a minute only, that he might have a word with Cherry, and give her the little trinket; then, recollecting he would see her again on Monday, he thought it would be best to communicate his mother's intention to Mason.

"My mother has been intending every day, for weeks, to drive over and see you, but one thing or another has occurred to prevent her. She hopes, however, on Monday to do so."

" I am very much obliged, and feel honoured by the intention. But we are but poor, hard-working people, and I think it does us no good, sir, to see too much of the gentry; it makes us dissatisfied with our lot, and we don't work so easily when we are discontented ; and may-be it would be better if your lady mother didn't come, sir, nor—you either, sir. You see, it can't do me nor my girl any good, and it may do us harm. I hope you don't think me—think me rude, sir ? and—I 'm ready, sir, if you are."

" No, Mason, I do not indeed think you— rude, or anything but honest and straightfor-ward ; but I think it might pain my mother if I told her you refused to accept her thanks for all the care you took of her son ; so, if you will see her on Monday, she shall not trouble you any more."

" It isn't trouble, sir,—that 's not it ; and— it 's not your lady mother, of course ; but—of course I 'm honoured in seeing her—but, but— well, sir, shall we go ? "

Cyril could hardly help smiling at poor Mason's anxiety to get rid of him. There clearly was no chance of having a word with

Cherry this time, or of giving her the locket. Well, perhaps it was best; and as Mason was standing at the door, waiting for and watching him, he held out his hand to the young girl, and bade her good-bye, then, mounting his horse, he and Mason went away together.

When they were gone, Cherry, with her finger resting on her rosy, pouting lip, and her foot tapping the floor with angry disappointment, tried in vain to console herself with the knowledge that she would see him again on Monday. But, then, on Monday his mother was to be with him, and of course her father would be there: moreover, by her father's manner and words she was perfectly aware he guessed at the truth, and would he, therefore, ever give her a chance of seeing Cyril again alone? The whole time of his visit had been a torture to her. She had not had a word, not a look, from him, only that one little touch of the hand, which was like an electric shock to her, and, for a second, sent a thrill of pleasure through her. He looked so handsome, so well dressed; the fine cloth, the white linen, the polished boots, the well-fitting gloves, all helped in their way to increase the girl's mad infatuation. Tears of vexation rose and glistened in her large eyes, as she mourned the opportunity lost of hearing him say some loving word to her. Then a sudden idea flashed through her brain; if he went home by the lower road she might overtake him if she went by way of the rocks—for road there was none, but by climbing over those dreadful jagged rocks she came in, at the distance of about a mile, almost four miles ahead of the road he took. She knew her father would be on his beat, so on that score she felt safe; and as quickly as her nervous fingers would permit, she prepared to put her plan into execution, and see Cyril, come what might.

She closed the door of the cottage, and, putting the key in her pocket, she started. It required the alacrity and activity of the chamois to clamber up and down the sharp-pointed rocks over which her way lay, but she did it with a quickness and security that seemed almost unnatural. In twenty minutes from the time she left home she found herself overlooking the road by which she knew Treherne must pass, with only a hedge between her and it. She thought at first of getting over it, and waiting in the road itself, but then a foolish dread of a very improbable occurrence decided her on remaining where she was. Her father, she thought, might be with him yet, and in that case she should see him in time to prevent herself being seen; so she stayed where she was. So impatient was she, or Cyril was really long in coming, that she began to think he must already have gone by. She wondered at last how long she might safely wait there. She could not stop till evening. Her father's movements were sometimes uncertain, he would come in when unlooked for, and not, perhaps, when he was expected; in short, she was beginning to get frightened at her own temerity, and almost to wish herself back again, for it seemed as if, after all she had done, she was not to be rewarded with a sight of him.

"He must have gone by Oswald Downs." she thought; "and I might as well have spared myself all these scratches and bruises, that in my hurry I could not escape. If I only knew the hour!"

After stretching her neck, and looking as far down the road as she could, she was about to turn back, with a heavy heart, the way she had come, when she heard the distant sound of a horse's feet echoing up the road. Her pulses beat almost as fast as the quick tread that had sent the blood up into her cheek. In a few seconds she saw Cyril coming along at a quick pace, and alone. Now she must scramble over the hedge, so as to prevent his passing without seeing her, which, at the rate his horse was trotting, was not an unlikely occurrence. She looked right and left in the hopes of seeing a gate or an opening by which she could pass, but in her fear and anxiety she saw neither, so she made an attempt to get over it, and was in its very midst when Cyril came up. He was passing on, looking neither to the right nor left, when the young girl's voice arrested him.

"Mr. Treherne!" Then much louder—"Mr. Treherne!"

He saw her now.

"Oh, if you please, sir, stop a minute! I want to speak to you."

"Cherry! how did you come there?" He reined in his horse, and then went close beside the hedge. "Is it really you? And what are you doing in the middle of that hedge?"

All scratched, and her best frock torn almost to shreds, poor Cherry looked an object for commiseration. She felt, too, in such a stupid, awkward position, she hardly knew whether to cry or to laugh.

"Here, let me help you," said Cyril, dismounting, and going to her rescue, for she found it impossible either to advance or recede.

After a scramble and breaking of branches to an extent that would have driven the owner of the field the hedge enclosed distracted, seeing a hole remained big enough for Cherry to pass out with ease, she stood on the road beside Cyril, with her eyes down, and her hands gathering together the tattered frock, that surely must have been made for the express purpose of getting into difficulties. Poor little Cherry! Like many others, she had yet to learn that will is the cause of woe.

"Well, have you nothing to say, Cherry? Don't look so cast down: I will give you a new dress. But what brought you into that hedge? Surely I left you at home, so how you got there is a mystery to me. You must have wings hidden somewhere under that little cape. Let me see—"

"I haven't wings, sir," said Cherry, in a petulant tone. She had expected sympathy for her troubles, and Mr. Treherne spoke rather too cheerfully. She wished she had not come. "I walked over by the rocks; it's a near way—and—now I'm going back again."

"Wait a moment. It is impossible you crossed those rough, slippery rocks for the sole purpose of getting fixed into a hedge and tearing your frock to pieces."

" I don't care for my frock."

" I did not say you did; but if your object
was merely to destroy it, you could have cut it
to ribbons at home."

" I didn't want to destroy it. Oh, why," she
broke out at last, with her lips quivering, and
her eyes filling, " why will you tease me! I
came—I came to see you, sir, because—"

" Well, Cherry, because—?"

" Because you said, a fortnight ago, this
would be the last time, and I could not bear
the thought of it!"

" But did I not tell you I should bring my
mother over to see you on Monday? I did
intend it to be the last time; but you see we
cannot always do the right thing even when
we try. The devil seems wonderfully fond of
affording us ways and means of indulging one's
inclination. I wonder if it is very wrong,
Cherry, to follow one's desires when they—"

" I don't know, sir," said Cherry, interrupting him. " I hope it isn't; that is, if your
desire is to come over to Shelton sometimes,"
she added, naïvely. " But I must go, sir," she
continued, glancing up at him for a moment. " I
have a long way to go to get home; the tide is
coming in, I can't go back by the rocks."

" Foolish child! And did you positively

come here merely to learn if I were coming on Monday ?"

"Not altogether, because I don't count Monday like seeing you; but to ask you to come once more—just once!" she added, her beautiful eyes pleading even more than her words.

Cyril seemed to hesitate a moment, and then he gave in; the temptation was too strong for him, and he promised. He was walking by her side slowly—they were going the right way for her—when she exclaimed, suddenly,—

"There's some one coming! How long is it since father left you? Which way did he go?"

"Don't be alarmed: your father left me quite half an hour ago; and he turned off to the left, going straight towards the sea. Look, it is not your father; the man is dressed in black. He is some one that does not know you, depend upon it."

"Don't leave me, please, sir, till he's passed."

So they continued their walk, and in a couple of minutes came on the man who had frightened Cherry down to pale cheeks and trembling limbs. He stared at both, and then at once addressed himself to Cyril.

"Can you tell me if I am on the right road for Sandcombe? Oh, Mr. Treherne. I think—I am not mistaken, am I ?"

"No,—I am Mr. Treherne; but you have the advantage of me, sir, for to my knowledge I never set eyes on you before. If you continue straight on you will find a sign-post about a mile or a mile and a half further on, indicating the road to Sandcome."

The person, the individual, the stranger, anything you like to call him, except gentleman, that addressed Cyril Treherne, was a man of middle stature, stout, with a sensual face, yet with an expression of humility and meekness pervading it. His features were small, with the exception of his mouth, and that was large, with thick, moist lips; his face was cleanly shaven; his hair—greasy and straight —was dark; his hands—none of the cleanest —were fat and podgy, with dimples where knuckles should be visible. He was dressed entirely in black, with a white necktie; the trousers were very glossy at the knee, perhaps from constant praying, perhaps from a troublesome habit of always rubbing his knees whenever he was sitting down. His whole appearance was anything but prepossessing,—even worse, it was such that most women would have made the same request Cherry did—not to be left within his power.

It is hard to explain what there is in some

faces so attractive, and in others so repulsive. You have only to look at some people without even speaking to them, single them out in a crowded room, and feel you can both like and trust them. So likewise can you in a glance point to those who repel, and give rise to mistrust and doubt. Such a one was the Reverend Samuel Snape, the Methodist minister of Sand-combe, and guide and director-general of Mrs. Henderson and her household, who, having had some hint that he might obtain some addition to his missionary fund in the direction of Shelton, had gone in search of it, and was now on his road home with a five-pound note more in his pocket than when he started. He accosted Mr. Treherne more with the object of finding out who that gentleman was, leading his horse and walking in a suspiciously slow way with (even in the distance he could tell) a young girl, than to learn his road, and before finishing his question he recognized the heir to Treherne Court; and, having shown his knowledge, he volunteered the same information concerning himself. He lifted his hat as he spoke, whether as a mark of respect to himself, or Treherne or Cherry, it would be difficult to say, but it seemed quite unnecessary; as he did so he showed the top of his head to be of a shiny baldness, and his forehead no bad shape. The man was evidently no fool—probably a knave.

"I have heard your name, sir," replied Cyril, haughtily. "That is your way, sir," and the young man pointed with his finger down the road he himself had just ridden over.

"You are not returning to Treherne, I suppose?" asked Mr. Snape, with a bland smile, thinking it would be a great stroke of fortune if he could be seen walking into Sandcombe with the young Squire of Treherne—an event that might possibly lead to that other so long desired of being invited to the Court.

"I am not accustomed to be questioned by tr—" ("tramps" he was going to say, but stopped himself in time) "strangers as to which way I am going. Good evening."

"Good evening, sir, good evening."

The Reverend Samuel bowed again, and smiled too, showing a set of long narrow teeth, that seemed to have descended from the gums nearly to the roots. That smile boded mischievous intentions; whether they would be effective or not remained to be seen; but he resolved if the fates were not against him to pay off that haughty young man who dared to talk to him in so arrogant a tone. However he walked on, and when a few minutes afterwards Cyril turned round he was no longer in sight.

"Now, Cherry, you are safe, and I will leave you. How long will it take you to get home?"

"Half an hour, if I run all the way," replied Cherry, dolefully.

"But you must not run all the way. You will not breathe properly for twenty-four hours at least if you do such a foolish thing."

"But I must, though, or I shall not get home till after six, and father may come in before that—he does sometimes."

"Then be off at once!" said Cyril, kissing her, as a matter of course; but very differently to the last time, and to Cherry it seemed cold and indifferent—a kiss without love, which in truth it was; for, though Cyril had won the girl's heart past reason or restraint, he loved her not himself. For all his folly and his thoughtlessness, his heart was true to Willie Thorpe.

So, on the whole, Cherry's escapade had not been fraught with pleasure. She walked on alone now, her heart heavy and her hopes disappointed; though she would have found it hard to say why, even to herself. Cyril had promised, independently of Monday, to see her again, so she might have been satisfied; but there was something in his manner, something wanting, that hurt her, and a cheerfulness about him she, in her sorry plight, had been unable to share or even like. Perhaps Miles Mason's outbreak had helped to bring him to his senses, and cooled down his ill-placed admiration, and so his embrace lacked the warmth the girl expected. He might have thought it well to go so far and no further, when he became aware of the depth of love poor Cherry was capable of feeling. It is easy to arouse passion, but not so easy to allay it, and he perhaps began to see he was on a dangerous path; however, whatever it was Cherry felt the difference, and was sad and weary accordingly. She forgot all about running; her one trouble quite deadened her others, and so she walked quietly, if not slowly, homewards.

About a quarter of an hour after Cyril had parted from her she again heard the ring of a horse's hoof along the road, coming at a rapid pace; as the sound neared, she turned to see who it was, and to her joy she recognized Cyril. She stood still, and he was soon by her side.

" See here," he said, taking the little box containing the chain and locket from his pocket, "I actually came over on purpose to give you this, and yet went away entirely forgetting it. Come close—do not be afraid, Bob won't kick—and I will put it on you."

Cherry, once again full of joy and hope, and her heart beating with happiness, received Cyril's gift with a blushing, smiling countenance.

"Oh, I thank you, sir; I thank you more than I can find words to express. This will ever be the most precious thing I shall possess." And she kissed the locket as she spoke.

"You might kiss the donor, I think," he said, smiling.

But too ready to give obedience, Cherry's lips were held up, and he stooped down and met them.

"Is your hair in it?" she asked, suddenly.

"No, little one, of course not!"

"Oh, do, do give me a little curl—do not refuse me; just one little bit to put in! You have plenty; you need not grudge it me."

"But I can't tear it out of my head. I'll bring you a piece on Monday."

"No, no, no; now; perhaps on Monday you may not have an opportunity of giving it me."

“ Well, then, on that next occasion.”

“ Oh, no; please now!　Have you not a knife ? ”

Cyril had a knife, so she asked him to bend down his head whilst she cut off a curl.　It was soon done, and a dozen such might have been taken without their being missed from his head.　One of his beauties was the quantity of rich-coloured yet fair hair.

Cherry now went home happy, and for the moment thoroughly satisfied.　She had advanced another step on that road that seen in perspective appears so fraught with bliss, but which has an invisible end—a deep gulf of misery, a gulf from which there is no escape but the grave.

Cyril had now to put his horse into a fast trot; he was late, and wished to get home. Within a few yards of where he had just parted with Cherry his eye caught sight of the figure of a man that he could have sworn was that of Snape, had he not, more than half an hour ago, seen him going at a good walking pace in advance of him; still he felt so convinced that he took the trouble of reining in his horse, and turned his head round to see.　True enough, there was Mr. Snape, now coming briskly along; but he would have passed by without appearing to see Cyril, if he had not himself been addressed.

"You seem to have made progress towards Sandcombe crab fashion, Mr.—Snake."

"Snape, sir, if you please; but, I beg your pardon, I am not clever at jokes." And Snape raised his hat.

"No, perhaps not, nor at minding your own business!"

Cyril felt morally convinced the man had been watching him. He wondered what he knew, how much he had seen. He could not ask him, so he once more started off on his way home, not drawing in rein till he reached the gates of Treherne Court.

"I think I may make something out of this," said Snape to himself, as he went cheerfully on. "I think Mrs. Henderson may work some good from such materials; and if I gain no tangible benefit by it, I may at any rate have the satisfaction of giving that young gentleman a few uncomfortable hours in return for his insolence." And, planning and plotting, he got along quite cheerily.

CHAPTER XIII.

If there is anything in general more stupid than another it is a school feast; doubly so to those who know neither the children nor the locality very perfectly. It would seem as if there must be some wonderful and unusual amount of good nature, of charitable sympathy with the less fortunate portion of our fellow-creatures, or something very weak in us, if we deliberately and freely go to one of those gatherings with nothing more in prospect than having to act the waiter to the best of our abilities; we must either have a good supply of the milk of human kindness in our composition or we must be wanting in the small quantity of moral courage that would enable us to say, No.

And yet at the great annual gathering at Stanmore there were those present who neither cared for nor knew the children, nor the districts they came from, and yet they were there, and, moreover, at their own earnest desire, with hope rising within them as the minutes flew by, till the moment came when it was either crushed out to the very death or fulfilled. It is so pleasant to go about for a few hours with a beating heart, anticipating every instant all sorts of pleasure and happiness, even at a charity-school feast, that it is not to be wondered if even such an opportunity is seized on by many for the crowning of their dearest wishes, when no better occasion presents itself. Few go to any gatherings—among the young, we mean—without having something in prospect that they hope may turn out as they wish.

So, at Stanmore on the Wednesday in question, besides the children—nearly two hundred in number, for they came from the villages all round within a circuit of three miles—there were at least a hundred other guests, and a quarter of them came to fulfil their own desires and hopes, regardless alike of charity boys and girls and hard-hearted fathers and selfish mothers. The day was propitious: it was one of those rare days we are occasionally favoured with in this prosperous country—a day that seems to have broken loose from its Southern

home, and, spending it with us, gives us a
taste of what we might enjoy five-sixths of the
year, were we not doomed by our position to
breathe our lives out in fog and rain and east
winds. The sun was shining out clearly in a
palish blue yet cloudless sky; there was the
least possible breeze, sufficient to temper the
heat and to prevent people who desired so
much to look well from having a reflecting
hue on their faces: for, perhaps, with all the
young ladies there assembled—the two Miss
Howards excepted—none dreamed of securing
themselves from such a contingency by the
application of *poudre de riz*. They were
mostly simple, natural English girls, who tried
to look their best, but knew nothing of
Rachaelism.

Sir Gilbert St. Aubyn, who loved show
intensely, and delighted in the lesser squires of
his neighbourhood seeing and admiring his
house and his plate, his gardens and hot-houses,
his wife and his son, his stables and his kennel,
was a victim on such an occasion as the present.
What could all that mass of puerile humanity
know or understand about his wealth and his
position? and though, as he entered tent after
tent, where they first assembled to be crammed
with fruit before the amusements prepared for

them were to commence, the children rose up, and, under the direction of proficient leaders, gave hearty cheers for the lord of the manor, he still felt it was a mere nursery doing him honour, a paltry, worthless imitation of the real homage from full-grown men and women which was his due.

So the affair to him was a bore, and he was heartily glad when his speech was over and the day past. He had neither hopes nor fears in the balance; neither pleasure nor pain in store for him.

Almost all the guests had arrived; the Trehernes were among the last. Cyril, anxious as he was to be there, wished the distribution of refreshment to be over first; he did not feel in a mood to be doling out strawberries and gooseberries to the thick-featured. heavy-looking crew of school-children: there were hands enough without his to minister to their voracious appetites; besides he had a kind of jealous dislike to seeing Willie Thorpe so employed, and it would have irritated him had he seen her flitting about in her pretty white muslin, done about with blue ribbons in all directions, attending to every one, and without the time to give him, perhaps, more than a passing look. Act the Second would be enough to endure, supposing he did not succeed in getting her to the opposite end of the grounds —to where the tents were pitched—before it began.

But Willie, who had arrived at Stanmore early in the day, was looking anxiously about for him whom for days she had been longing and hoping to see ; and as carriage after carriage drove up, and yet he came not, her heart began to feel heavy, and the day seemed to grow dull and all around uninteresting. She went in to do her part and help to distribute fruit and biscuits to the ever-hungry mouths of village children in a mechanical, silent manner that proved how far her thoughts were from her occupation. It was so hot, too, in those tents, and the buzz of voices, the clatter of feet kicking about, the misty atmosphere from the many people, all confusing and oppressive, made Willie feel her head light and dizzy. She slipped out at last, unseen by any but Harriet Henderson, who was one of those people that always saw what no one wished her to see, and heard what never was meant nor desired to reach her ears. Not that Willie cared two straws who saw her; she felt unhappy, and so longed to get away and alone to indulge in her disappointment. Perhaps, after

all, Lady St. Aubyn had not invited the
Trehernes. At that moment she would have
welcomed even Mrs. Treherne—any one who
could have given her news of Cyril. She began
to rebel at her father's hard restrictions, as
she sat under the shade of a large beech, far
away from every one, and only the buzzing echo
of many voices reaching her: if he thought
Cyril good enough for her husband, surely
there could be no harm in their meeting on
such occasions as this. Many married at her
age; she was not such a child after all, and
why should she be kept in tighter reins than
others? Willie Thorpe was beginning to learn
the lesson that is taught by the love that grows
stronger and stronger, to the exclusion of any
other. Up to within a very short time back
Mr. Thorpe held the first place in his child's
heart, and it was not in a moment he was
displaced; it was by degrees, yet therefore
the more indubitably. Had her father been as
indulgent on this point as he had been on all
others, Cyril and he might have been ever side
by side; but, as it was, she felt the one love, as
it hourly increased in depth and strength,
slowly but surely lessening the other.

"I had better never have seen him, never have
gone to Treherne, never have gone anywhere

till papa thought me old enough to marry, or
the promise given to poor mamma fulfilled,
than lead this sort of life for the next year
to come !" she murmured to herself.   Then
trying, it would seem, to vex herself as much
as possible, and render everything in its least
pleasing colour, she went on,—"Cyril himself
ought to stand out against it; he ought to say
that he won't give up seeing me, and if he do
not, then I am sure he does not love me, that's
all !"

And with flushed cheeks, and her laughing
blue eyes looking almost fierce, she resolved to
tell Cyril this the first opportunity.   It was not
far off, if she chose to avail herself of it, for
Cyril stood behind her, watching her usually
beaming, bright face, and wondered what
could have ruffled her into even a seeming
anger.

"How long, Willie, am I to stand here without even a glance of recognition ?" he said at
last, thinking he might be losing a few precious
moments that he might enjoy with her in
peace, if he did not interrupt her reverie.

"Oh, Cyril, you are come !" she exclaimed,
springing to her feet. "I am so glad ! I came
here to be alone ; I was so afraid you were not
coming.   Why are you so late ?"

And the cloud passed off her face, and it was once more all smiles and love and happiness.

" My own, my darling !" he whispered, and for one moment he wrapped her in his strong arms, and pressed her to his heart, " I have been looking for you for at least half an hour. I inquired of every one—your father excepted —and no one could tell me anything about you."

" I did not want any one to know : I wanted to be alone. I felt bored and tired and cross."

" And now—? "

" Now I am not—that 's all," and she looked up with a smile so full of contented love that Cyril's heart beat with happiness.

" I suppose we may sit here a little together, without fear of scoldings or cross looks afterwards. At any rate let us risk it, for I never get a word with you alone, Willie; we are kept as much apart as if your father had refused his consent to our marriage."

Willie was silent : now Cyril was with her she felt happy, and wavered as to telling him what her thoughts had been when he interrupted them. They were sitting side by side under the great beech, almost hidden by the sweeping branches that spread around, touching the ground. One little hand was imprisoned ;

the other Willie was pulling up bits of grass with. Her ideas were travelling fast backwards and forwards; she was undecided what to say, so she made no reply; yet she longed for him to know that she thought her father's prohibition as harsh and needless as he did.

"Imagine," he continued, "my jumping at an invitation to a charity-school feast as the only means of seeing you for a month to come! Do you know, Willie, your father made Lady St. Aubyn promise she would not ask me whilst you were here? It was Charley gave me the invitation."

"No, I did not, indeed; but I shall like Charley immensely from this time!"

Willie said this in a tone that implied she thought that a valuable recompense to any one, and sufficient to wipe out any debt of gratitude.

"It may be all very well for you to go on like this for another year, but I cannot,—I cannot indeed, Willie. You have no end of things you can occupy yourself with."

"No, I have not; what have I?"

"You have needle-work, and music, and reading, and then you have Dust and Snow, and you have your father, whom, I suppose, you love better than me, or you would not submit without an attempt, at least, at a remonstrance to his unjust determination."

"I don't love him better than you!" exclaimed Willie, pained into the admission by Cyril's taunt.

"Then why, Willie," he said, coming yet a little nearer, and bending fondly over her, "why not tell him he must not keep us so apart? Tell him he must let us meet in his house, and in my father's, and wherever chance may admit of it. Will you ask him this, Willie, or shall I?"

"No, no; I will speak to him."

An hour ago she was upbraiding Cyril in her heart for his not endeavouring to turn her father from his decision, and, now that of his own accord he proposed to do so, she was the one to prevent him.

"And if he refuse you must let me go away altogether. You must let me travel, Willie; for I feel, darling, I cannot stay here and not see you."

So Willie determined to speak to her father, and plead for Cyril and herself with all the fervency possible.

"We had better go now and join the rest, or we shall be having some one sent in search of us," she said, after they had been there more

than an hour, though it appeared a very short
one to both.

Reluctantly they left their retreat ; for it had
been a happy time to both, and it is so difficult
to feel sure of a happy hour in the future.
Willie had forgotten all her vexation from the
moment Cyril joined her ; and he, in the
pure enjoyment of her love, let no troubling
thoughts arise. Cherry never once crossed his
mind ; the lock of hair,—the few minutes he
managed to steal away with her on the Monday when he had gone over to Shelton with
his mother,—the promise extracted from him to
see her again,—the scared look when he told
her he was going to leave Treherne for a time,—
none of these recollections rose up to mar the
happiness of the moment. He loved Willie
with all the strength and intensity of which a
man's heart is capable. He cared for Cherry
but as a pretty, rustic child,—a plaything that
might, had she not been so sadly earnest in
her love, have helped him through his year of
probation ; but he knew her wild, uncurbed
passions must lead to trouble if he continued
seeing her, and he determined nothing should
induce him to go again to Shelton. In her
presence he was weak ; he made the last promise hastily,—she clung to him till he gave it,

and her father was almost within hearing. So it was with a heart free from care, and full of gratified love, that he, with Willie by him, walked round by the plantation to the flower-garden, and then on to the lawn, where all kinds of noisy games were going on. You could, however, detect at once the presence here and there of a teacher by the subdued manner of the children within their sight, and the half-shy look with which they answered when spoken to. They are terrible wet blankets everywhere, whether as a governess in a private family or school-teacher.

"Where have you been, Miss Thorpe?" asked Miss Howard, as Willie and Treherne joined a group that were holding counsel as to the propriety of having a little amusement themselves in the shape of a game at croquet.

"I have been enjoying my own company," she replied, smiling, "till Mr. Treherne happened to discover my retreat, and then we came to join you."

"They have been a long time about finding their way to us," said Miss Mary Howard, laughing, and in an under-tone to Miss Henderson.

"Yes, I think it quite shocking to see the boldness of—some girls. I suppose in this case

it arises from the want of a mother's care," was
the rejoinder in a higher key.

"We were debating the question of a game
at croquet, Miss Thorpe," said Captain Mayne,
who looked handsome enough, but too much
resembling the pink and white complexion and
back hair of the wax heads in a hairdresser's
window; "but we are not sure if, under the
circumstances, it is the proper thing to do."

"Considering the mission we are on here,"
said Willie, "I am not sure that it is, though
it would be nice enough, and better than standing doing nothing."

"We are surely not wanted simply to look
on that batch of children playing 'Hunt the
slipper,' and that other at 'Blind man's buff,'
or to form part of the audience of that magni-
ficent-looking magician."

"I wonder," said a tall, fair girl, standing
with the rest, "how it is all the children do
not want to see the conjuring: surely they
must prefer it to those stupid games."

"Oh, but Lady St. Aubyn arranged for fifty
at a time to witness it," said Willie, "or, of
course, the whole of them would rush to it."

"So that poor, wretched man must go through
his tricks three or four times!" remarked Miss
Howard.

"Holloa, Treherne! I 'm tho glad you 're come, old fellow," cried Charley St. Aubyn, coming up. "I thaw your mother, but I couldn't find you, and I wouldn't athk where you were because papa Th—oh! Mith Thorpe, how do you do?" said poor Charley, suddenly pulling himself up, for he caught sight of Willie's laughing blue eyes just in time to prevent his committing a complete blunder.

"Why, Mr. St. Aubyn," said Willie, enjoying his confusion, and perfectly understanding his greeting to Cyril, "you saw me when we arrived, and we lunched together; still, how do you do? I suppose you cannot ask a question that clearly shows a great interest too often."

"To be thure—yeth, I remember; I didn't mean to thay, 'How d'ye do?' but 'I hope you 're not tired.'"

"I don't think Miss Thorpe can be tired; at least, not from what she has done," said Mary Howard.

"Doing nothing I find awfully fatiguing at times," drawled out a handsome youth between eighteen and nineteen, brother to the tall, fair girl, who clearly had a very favourable opinion of himself.

"Try some other employment, Delafield,"

said Cyril; "it's quite time you should begin."

"So I will, my dear fellow. Let it be the game of croquet we have lost so much time in discussing."

"There are eight of us. We really might play a game, I think," said Captain Mayne. "Come, Miss Howard, will you nail your flag to my mast, and let us meet the enemy with our united strength?"

Miss Howard was charmed. She admired Captain Mayne's pink-and-white beauty; and having found, notwithstanding her best endeavours, she had failed in winning anything more than common civility from the two great catches in her part of the county, Cyril Treherne and Charles St. Aubyn, she thought she might, *faute de mieux*, make herself contented to become Mrs. Mayne. They would be re-marked as a handsome couple, at any rate for some few years to come, however little celebrated they would be for their wealth. So they all paired off, and beat a retreat to the croquet ground, a beautifully oblong piece of velvety turf, smooth, even, and soft; sheltered and enclosed by some magnificent shrubs, and double seats arranged in various corners.

They soon commenced the battle, and were

in the very thick of it, no one side being in a much better position than another, when a stoutish black figure appeared, coming in by a little narrow path behind where Willie and Cyril were standing, Miss Howard and Captain Mayne being near them. The intruder watched the game in silence for a minute or two; then the players absorbed his attention. On seeing Cyril Treherne he gave a slight start: from that time on he alone occupied him, and he had a fair opportunity of noting those hundred and one little attentions that men in love are apt to pay to the lady of their choice, and which they imagine are neither visible to, nor understood by, any other than the one to whom they are offered; so the man saw, more than once, Willie's little hand held captive, and saw the expression which accompanied a whispered word every now and then. He seemed immensely interested in this couple: neither they nor any of the others, with the exception of Miss Henderson, had heeded him; indeed, but one or two had seen him. Presently, as if he had observed enough, he crossed over to the other side and shook hands with Miss Henderson, taking off his hat twice,—once, no doubt, to her, and once to the company in general. After speaking a few words to the young lady, he returned to his original side, and again went off his hat.

"Mr. Treherne," he said, "I am glad, sir, to renew my acquaintance with you. You do not seem to remember me," he continued, as Cyril, having glanced at his smooth black suit and bald head, resolved to have a Tichborne memory, and with an inclination, scarcely to be called a bow, he turned round and addressed some casual remark to Miss Howard. "I had the pleasure of meeting you on the Shelton road last Saturday, when you were, like a true knight-errant, decorating the pretty daughter of Miles Mason."

"What d—d stuff are you talking? Who are you, and where do you come from, that you dare intrude yourself and your stupid inventions in the presence of these ladies?"

Cyril Treherne spoke loudly from anger— louder than he intended; his face was pale with rage and vexation, yet not paler than Willie Thorpe's, who, looking from the one to the other, hardly understood what was said, but feeling that a sudden darkness was shadowing over the brightness of her life. If Cyril did not know the man, why then that anger?

The game stopped as if by general consent. Truly Snape had taken his revenge. Miss

Henderson, who had heard—as all present had done—Cyril's violent language, came hastily over to where he was, and said,—

"Oh, Mr. Treherne, please do not talk so! This is Mr. Snape; do you not know him—our dear minister and guide, who never errs in—anything. I th-in-k he must have seen you, though I quite understand your—reluctance to —to having any act you committed thus publicly alluded to."

"Yes, sir, as Miss Henderson says," chimed in the Reverend Samuel, "I can *quite* understand your reluctance to listen to me, or perhaps recognize me; but, young man, as a minister of God, it is my duty to chide you when I see you thus going down hill to hell as fast as your evil passions—more uncurbable than four thorough-breds—are carrying you! I must reprove you, and—"

"Go to—!" Cyril. fortunately for ears polite, left out the locality to which he desired to send Mr. Snape: and then, turning round to Charles St. Aubyn, said, "Charley, shall I kick this psalm-singing hypocrite out of this place, or will you?"

"You may,—ith your affair: only I muth thay ith very hard to have our game thopped by thuth a row,—ith it not, Mith Athley?"

"Well, I don't know: I think. on the whole,

it is rather more exciting; only I did not hear the beginning, and so do not quite know what it is about."

"No more do I; only Treherne wanth to kick that black gentleman out, and I thuppothe the black gentleman would rather not."

"Oh, my dear Mr. Snape, pray come away! come with me! It is awful to think of your pure ears hearing such profane language! I wonder the earth does not open and swallow up people who talk so."

"Ah, my dear Miss Henderson," said Snape, bowing to every one, and then allowing himself to be led away, not with his usual solemn walk, but at a quick pace, as if with a certain dread a kick might yet come to hasten him, "this is a wicked world, and I am afraid the earth would cease to bring forth if it opened every time bad words were used or evil deeds done, for it would be incessantly gaping. Are we— quite out of reach of that violent young man— that hardened sinner?"

Harriet Henderson looked back. "Oh, quite; you are safe!"

The Reverend Snape drew a long breath; he was rather what is vulgarly called blown, and he stood still a moment to pant and puff and gain a little breath.

" A shocking young man ! " he said, at last ; " my life was not safe whilst within his reach. So that's the young lady he is engaged to ? " Harriet nodded her head. " A pert-looking girl, I think, but pretty—no doubt pretty ; so is the other. My dear Miss Henderson, where is your mamma ? "

" She was helping to place the buns round the table in the big tent when I left her."

" Let us seek her ; I would consign you to her care. I must return home at once, and I will call and see you to-morrow morning, between eleven and twelve."

CHAPTER XIV.

A CLOUD hung heavily over poor little Willie Thorpe's heart when she went to bed that night. There had been no opportunity for her to have an explanation with Cyril. Mr. Thorpe joined his daughter almost immediately after Mr. Snape had vanished, and, whether by accident or with premeditation, hardly left her side for a minute, till, just as Mrs. Treherne was bidding her hostess good-bye, Lady St. Aubyn looked round for Sir Gilbert, to ascertain if the lamps were lighted along the carriage-road through the park, as it proved to be a dark night, and the deer sometimes strayed across the road, which might cause accidents if there were not sufficient light. But Sir Gilbert was not to be seen, indeed he seldom was when he was wanted, so Lady St. Aubyn begged Mr. Thorpe to do the commission for her. Then Willie stole round to Cyril, who on his side had not done much to bring about a *tête-à-tête*, and, sliding her hand into his, unobserved in the dim light that the lamp gave, and which threw shadows on everything, she said,—

"When shall I see you, Cyril?"

"As soon as I can, my darling."

"I want to ask you something. That horrid man, Cyril!—his face haunts me, and—all he said!"

"It was not true, my own Willie." As Cyril spoke his expression changed from one of love to one of anger. "I never saw that man before—"

"It's all right, Lady St. Aubyn; the lamps were already lighted," said Mr. Thorpe, coming back, and at once acting as a repellent between his daughter and Treherne.

And so they parted. Willie found no comfort in the few hurried words Cyril had spoken. Thus the first disturbance of the hitherto unruffled waters of her life took place. It is a moment that must come to us all, yet it seems hard when it comes so early. We all know the trite saying that "Man is born to trouble." When that was spoken women were not much thought of; they were considered simply as a necessary ingredient to make up life, part of

the furniture, without which the world could
not be perfect, **but,** like the lower animals,
were not thought worthy **of** a hereafter, so
their pains and sorrows did not merit the least
consideration. But we have learnt a little more
than even that very wise author, who, with all
his fleshly failings, was considered almost god-
like as to knowledge, and we now admit that
women not alone suffer as well as men, but we
recognize their responsibility and their power
and influence, and no doubt, could we have
been behind the scenes, we should have found
Solomon as easily twisted round the finger of
his favourite wife as a clever man is in modern
times by the woman he loves, though he was
too sensible to see it, and too wise to acknow-
ledge it.

So Willie's troubles began after seventeen
years and a few months of unmingled happiness.　I suppose she was born to it, as man is;
but she did not take to it easily, as one might
imagine people who are fated to certain things
would.　She lay awake with old Snape's words
ringing in her ears.

"Like a knight-errant decorating the pretty
daughter of Miles Mason"!　Who was Miles
Mason; and how could Cyril decorate his
daughter?　There seemed hardly any sense in

it, yet every word was full of bitterness to the poor girl. *La nuit porte conseil*, and Willie determined the very next morning to speak to her father, and not wait till they returned to Yardley Wood. She could not endure the suspense; she could not live, she thought, through another night of doubt; she would speak to her father, and then write to Cyril to come to her, and she would hear all about this story of " decorating Miles Mason's daughter." Surely people did not decorate girls unless they had done some worthy deed, some brave action! Could this Miles Mason be the man who had helped to save Cyril on the night his yacht was wrecked? Ah, a light was gradually breaking in on her bewildered brain. And could the daughter be the same that tended him in the cottage? It might; and, if so, what more natural than that Cyril should show her in some marked way that he thanked her for her care? But then, if so, why did he deny it; and why did he seem so angry when that horrid, fat, vulgar man said he knew him?

Poor Willie! She was getting adrift again on the sea of doubt. She could make nothing of it, so finally she cried herself to sleep, awaking in the morning with swollen eyes and two dark rims round them, and a splitting headache to boot, thus feeling even more desponding than before.

Her appearance at breakfast was hailed with inquiries as to what was the matter with her. The table was well filled, and many eyes were turned on her when Lady St. Aubyn remarked on her miserable looks.

"You seem, Willie, as if you had been dissipating last night."

"Why, child, what is the matter?" asked her father.

"Nothing at all. I have an atrocious headache, caused by not being able to sleep, I suppose. I shall be all right after breakfast," she added, trying to look cheery, but failing completely.

"Want of sleep makes one look horribly seedy, doesn't it, Miss Thorpe?" said young Delafield.

"I dare say it does," replied Willie. "I 'll try and sleep to-night, so as not to look seedy to-morrow. You must have slept too much, Mr. Delafield, you look so fresh: or else you were too lazy to help yesterday, and so were not in want of rest."

"That 's just exactly what it was. But I did do croquet, did I not? I played vigorously till that extraordinary interruption. By-the-bye, aunt, who was that sanctimonious, stout old party who upset Mr. Treherne's equanimity by declaring he had seen him decking some fair daughter of Eve, or some other person's. on the high road. Treherne used strong language, by George! in reply."

"I really do not know who you can mean. I saw no one especially sanctimonious, unless Miss Henderson, and you could not mistake her for a stout old party." was the laughing reply.

"That's very cruel of you, Lady St. Aubyn," said little Mr. Dawson. "Poor Miss Henderson! I really do believe she wishes to be a saint, if possible."

"I am glad you put in that 'if possible.'" said Mrs. Prendergast, Lady St. Aubyn's sister, who, like herself, rather ridiculed the over self-righteousness of some of the Sandcombe people. "I doubt any saint ever permitting any claim to goodness in its true sense being recorded against the name of that young lady. She and her mother are the most detestable, overbearing people I ever met."

"Really, Maria, you are quite vicious. Did either mother or daughter sit upon your dress yesterday, or tear your lace?" asked Lady St. Aubyn, jokingly.

"No, neither calamity occurred."

"But what was all this about Treherne and an unknown individual?" at last asked Mr. Thorpe, who had been waiting impatiently for a pause to enable him to speak.

"Miss Henderson knew the man, aunty," said Constance Delafield, "and she said who he was. She was telling Mr. Treherne, who declared he did not know him. I think she said he was a deer-guide, whatever that may be."

"A deer-guide! what's that?" said several voices, amidst much laughter.

"Oh, some of your Devonshire offices, I take it," said General Delafield.

"What was the man like?" asked Mr. Thorpe.

"Horrible podgy," said Frank Delafield: "short, a round face, shining and bare, like his pate; small, nasty eyes; a watery mouth. That's his appearance, Mr. Thorpe: his dress all black, a white choker, and a hat that looked in a bad condition. I should think, from the way he stumped off with Miss Henderson, that he was not overburdened with courage; indeed I should say Mr. Treherne put him in an awful fright."

"Did you not see him, Willie?" asked her father.

During the whole of this conversation **Willie** had remained perfectly silent. She went on with her breakfast—it was a very light one—as if no one were present; and though she drank in with greedy ears every word that was said, she appeared almost unconscious that any one was speaking. She looked up when her father addressed her, her face was pale and her eyes heavy; to the father she looked very ill, but he was nervous and always anxious about her, and he exaggerated the evil.

"Oh, yes, papa, I saw him," was the answer. "Mr. Delafield has described him very well, I think."

She tried to speak cheerfully, and with a tone of indifference; but her eyes wandered round the table in search of Charley St. Aubyn. She had looked before, and not seen him, but she fancied she might, with all the faces there, have missed him; but he had not yet made his appearance."

"And do you not know who he was?"

"Not in the least."

In came Charley now, full of excuses and apologies for his being so late; but something went wrong, in the most aggravating manner, with his toilet, and hence his coming in when every one else had finished.

"We'll forgive you, Charley, if you can tell us who some mysterious visitor was that came yesterday, and seems to have spoilt more games than that of croquet. I think, from the description, he must have been one of the school-teachers," said Mrs. Prendergast.

"He certainly put an end to *our* game," said Frank; "but I for one don't owe him a grudge on that score, for I think we should have lost; so, as it was, we had the benefit of a doubt."

"How mean of you!" said Willie, trying now to talk, for fear of drawing more attention to herself by silence, but she could not get a cheerful expression over her face. She felt her mouth rebellious; you may command the eye, but the mouth will have its own way.

"Now, what is mean?—I appeal to you all, what is mean—in that? I declare, Miss Thorpe, you are very hard on me!"

"Hold your tongue, Frank, if you can, for a few minutes, and let us hear Charley answer his aunt," said the lad's father.

"I know whom you mean. It was old Thnape—holy Thnape!"

"Holy Snape!" exclaimed Sir Gilbert St. Aubyn. "Who asked him here?"

No one answered.

"Snape!" said several voices. "What

name!" "Mr. Snape!" said Lady St. Aubyn. But all were speaking together.

"Why, isn't that the Methodist fellow at Sandcombe?" asked Mr. Thorpe.

"The deer-guide!" said young Delafield, roaring. "Miss Henderson's ' deer-guide '! Your hearing is getting defective, my dear Conny."

"Well, I declare she said so," replied Miss Delafield, indignantly.

"You are very likely to be right, Constance," said Lady St. Aubyn; "for Miss Henderson always speaks of him as ' our dear Mr. Snape,' or ' our dear minister ' or ' dear guide.'"

"And why should Mr. Snape's appearance cause such a hubbub as it appears to have done?" again inquired Mr. Thorpe, who till now had had no answer to his previous question.

"Well, he pretended to know Treherne, and Treherne pretended not to know him; and then Treherne propothed my kicking him out, and I propothed that he thould do it himthelf, and then the old fellow bolted with Mith Henderthon."

"But did Treherne not know him?" inquired Mr. Thorpe.

"I thuppothe not, as he thaid he didn't."

"No, papa, he did not."

Willie spoke out so distinctly that all eyes were turned on her.

Mr. Thorpe was silent; he saw Willie was struggling to keep down an outburst of tears, by the colour that quickly mounted her cheek and the quivering lip she was endeavouring to control. It was only by speaking almost harshly that she succeeded in uttering the few words she did without breaking down.

" I propoth, ath you all are so very curiouth about Thnape, that we thend over for Treherne, and make him tell uth all he can about the holy man he won't know."

" A capital idea ! " said Frank Delafield.

" And you ride over and fetch him, Frank," said Lady St. Aubyn, who understood her son's intended piece of good nature.

" Well, I will; but I won't go alone, it's horribly boring to ride no end of miles by oneself. Who 'll go with me ? Don't all speak at once," he continued, as no one proffered his company.

" I will go with you," said his sister, at last.

And then followed, " So will I ! " from various other voices; but Willie's was not amongst them, though she was longing to say she would go also.

" That will be awfully jolly ! " cried Frank.

“I’ll bless old Snapes; let’s all bless him for having given rise to an idea for occupying nearly half a day. How far is it from this to Treherne?”

“About six miles,” said Sir Gilbert.

“Positively nothing more than a good walk,” said Mr. Prendergast. “I will walk over and meet you there. Will any of you join me?”

One stray man from sheer shame said he would, but suggested it would be very hot.

“Then the pedestrians ought to start an hour before us,” said Lady St. Aubyn. “Willie, you are going? You have your habit, dear, with you, have you not?”

“Yes. You know we rode over here,” she replied, with a smile of gratitude, “so I have my habit and horse too.”

“So much the better, for I doubt if Sir Gilbert’s stables would quite supply as many horses as it seems may be wanted. I will go myself, if any one will drive with me.”

“I will drive with you,” said Willie, instantly. “I do not care about riding: and perhaps Miss Delafield will ride Peri; she is very quiet and gentle.”

“No, Miss Thorpe, thank you; I have not

my habit, so I cannot if I would, and I am afraid I would not if I could. I am so stupidly timid that, unless I know my horse well, I am expecting at every movement of his head or ears that he is going to bolt."

"Yes, Conny's an awful idiot," said her polite brother. "She gets in such a funk that it spoils every one's pleasure; and she's almost as bad driving, so look out, aunt, if you take her with you. She'll pinch your arms black and blue before you reach Treherne, if the horses are the least inclined to be fresh."

"You are a disagreeable, rude boy," said Constance Delafield, very much vexed. "And, besides, you are saying things that are not true. I never pinch people!"

"Don't you, though! Do you recollect poor Major—"

"Frank, hold your tongue, and don't tease your sister!" said the general, coming to his daughter's rescue.

"And it is past eleven now, good people," said Mrs. Prendergast; "if you really are going you had better make up your minds and settle the hour."

"Are you sure you are up to going, Willie? — it is hot work riding in the middle of the day," asked Mr. Thorpe, as, all having risen from the breakfast table, they were, in one large group, discussing what hour and by what means they were to go. And Willie was among them, but a listener only.

"Quite, papa. I never feel too hot riding; besides, if I look tired I am not so. I want to speak to you for a moment. Will you come out with me? I will get my hat and wait for you in the hall."

Mr. Thorpe nodded, and Willie went out of the room, and was running upstairs when she met Charles St. Aubyn.

"Where are you going to?" he asked.

"Only for my hat. I am going for a walk with papa."

"But you are going to Treherne thith afternoon?"

She nodded.

"And you will ride?"

She again assented in the same way.

"And was I right to propothe going?"

Another nod. Then he was going down, when she put her hand on his arm.

"Do you think, Charley, that man—did see Cyril with—any one?"

Her Hebe face wore such a melancholy expression, yet with such a pleading look, that Charley, without hesitation, said,—

"I am *thertain* he didn't!"

"I am so glad! Thank you, dear Charley!"
And she ran upstairs with part of the load
removed from her heart.

"That 'th pleathant!" muttered Charley to
himself, as Willie left him, "and I am dear,
too! Now thuppothing there ith thomething in
what that beatht thaid! I think I will tell
Treherne: the ith thuch a jolly little thing I
would do anything for her; and Treherne
mutht tell another lie if obliged—the ith
worth it!"

When Mr. Thorpe joined his daughter, he
fancied he must have been mistaken about her
looking so ill at breakfast. She looked bright
enough now. Perhaps there was the reflection
from the trees thrown into the room, or the sun
shining through the curtains, or some other cause
for her having seemed so pale before; at any
rate she appeared much more like herself than
she did then. The truth was that, like all very
young people, especially those fresh to trouble,
she no sooner saw a gleam of sunshine pierce
through the cloud that had darkened her life
for the last few hours than she widened the
aperture and let the light shine in with all the
fulness of its warmth and brightness. She was
sure the whole thing was a mistake, and she

was quite certain the moment she spoke to
her father and told him she wished a
different plan pursued with regard to Cyril
he would consent at once to their meeting
more freely and more frequently. Hope is so
easily buoyed up in our extreme youth; we
understand life so little,—of human nature, of
evil, even less. That depression is generally
but temporary, every sunrise and every sunset
altering the phase of events, though they may
in reality be steadily working on to some
sorrowful ending a momentary prevision
had allowed us to see.

"Well, Willie, what is it, dear, you wish to
say to me?"

Willie had walked in silence by her father's
side for several minutes before he spoke. She
did not find it so easy to say all she wished
when it came to the point, and yet, whilst she
was putting on her hat, she had arranged the
exact words with which she intended to open
the subject. Now she could not recollect the
least what they were.

"I want to speak to you about Cyril, papa,"
came out at last.

"Well, dear, what about him?"

"He is not happy—nor am I!"

Mr. Thorpe looked at his child: his impression a minute before had been that she was happy; then before that again that she was not: now he saw nothing but a flushed cheek.

"And yet, Willie, you were desirous that Cyril's offer should not be rejected. You see how right I was, child, not to allow an engagement before the expiration of a year."

"It is not that, papa," said Willie, speaking quickly. Was her father wilfully misunderstanding her, she wondered; or did he really imagine she did not care for Cyril? "It is not that; on the contrary, it is that he does not like the restraint you put on our seeing each other, and," she continued, gaining courage now the ice was broken, "and I too don't like it. I want you to let him come to Yardley Wood as often as he likes, and for us to visit more frequently at Treherne. Will you, papa?"

"No, Willie; not till the year is over. In the first place, I want to be sure that Cyril Treherne is worthy of you, before I promise to give you to him; and I must see and judge for myself, with my own eyes and my own senses."

"But how can you see anything if he never comes?" asked Willie, feeling angry and vexed with her father. "How can I learn more of his character than I do, if I am not allowed to be with him ?"

" There is no need for you to learn more; anything you did learn would have no effect. You are not old enough to judge for yourself: when you are, you shall do so."

" Many girls of my age are married."

" Perhaps so; but that does not make it advisable."

" But they must know what they like and what they do not."

" Not always."

" I do, at any rate."

" You think so, Willie, I dare say. But do not let us dispute over the subject, my child. It is my deep anxiety and love for you that make me seem to you, perhaps, over cautious; therefore you must bear with it. I have none to share the responsibility with me. If your marriage turned out badly, who would be to blame but myself? No, Willie, you must let me act in this matter as my conscience and my heart direct me. The time will soon pass, and then you may choose for yourself; but now, for the present, I must choose for you."

" He says, papa, he will go away if you will not give in."

" Then he must go."

"How will that further your object? How can you learn more of him if he leaves England?"

"I must take my chance. Events arise sometimes unexpected and unforeseen; but in any case you will be a year older."

"I am going over to Treherne to-day," said Willie, in a defiant tone, yet half questioningly, for she began to fear her father might refuse.

"I have no objection to your doing so. I do not wish to prohibit your meeting as ordinary acquaintances; but what I will not consent to is your meeting more frequently, or as engaged people. You must both be free till the year has expired."

Without opening her lips again, Willie returned with her father to the house. A spirit of rebellion gaining possession of her, she felt herself revolting against her father's will, and, in spite of him, she determined to see Cyril as often as possible. For the first time in her life she wished herself away from that father who, till within a few months back, had been her idol on earth; who, even during the first blooming of her young love, was thought of and considered, and who gained from her a promise Cyril had been unable to surmount by obtaining a counter one. And now, with opposition, and almost defiance, seething in her breast, and passionate love stirring up her heart to rebellion, she prepared for the ride that was to bring her to the side of him for whom she was ready to throw to the winds her childhood's memories and affections. To her life was only now beginning; it never does begin till we can pick out days and hours that are landmarks of happy or sorrowful events. It is hardly to be called life, if the current of existence flows on smoothly and uninterruptedly, without storms or sunshine, without rocks or even stones to break the monotony of its course; without them life is mere vegetation. Yet how many such there are. and moreover they are satisfied! It is true, if they have no great pleasures, neither know they much of pain; and this with some natures harmonizes. They are not capable of feeling deep love or deep hate; none of their emotions are intense; passion they know not in any shape, and they go on to the end quietly and calmly. knowing little, feeling little, yet believing all things, especially of that world beyond, which deep thinkers, those who dare try to fathom the mysteries behind the veil, see and ponder over. in a different spirit. Truly faith is a gift, whether in people or things or eternity; we cannot will to believe, though we may convince ourselves that to doubt is wrong.

Willie had full faith in Cyril again, though it had been for a moment shaken, chiefly because she had for the time being cast aside the support which, till now, had fostered, cherished, and shielded her with almost a woman's tenderness and love. She doubted now this love, and knew that her doubting was wrong. She felt as she was galloping through the fresh breeze that she was doing her father an injustice, but she did it all the same, and felt a pleasure in it too. A woman must lean on some one, and she had a ready prop to hand. They generally have before finding the courage to cast aside the old one.

CHAPTER XV.

Mrs. and Miss Henderson were sitting together in their drawing-room, very much about the same time and on the same day as the party at Stanmore Park were discussing the *boule-versement* occasioned by Mr. Snape at the school feast. The mother was reading 'Crumbs for Christians,' and the daughter was sewing together some bits of list for an old woman's cape.

"I wonder our dear minister is not yet come," said Mrs. Henderson, putting down her book for the fourth or fifth time, and looking at the clock. "Do you think, Harriet, anything can have happened to him?"

"I should think not; what is there likely to happen?"

"That irreligious young man!—that poor blind sinner!—he might have met him, and might have—have done him some harm."

"I don't think that very likely: you mean Mr. Treherne, I suppose. I don't believe he would take any notice of him, supposing he did meet him. He was angry yesterday, because of Miss Thorpe's presence. I dare say something has occurred to prevent him coming as early as he said, and he will be here, perhaps. this afternoon."

"Then we must give up driving over to Badstow Cliff to-day; at any rate till after he has been."

"As you like, mamma," answered Miss Henderson, going on with her stitching.

Harriet Henderson was one of those beings of whom we were just now speaking, without great power of feeling, who took things as they came. If a rough wave threatened to strike her she bent her head and let it pass over her; if a rock stood in her narrow walk, she would go slowly and carefully over it, so as not to hurt herself. There would be no shock to the nerves by her attempting to breast the one, or dash against the other. She was never likely to love very deeply, or to be loved; but she was, in her own way, happy and contented, without sufficient mind for ambition, yet enough of opinion to think herself superior to her neighbours—her dear Mr. Snape excepted

—and satisfied to go on her even course with the blessed belief of a beatified future. Little disappointments were rather courted and gloried in in this godly household. They were reckoned as those crosses that help to purify the purgeable Christian, for in the Henderson mind there were persons without the pale altogether, whom nothing could make clean or pure. It is fortunate for us less pious, less devout members of the Christian community that we do not accept the doctrine of hell-fire and everlasting damnation as the end of those who do not think with the Henderson school, but that we embrace and hold fast the faith in a merciful and loving God, a heavenly Father, who, more indulgent than an earthly father, forgives the sinner and pardons the wrong-doer, as a fond mother will excuse and absolve—aye, and sometimes from sheer love justify—the faults of her erring child. But the Snapes and Hendersons of this world have no mercy, no pity; hard, harsh, and unyielding, they damn you on your evidence, and leave you to quiver and quake in your shoes—if you have any, and they will not give you any if you have not—wondering whether they or you are right, and whether God is the great, almighty, perfect Spirit over- .

ruling all things with a justice the human mind is too narrow to grasp, or whether He is the God of revenge and pitiless justice they try to make you believe Him to be.

Ah, me! These tremendous differences are horribly perplexing. All think themselves right; on the first blush of it one would pronounce that to be impossible; a multitude of different views cannot all be right; reason, common sense, both go against such an hypothesis. And yet, when we inquire carefully but rationally into the question, does it not appear that after all each one *is* right, from the pagan down to the Plymouth Brother, and that every one without let or hindrance will meet in that after-life, which we hope in from love, but fear from hate? According to your faith be it unto you! Yes, there is the great solution to our difficulty. The heathen believes in the carved model of ugly humanity for a god, for he is born to it, bred to it, and dies—very often—for it. The Christian believes in the efficacy of water to produce the soul's salvation; one sinner dips his fingers into rain or river water and splashes it in the face of another, and so brings about such a change that transubstantiation is nothing to it. Do you believe that in the sight of God, the almighty Creator of all works around us, the supreme Spirit overruling our every thought and action, a charitable act is less acceptable if it issue from the hand of the man who believes in wood or from the hand of the man who believes in water? All God's creatures are as one great family to Him; the black and the white, the rich and the poor, the sun-worshippers and the water-worshippers, the believing and the doubting, the fool and the scholar, the good and the bad, they are His children; and as in every household punishment is meted out to the wrong-doer, so it is with the family of the earth. We all suffer here for our misdeeds (God knows, bitterly enough) not to require further misery hereafter!

"How much have you received this week for the Blanket Club, my dear?" asked Mrs. Henderson, who, with Miss Harriet, had just returned from the dining-room, where they had been enjoying a simple meal, consisting of all the good things of this earth that are to be had in the fruitful month of August.

"Only two and tenpence, mamma, and part of that was paying up arrears. The more children there are in a family, the less inclined do they seem to subscribe."

Miss Henderson seemed forgetful of the fact that many mouths diminish the capacity for laying by even a penny a week as a winter store against the biting frost. With the pence to buy a loaf of bread, and hungry children crying for it, it is not, with the thermometer at 80° in the shade, so easy to place it in others' hands against the day of cold. The poor are too apt to accept the gospel statement that the morrow will take care of itself, and there is no need to take thought for it.

"And yet the worst payers are the greatest beggars," said Mrs. Henderson.

"Very true; but I never will encourage begging: I always tell them to seek work," added this charitable daughter of a charitable mother. "I think Sandcombe is getting a little better, though, in that respect; at least they do not come here so often."

"I suppose they have given up coming because they find it useless," said the mother, innocently. "There's the bell," she continued, after a pause; "that is our dear Mr. Snape, I doubt not. It is only half-past two. I dare say, after all, we shall be able to go to Badstow."

Presently the portly figure of the Rev. Samuel Snape appeared, duly announced by James, the one man in the indoor establishment of Sandcombe House, who, like his employers, was in name a sinner, but a saint in his own estimation. He had an extra grave and important air whenever he announced his beloved minister. Snape was adored in the household, and the mere mention of his name required a special reverence of tone. He closed the door softly, as if a bang would have roused some evil spirit and angered the angels that, in James's narrow mind, were ever hovering around and watching over that godly man.

"My dear friends, I am rejoiced to see you. Not fatigued from yesterday, I hope? It was a noisy, riotous gathering, and I regret to say I heard no hymns sung, no prayers offered up in thanksgiving for the blessings that are so bountifully showered down on that family."

"No, my dear Mr. Snape; and when, after the children had finished their tea and cakes, I suggested to Lady St. Aubyn that we should go down on our bended knees and offer up a song of praise for all the mercies vouchsafed us, she said, in an unbecoming, indecorous tone, 'My dear Mrs. Henderson, let the poor children enjoy this one feast without psalm-singing.' Of course I could not stop and argue with the lady of the house before all those children; but I do think, my dear Mr. Snape, you might point out to her the shocking effects of such a bad example, and the misery that falls on all who do not, when they can, instil godly principles into the young."

"Yes, yes, I will when I get an opportunity; but you see the St. Aubyns do not attend my chapel, and therefore I am not responsible for their want of godliness. They had all the children from our school, so of course I was there; and, though I cannot say I enjoyed myself particularly, I am very glad I went, very glad, for through the merciful interposition of Providence I may be the humble instrument of saving a poor erring soul from destruction."

"Why, what do you mean?" asked both ladies in a breath.

"Well, I must first tell you of a circumstance that happened last Saturday, and then perhaps you will better understand the rest of the story."

Here the Rev. Samuel detailed his meeting with Cyril Treherne on the Shelton road, and of his having scrambled through the broken hedge, where Cherry, by her passage, had made a sufficient gap to enable him to get through, and retracing his steps to witness their last farewell and the gift of the locket and chain.

"Then that is what you alluded to yesterday?" asked Miss Harriet, with eager interest.

"And it was true, then?" inquired the mother.

"Most true. And now I will tell you what I have done, and why it is I am only now here instead of this morning, as I had intended and told you. A blessed thought struck me when I opened my eyes this morning, that I should go over to Shelton, and endeavour to trace out this poor erring, misguided young person, and save her, in spite of the devil who is busily working for her destruction. As I have often told you, my dear friends, we may frustrate the evil designs of the wicked one if we will but try, and so I resolved to try : and, having hastily swallowed a cup of cocoa, I started off soon after seven, and at about nine o'clock I found myself in front of the Coventry Arms at Shelton. You know where the village lies ? No ? Well, at the foot of the hills on the shore, not far from Prawle Point, where Mr. Treherne's yacht was wrecked some little time back."

"Oh !" exclaimed the mother and daughter; "oh, I think I see !"

These good people are so marvellously quick. It would take a sinner a long time to see the shadow of wrong in the little they had as yet heard from the pious flesh before them; but a saint is much clearer sighted—sees, hears, and condemns before the sinner has yet made out what there was on the other side to palliate or excuse the error.

"Well, I went into the Coventry Arms, and began talking with the man who was cleaning the place up. It was too early for customers, and I soon gathered from him that it was to the cottgae of one Miles Mason that Mr. Treherne had been taken on the night of the wreck, and where he had remained for a few days till able to get home. Now I knew, as I told him yesterday, that the girl I had seen on the road with him was Miles Mason's daughter, for a peasant at work in a field told me; so, wishing my friend good morning, I made my way according to the directions I received to the cottage by the shore, pointed out to me as belonging to the girl's father."

"And you saw her there?"

"Wait a bit, you shall hear all. Yes, I found her at home, and fortunately alone. She was attending to some household matters, but came forward at once and asked me whom I wanted. I told her, herself. For a moment she lost her colour, but then it came back and she was red to the roots of her hair."

" Is she pretty ?" asked Miss Harriet.

" Don't interrupt, Harriet," said Mrs. Henderson.

" Yes, I suppose in an earthly sense she is ; but her mind—oh, my dear friends, how awful it is to see such terrible sinners moving about amongst us !   How it is that we are not defiled by breathing the same air with them is only due to the mercies of a great Redeemer, whose blood keeps flowing over us, and cleansing us from such evil and pestilential influences; were we not so purified, we should be a mass of corruption!   But, to return to my morning's work, I at once broached the subject of Mr. Treherne's conduct, and I told her he was about to be married, and that therefore what I witnessed became a thousand times more culpable and sinful than were he free; and that she would have nought to look forward to hereafter but a tormenting and everlasting fire if she ever saw him again."

" He is not in reality about to be married,' ventured to say Mrs. Henderson ; " there is no engagement, you know, though I suppose it may end in one : so it is all the same."

"Quite.   It was necessary to speak firmly to

her, for I saw a glitter in her eyes—extraordinary eyes they are too—that half alarmed me. She looked as if she could have sprung on me like a wild cat. I could not get her to speak beyond requesting me to go; and, as I felt at that moment I could not move her to an admission of repentance, I thought it best to do so; and I determined to ask you, my two dear friends, to take the matter in hand, and see what you can do with this poor fallen creature!"

"Do you think then, my dear Mr. Snape, that—go out of the room my dear Harriet, I wish to confer alone, forone moment, with our dear minister." Miss Harriet retired like a dutiful daughter, and then Mrs. Henderson continued, "Do you think then, that—that the poor thing—has really—fallen?"

"I never wish to think any one worse than she really is, still less to state her to be so; but—I confess, I do—I have my doubts—"

"Dear, good man! say no more! I understand. Yes, we will go—we will go to-morrow early, and with the help of the Holy Spirit drag this poor soul from out the jaws of hell!"

"And now," went on Mr. Snape, who had exchanged a look of Christian admiration with his dear follower, "about Mr. Treherne. I pondered well over what ought to be my line of action in reference to him, during my walk home, and I resolved—as being the right thing to do—to speak to Mr. Thorpe, should there be any continuance of this sinful acquaintance."

"Oh, do not do that—do not tell Mr. Thorpe!" said Mrs. Henderson, with an energy unusual to her, and doubly so when conferring with Snape; she rarely ventured the slightest dissent from any of his propositions or opinions.

"And why not?"

"Because it seems to me as if—as if there were hardly grounds enough to go to him on, and you know—they are not engaged, and he might say it was no affair of his."

"But he would not let his daughter marry him."

"I don't know. They are fond of each other, I hear, and—and the world *is* so wicked!" sighed the lady, "that he might not consider that a sufficient reason for breaking off a marriage that has not yet arrived at its first stage—an engagement. I would wait a little, I think. Come in, Harriet dear; our secrets are over," said her mother, with a Christian smile.

"I have promised our dear Mr. Snape to go over to Shelton to-morrow. You see no objection to Harriet's going with me?" she asked of her unerring guide.

"No, no, none in the least. And now, dear friends, I will leave you, though not with so rejoicing a spirit as usual; for I generally feel so refreshed and strengthened, so as to meet any coming duties or trials of which my life is composed, after spending an hour with you. But we must accept the little crosses of our daily existence with cheerfulness, and the greater disappointments with resignation, well knowing they work together for our good, and that they are sent to us in mercy to prevent our clinging too much to the vanities and wickedness of the world. Bear this in mind, my beloved sisters, and—bless you!" And Snape raised his stout right hand in the position for a benediction.

"Have a glass of wine and a biscuit before you go," suggested Mrs. Henderson, after the solemn pause such an occasion demands. "I dare say you ate very little luncheon, with all this worry and anxiety."

"I have had nothing since my cup of cocoa at seven this morning," said the Reverend Samuel, in a pitiful tone.

"Nothing but a cup of cocoa! Oh, Mr. Snape!" cried Harriet.

"Go, my dear, at once and tell James. Quick! have the cold tongue and the pickled salmon and the chicken pie brought up; and some bottled ale and the brown sherry—it's more strengthening than the pale. How could you sit here all this time and not ask for luncheon?"

And Mrs. Henderson looked softly reproachful at her guest. In a very few minutes the table in the dining-room was laden with the good things that very soon were transferred to the capacious inside of Mr. Snape, who, after eating enough for half a dozen ordinary people, and drinking the bottled beer and brown sherry as if he had a fever, rose, with the rejoicing spirit he regretted not having with an empty stomach. He was strengthened no doubt as well, and was able to meet the troubles of all the united parishes, had he been called on to do so. And then he departed, with the body refreshed and the mind content, and with a vague, uncertain, dreamy idea that Mrs. Henderson and her daughter were both more careful of him and his wants than any other of his followers, and that it might arise from some motive he had not fathomed, or thought of trying to fathom, but that it might be advisable to attempt to do so; and, if he did, might he not discover something that would repay him the trouble ?—something that would be a meet reward for his life, which he thought had been praiseworthy in the extreme, self-denying, unselfish, charitable, and holy. Perhaps he was right as the world goes ; at any rate it never does any harm to think well of oneself ; and it has this advantage, it often makes others think well of us.

And Mrs. Henderson and her daughter, had they thoughts similar to those that were but shadowed out in the mind of the Rev. Samuel Snape ? Did anything approaching them rise in their minds ? Had they ever thought of this great example, this pure-minded, unselfish, godly man ever being anything more to them than their dear minister and guide ? Had Mrs. Henderson ever pictured him as her dear companion and protector, or as that of her child ? Had Miss Henderson ever dreamt of becoming Mrs. Snape, and being a helpmeet and devoted wife of this paragon ; or had she ever visioned him as a father ? I think we may safely say No to the latter ; but women's minds are so strange, their hearts so difficult to fathom, that beyond asserting Harriet Henderson never pictured Mr. Snape as her stepfather I would vouch for no more.

The two ladies were so occupied with their own thoughts that the drive to Badstow was utterly forgotten, and dinner-time came round before they exchanged a word ; and then it was not Mr. Snape they discussed, but the coast-guardsman's daughter, whom on the morrow they had resolved to interview, and, with Christian-like intentions, to cut to the quick, if words and looks could perform such an operation.

It was well for Cherry Mason she was not aware of the premeditated visit, or perhaps it was well for Mrs. and Miss Henderson, for assuredly had she been she would have been absent, and their drive would have proved fruitless : but the poor child knew not what a day was to bring forth.

CHAPTER XVI.

A DARKNESS had spread over the existence of
Cherry Mason that no time was ever to
lighten, no sunshine was ever to pierce;
there it would remain overshadowing her life
till she passed away from under it to that
mystic future beyond the grave, where let us
hope that some recompense greets those whose
sorrows have been heaviest here—something to
make up to them for having had to live *malgré*
themselves, having to suffer—aye, how bitterly
sometimes!—for others' faults.

She sat brooding over that hateful man's
words, the few, at least, she recollected; for all
the rest passed away as do shadows in the
shade. Mr. Treherne was going to be married!
He was to belong to some one else; some
one else would love him,—not as *she* did,
that was impossible; and, worse still, he would
love another. Then hope would spring up,
and she would cast aside the belief in this

coarse, brutal man. What did he know of Mr. Treherne's affairs? Clearly Mr. Treherne did not know him when he stopped him the other day to ask him the way; then why should it be true? But then came reason—a hard, stern master—was it not likely to be true? Was it not the most probable thing in the world that a gentleman like him should marry? Oh, who could it be? Was she young and pretty? she wondered. She hoped not; it would be easier to bear were she old and ugly.

So Cherry sat all the rest of that day dispirited and weary of her young life. Her home, too, had undergone a change. Her father was no longer so cheerful as before Cyril Treherne had crossed his threshold, and left there a weed that was growing up fast and choking up every vein of happiness in his cottage home. He grumbled, and not without cause, that his meals were not so well prepared, his clothes not so carefully mended; in short, he felt that he was neglected because another occupied his child's every thought. And that is not a pleasant discovery to make, not easy to bear, when you feel you are almost left out in the memory of the one to whom you have devoted all your affection; and it does not often happen that one is so completely forgotten as Miles was, for the last week, at any rate, by his daughter. In the course of nature he had looked to some day having to resign her and her heart's greatest love to another; but that change comes generally by degrees, and is foreseen. It was not so in this instance. Then Miles had learned from George Cooper of his rejection, and this was a deep disappointment to him ; he had hoped, past reason, that Cherry would accept honest, upright George, if he offered. He and George's father had so often talked the matter over together, and were so satisfied that Cherry must like George that the blow fell heavily ; and a stronger fear rose up in his breast as to what power this man, this stranger who owed his life to him, had gained over his only child.

But since yesterday morning, when Snape had paid his unwelcome visit, Cherry had been regardless even of her father's displeasure. She made no reply to him when, coming home tired and wearied from his daily duty, he found not only no supper prepared, but none in the house, and swore at her for the first time in his life. The oath was no sooner out than he repented himself of his violence, and said something approaching an apology for his temper; but the kind word was not more heeded than the harsh one. And Miles Mason, for the first time since he laid Cherry's mother in the grave up in Shelton churchyard, went to the Coventry Arms, and drank—eat he could not —and the liquor soon told on his unaccustomed brain. Then, half drunk as he was, he heard them talking of Snape's visit, and he believed it was Cyril. His head was too stupefied to make out the right story, and in that state, with a mistaken impression, he returned home and broke forth into such a torrent of abuse that poor Cherry, frightened at last into seeing the state her father was in, caused, she now knew, by her own neglect, escaped from the house and rushed heedlessly down towards the sea, sheltering and hiding herself among the slippery rocks, wet still from the just-receded sea.

It did not take long for Miles to return to his senses; and then, ashamed and abashed, he went out to seek his child, that through his conduct—though she had been the first cause— had been driven from her home. He called her by name when he neared the sea; he had been to the village and to George's mother, and to one or two other cottages where she might have gone, and, hearing no tidings of her, he with a heavy, fearing heart went in the other direction. Then, as he called her, his strong, clear voice reached her ear instantly, but she was afraid to reply till, as he neared her retreat, she thought she detected an anxious and not an angry tone; and then she answered him, and came forth and joined him, and with her hand in his they silently returned home. Then he kissed her, and bade her good-night, and so they separated till the morrow.

And over all this, and over Snape's words, was Cherry brooding, when, at about eleven o'clock, there was a knock at the door, and the girl, who loved the back room better than the little cheerful parlour, for the memory of the hours she passed there by Cyril's side, learning first to read the heart's lessons, was sitting listlessly by the window with her hands unemployed, clasped together and resting on her lap, when she heard the sound, and, springing to her feet, she ran into the front room, with an undefined hope, expressed more by the beating of her heart than any thought that Cyril was there. He had promised he would see her again, so it might be he.

The eager, expectant look in her large brown eyes died away instantly as she saw two ladies filling up the little doorway. Hard-looking women; no promise of kindly words or sympathy in their faces. Could they be **any relations** of the man **who** yesterday cut **her through to** the heart's core by **his news?** She wondered now, for the first time, **what** had brought **him** to her: **was it simply** for the pleasure **of** torturing her, **or had he been sent?** All this passed through **her mind** like lightning; **and** now she **was at the door, and must** speak.

"What do you want?" she asked, abruptly.

"Are you the daughter of a man called Mason, a coastguardsman?"

"Yes," replied the girl to the elder lady's inquiry.

"I want, then, to speak to you, my good girl. I want to ask you one or two questions. We may come in, I suppose?"

Cherry had stood like a sentinel at the door, as if with the intention of preventing the two ladies from entering.

"What is it you want? Who do you come from?" she asked, petulantly, but moving slightly aside as she spoke.

"We want your good only, poor thing! and we come from one whose goodness you may as yet not know, but—"

"Not from Mr. Treherne?" she asked, in an agitated manner, interrupting Mrs. Henderson.

To poor Cherry's simple mind there was but one whose goodness she considered passing all others.

"God forbid!" ejaculated the pious woman. "But I came because of him,—because of the shocking story I heard yesterday from that holy man, the Reverend Samuel Snape, who—"

"Snape! Is that the creature who came yesterday, and told me a lie—yes, a wicked, cruel lie?"

"Hush, hush, poor lost sinner! or God in His wrath may strike you dead here on the spot for uttering such blasphemy."

"I don't know what blasphemy is, and I don't care; but I do know that I hate that wicked man who came here yesterday, and I hate you if you come from him!"

"And if we do not come from him?" asked Miss Henderson.

Both ladies were now comfortably seated; they had managed to make Cherry back almost unconsciously, till they were in possession of two easy-chairs, and in this firm position they considered they had the poor girl at bay.

"If you don't come from him, what do you want?"

"To save you!" It was Mrs. Henderson who replied.

"And to spare that poor innocent young lady, who is so soon to be Mr. Treherne's wife, the sorrow and disgrace that must follow if you ever permit him to speak to you again."

The daughter, younger and with the heart's feelings less withered than her mother's, spoke. She knew by instinct how such words would tell, though to love as Cherry loved she was not born to understand. A little faint, piteous cry escaped their victim. Such words agonized as would the most excruciating torture; but to these women she felt so intense a repugnance that she endeavoured to smother her pain, rather than permit them to be witnesses of it.

"I don't know what you mean," she said, at last.

"Then I will tell you. Hush, Harriet!" said Mrs. Henderson, as her daughter was about to interrupt her, that young lady thinking she could let fly sharper and more stinging arrows than her mother,—daughters are very apt to think they can say and do most things better than their mothers after a certain age; "allow me to speak. You know, poor blinded sinner, that you have been breaking God's laws, and risking not alone your own salvation, but the salvation of that misguided young man, and—"

"I have *not* broken God's laws! You have no right to speak so to me!"

"You will end by the devil getting hold of you, and tortures past description, and too awful to imagine, being your portion hereafter, if you do not follow the advice I came here to offer. Think, poor miserable worm that you are—that we all are—what comes after this world: life is so short, eternity so long, pleasures so trifling, pains so fearful! Ah! stay your wicked course in time; learn from those who are but too eager to help you what the Gospel tells you—that a camel can as easily go through the eye of a needle as a sinner into the kingdom of heaven."

"A rich man, mamma!"

"And if you do not go to heaven," continued Mrs. Henderson, regardless of her daughter's correction, "where do you think you will go to?"

"I don't know, and don't care. Will you, *please*, leave me?"

"What! are you still unrepentant? Are you still the hardened, reckless creature you were before you heard the truth?"

"I don't know what I am, ma'am, and I don't think it much matters, at least to you. I want to go on with my work."

"Where is your father, young woman?"

"He is out."

"I shall wait, then, till he comes in. I can make no impression, it seems, on you; so I will see whether he will not listen to me, and force you to be saved in spite of yourself."

Cherry quailed at this threat, the one of all others that could have any influence on her. For these women to speak of her to her father as they had spoken to her of herself, would be fatal to the hope she still clung to of again seeing Cyril. Oh, that unlucky chance of her following him that Saturday! And yet, even now, when it seemed to have caused the crushing of her happiness, she would not undo it— memory was too sweet. So, to avert what she thought a terrible evil, Cherry faced out a lie.

"Father won't be home till bedtime; it's his day out."

"Then he will be in to-morrow?"

"Yes."

"Then, young woman, I will come again to-morrow. I will not shrink from the duty that has been thrust upon me. I will endeavour to awaken your soul to the heinousness of your guilt, and convince you of your wickedness! Remember, you will have no peace till you are pardoned; and no pardon

is granted without sincere repentance. I want
to lead you to the Physician who can heal all
diseases; who, though polluted as you are,
can yet cleanse you with His precious blood;
who will 'take away the heart of stone,' and
can give you a new heart, that will love Him
who gave so much and endured so much for
sinners like unto you. Pardon is what you
most need, and until you obtain it you can
do nothing right; and what we most need
God offers for our acceptance. Pardon is ever
ready for us if we but seek it; and, poor
sinner, there is no time for you to lose. 'To-
day,' says the Holy Ghost. And supposing
you turn a deaf ear to what I am saying, and
refuse to think over my words when I am
gone, and supposing you die in your terrible
sin, unrepentant, what is there for you in
eternity but everlasting tortures? Is it not
better, then, laden as you are, weary as you
must be of the guilt that has defiled you, to
go meekly to Jesus and unburden yourself of
all your sins, and have them blotted out for
ever, and the Holy Spirit filling up those gaps
that were filled with filthy sin before? Ah,
my poor erring girl! open your eyes to the
true state of your soul, and then there will be
hope for you here and hereafter. Repent

quickly, whilst you may, for if you put it off it may be too late!"

"I don't know in what way I am so awfully wicked!" exclaimed Cherry, half bewildered with Mrs. Henderson's oration. "I have done nothing that I know of,—at least nothing so very wrong."

"Heaven forgive you! Are you so utterly ignorant as not to know the Ten Commandments?"

"Yes, ma'am, I know them."

"And don't you know that if you break one you break all?"

Cherry thought for a moment. She thought she had once heard something to that effect, but it had not made any deep impression on her; and then she ran her mind quickly over the ten laws, and came to the conclusion she was not so innocent as she had imagined. She had broken more than one: she had sometimes failed in the fourth, perhaps latterly in the fifth; in the ninth, perhaps; and now decidedly she broke the tenth. Yes, there was no doubt she was guilty of the charge: and so, not being able to defend herself, she remained silent.

"You admit your wickedness, young woman?"

" I suppose so, in the way you put it. I have sometimes failed in keeping the Sunday as holy as perhaps I ought; and I have once—but I don't believe more than once—failed in duty and obedience to my father, and—"

" There—stop! I do not want you to confess your sins to me: I only desire to bring you to see them in the proper light, and to make you stay your reckless, self-destroying line of conduct. Come, Harriet, let us go now. I trust and pray our visit has not been wholly without some good—if but little—result. I shall pray for you, young woman, that you may be led to see the error of your ways, and that you will for the future lead a virtuous and respectable life. It is a pity you cannot get into a situation. Perhaps, if I find you following the path of rectitude I may exert myself to obtain a place for you in some Christian family.'

" Thank you; but I do not wish to leave my home. And as to leading a virtuous life—as you said just now—I've never done anything else."

" What! is it possible you are still so hardened as to brazen out your guilt, after all I have been saying to you?"

" There is no guilt that I know of."

" No guilt, wretched sinner! Do you know what guilt means ?"

" Yes, I do. Trying to destroy an honest, virtuous girl's character, as you are endeavouring to do, that is guilt."

" You are an impertinent good-for-nothing!" exclaimed Mrs. Henderson, roused by the girl's words to an anger that if she ever felt she rarely allowed to be seen. " You are a sinful, wicked girl, and I will take no more trouble about you. You may do as you please, and if you want help never come to me, for I will not give it you. But I will take such steps as will put an end to the vicious life you are now leading."

Without waiting for an answer, which might not have been made if she had, Mrs. Henderson, preceded by her daughter, left Miles Mason's cottage, shaking—as she afterwards expressed herself to Mr. Snape—the dust from off her feet.

When they were gone it all seemed like an ugly dream to Cherry. She could not understand why any one should be so interested about her as to find her out, and talk as these two ladies and that horrid fat man had done. Who were they all; and what did they want? She puzzled her poor brain for long, but made nothing clearer. She felt, however, thankful that, from the elder lady's parting words, she was not likely to be troubled with them any more, and that her father would not be made more angry on the subject than he was already, by the chattering of these people.

And then, when she had done wondering over all this, she fell a-thinking again of Cyril, and what the man in black had told her and the ladies confirmed, and she determined to ascertain by some means the truth. This resolution seemed to calm her a little, and she tried to set about preparing for her father's return home, and so avoid a repetition of the scene of the previous night. And so " will " was again to " cause woe " to poor Cherry !

CHAPTER XVII.

THERE are certain moments in every one's life that are terribly perplexing; when the clearest mind may err in its decision. when inward suffering may, through its very pain, cause us to mistake the right course: the weaker the mind, the quicker the conclusion arrived at. Hence, women jump at a plan of action almost instantaneously, even under the most difficult circumstances, and then, though they may be right, they are right more by chance than by a correct appreciation of the position. To deliberate or act with caution is not in their power. All their decisions are influenced by feeling, and the effects are scarcely to be thrust before them as a reproach to their discernment; yet how apt we are, if the current of events prove adverse, in consequence of a mistaken judgment, to turn round on those who, having acted for the best, yet failed in attaining the desired end. Men pause and reason, and, if for others, act wisely; rarely, however, do they do so when the matter concerns themselves.

Mr. Thorpe took all the time there was before him—it was not much—to ponder over and weigh in all its bearings the request made to him by his child that she might see Cyril Treherne more frequently, and meet him on that intimate footing usually enjoyed by those who have made up their minds to become man and wife. Willie did not use those words, but that was in fact what her request implied. And her father had, then and there, distinctly refused; but he did so fully intending to consider well whether it would be wise to adhere to that decision. He thus kept the power in his own hands, which he would have let slip had he hinted to her it was possible he could waver. He had not long to make up his mind; a short hour, and then they were to start for Treherne; and he knew quite well that jolting along on horseback, with a number of others chattering nonsense around him, would not help his brain to view so important a matter calmly and steadily. So he must make up his mind before leaving Stanmore; and he strolled for that purpose far away from all sound of

human voices into the pretty little wooded
glen that stretched from the end of the
shrubbery walk to where the high road to
Plymouth bordered the property. Then, with
his cigar in his mouth, he chose a soft turfy
bank, and lying down with his hat placed half
over his face, to shelter his eyes from the sunlight that danced through the waving boughs
of the slender fir and the sturdy oak, he
gradually composed his anxious mind to consider and decide what he should cede, what he
should hold firm to.

Some innate, inexplicable feeling made him
conscious that, as he decided, so would the
current of his child's future flow smoothly or
roughly. Her tone, her manner, her expression
when talking to him, probably caused him to
feel this; and as the burden of responsibility
increased, so did his clear judgment become
dimmed, and his power of arriving at a correct
decision lessen. How often it happens the
more anxious we are to do a thing well the
less we succeed!—our powers become, as it
were, paralyzed, and we want the coolness
indifference gives to arrive at the desired end.
And so Mr. Thorpe, finishing his cigar and
meditations, rose determined to keep Willie
bound to her promise, yet, at the same time,

he felt dissatisfied and discontented with himself.

It was not till they were cantering across the tract of moorland that lies between Stanmore and Treherne Court, and that Frank Delafield said something as to what Mr. Snape's feelings would be, could he know his presence yesterday had given rise to such turmoil, and that the formidable party then making for Treherne were intent solely on the clearing up of the mystification to which he had given birth, that Mr. Thorpe recollected the Snape episode. It had passed from his mind, pushed aside by what had appeared to him of so much importance; but now it all rose up before him, and he felt more certain than ever he was right in adhering to his original resolve. If anything were wrong in the matter, he at any rate could save his child from sorrow falling to her share in consequence. As he argued, so he thought; he was not endeavouring to drown conflicting ideas, but to look at all unbiased; and he felt certain his decision was as it should be.

And Willie? Holding in Peri's head with a firm, steady hand, a determined, obstinate spirit got possession of her, making her show, in her command over her horse, that she meant to be master: with lips compressed, and sitting so steadily that even when trotting she seemed one with her horse, she rode on fast and yet faster, keeping the lead and flying, with her rebellious mood every moment becoming less controllable; answering, when spoken to, in monosyllables, and sometimes not correctly, so occupied was she with all she had to say to Cyril.

She bitterly resented her father's conduct; she accused him of want of affection for her, and of being guided solely by selfish motives; she asked nothing of him that he had any right to refuse; she would retract her own promise to him, she would have her secrets with Cyril; in short, she wound herself up to a state of almost indifference as to what might happen, never, however, imagining anything worse than holding secret communication with Cyril, meeting him by stealth if she could not do so openly and freely, and deliberately defying her father.

They were at the gates now of the old Court; handsome, massive iron gates with an ivy-clad archway spanning the road above them, with a lodge on either side, and the splendid beech avenue stretching straight away up towards the house, the branches meeting overhead, forming a tunnel of verdure cool and delicious after the glare and heat of the exposed table-land they had ridden over.

Lady St. Aubyn's carriage had already arrived, so the family was aware of the influx of visitors about to come. Mrs. Treherne was standing in the hall, the doors wide open, awaiting the cavalcade. The admiral was with the ladies in the dining-room, getting them some iced drinks; whilst Cyril stood a little away beyond the covered entrance, with his eyes already fixed on the pretty, slight figure that still headed the party. She gave a little touch to Peri, and lightly moved the rein to make her hasten on still faster, as she caught sight of Cyril; the next minute she pulled up, and Cyril, taking her round the waist, lifted her off the horse.

"My darling!" he whispered, "this is unexpected!"

"Oh, Cyril, I have so much to say to you, and I must say it; so do manage to get away with me presently. Tell some one to take special care of Peri," she continued, as the others were now around her, and she passed by Cyril to greet Mrs. Treherne.

For the first time she felt a liking for her future mother-in-law. Hitherto she had thought her so dreadfully religious and good, and rather too fond of offering advice; but her disagreement with her father had left a vacancy in her heart that Mrs. Treherne for the time being seemed to fill up; besides, she wanted support, and she wanted help in case Cyril should persist in going away, to induce him to give it up, and she knew his mother would but too gladly give her that help; so she greeted her almost affectionately. And Mrs. Treherne, if in some things she was a hard woman, was at any rate an affectionate, devoted mother; so she met Willie more than half way, and felt her heart beat warmly towards the young girl she hoped would prove as loving and faithful a wife as in her great love she believed her son deserved.

All were more than willing to follow Lady St. Aubyn's example and take some iced soda-water with sherry after their long and dusty ride. Mrs. Treherne took them into the dining-room, and, after attending to their requirements, sat herself down in the recess of the large oriel window, fanning herself with that morning's *Western News*.

"I cannot think why you did not tell me yesterday you meditated this descent upon us; I would have had luncheon ready for you."

"We had no notion of this invasion, my dear Mrs. Treherne, till I forget who, but some one at breakfast this morning suggested Frank's riding over to ask Cyril some stupid questions about a still more stupid person."

"No, mother, to bring him back with him; and then, when we had him under lock and key, quethtion him ath to all he knowth of that —that Thankth!" said Charles St. Aubyn.

At the name of Snake, as Charles persisted in calling him, Cyril's cheek paled slightly: both Willie and her father observed it; the one with a sinking dread, the other with a kind of pleasure, for it supported him in the notion that his decision made that morning was correct. If anything was going on wrong, he became doubly right in not allowing matters to progress further.

"Snakes!" cried Mrs. Treherne, "you mean Snape! What do you want to know about him? I know him, and can tell you anything."

Cyril had had half a mind that morning to make his father his confidant, and so enlist his help out of the scrape he felt he was drifting into. But, though he loved his father sincerely, he had not been in the habit of treating him as a friend, so he found it hard to do so when he wished; he let the opportunity pass, and now regretted it.

"I can tell you a great deal more about Snape than madam," cried the admiral, unwittingly coming to his son's aid; "she only knows the fair outside—"

"Fat outside!" interrupted Frank Delafield.

"All right, young fellow," continued the admiral; "the fat, fair outside, and nothing of the ugly interior. In the first place, he is the Methodist minister of Sandcombe, and juggles money out of every woman's pocket that he can get his hand into, and then spends it on his own inside. Excuse me, ladies, but it is the fact."

"Admiral, admiral!" cried his wife, "you are very wrong to speak of a really good man in that shocking manner. I do not think there ever existed a better or more generous being—"

"But, Mrs. Treherne, I do not think we have arrived at the solution of our difficulty by hearing Snape's good qualities, because we most of us have heard good—or bad of him. We wanted to know how your son made his acquaintance," said Mr. Thorpe.

"I am hardly accountable to any one as to

how or with whom I make acquaintance," said
Cyril, a little too haughtily.

"I don't think Cyril knows him," said Mrs.
Treherne.

"Let us get out of this room," cried the
admiral, in the same breath: "it smells of
pickled salmon and pineapple—a horrible mixture. Come, Lady St. Aubyn, let us sit in the
large drawing-room: it is the only cool place,
excepting the hall."

"And let Snape be d—d! eh, admiral?"
laughingly said Sir Gilbert St. Aubyn, in an
under-tone. "You won't mention the fellow's
name again, Charlotte, if you take my advice;
there is clearly something in it that arouses ill-
feeling."

As they were all strolling out from the dining-
room, Cyril and Willie passed on unnoticed
through the drawing-room into the conservatory, and so into the garden.

"Cyril, I am not happy," began the young
girl, when they were out of sight and hearing.
"I feel as if a whole world of sorrow had suddenly fallen on me, and it is all because papa
will not listen to any change: he says I may
see you as I see others, and so on, and tells me
it is for my good, but I don't think so. But,
Cyril—dear Cyril," and the deep blue eyes

were raised pleadingly to his, " you won't go away—will you ?"

" My own little Willie, if I am not to see you, am I not as well away as here—indeed better ? Think, darling, the pain it is to me to know you are within a couple of hours of me, and yet that I may not see you ? I cannot bear it, darling."

Willie was silent. Rapid thoughts chased one another through her brain. Was it not selfish in him to go, if she wished him to stay ? Was it not more selfish still in her desiring he should stay, when she could offer him nothing in exchange for his giving it up ? Would it be better for him to be absent ? He might forget her, yet she hardly feared that.

" Cyril," she exclaimed suddenly, after many minutes' pause, " do explain to me what that man meant yesterday. We really came over for that. It was so kind of Charley to manage it : I am sure he proposed it only to get you back to Stanmore."

" Well, it was a strange way of setting about it," replied Cyril, a little bitterly.

Willie looked up.

" You are not vexed about it, are you ?"

" I have nothing to be vexed about; only

they all seem to have been amusing themselves at my expense."

"But, Cyril, do you know this horrid man
they call Snape?"

"It would be very odd if I did not know
him by this," was the reply.

"Well, but you know what I mean. Did
you—did he meet you the other day near to
Shelton, and—was some one with you?"

It was fully a minute before Cyril replied,
and Willie watched and waited with a beating
heart for his answer. In that moment a
struggle went on in Cyril Treherne. Had he
followed his first impulse he would have told
her the whole story, without keeping back
anything; but the after-thought was that it
would be giving her useless pain, for he knew
full well he did not care two straws for Cherry
Mason, and so what good would it do beyond
saving him the denial of Snape's statement?

"No, Willie, I did not meet this man near
to Shelton."

It was Willie's turn to pause now. Perhaps
it was not near Shelton; it might have been at
Shelton. Perhaps he did not meet him; it
might have been Snape overtook him. Could
he, she wondered, prevaricate? No, came the
instant reply. Her generous nature could

admit of no such grievous fault in one she loved so well.

"You were a long time answering," she said at last.

"I was. I wondered how *you* could ask me such a question, when you heard me tell the man himself I never had seen him before."

"Forgive, me dear, dear Cyril!" exclaimed Willie, cut to the quick by his reproach, well merited she believed. "I was sure you did not know him, and I do not know why I asked you. I have not grieved you, have I, Cyril?" and she put her hand coaxingly on his arm.

"No, my own darling, no; let us forget all about this matter, and never allude to it again."

"And will you promise, Cyril, never to have any secret from me, no matter what it may be? I would always rather know disagreeable things than that they should exist and I be kept in ignorance of them."

"I asked you for a promise, Willie, some little time ago, and you told me you could not give it me."

"I did; but then you asked me to contradict myself. I had already made a promise that prevented my doing what you asked; but I will promise never to have a secret from you. Will you make the same to me?"

"Yes, darling, I will. Though I do not think it a wise promise to give, there are so many things might happen that the knowledge of would unnecessarily pain you, still—"

"Still you promise?"

"What an exacting little thing you are!"

"I love you, Cyril."

Willie almost whispered the words, and in a tone as if to exculpate herself for her seeming exaction, and, though uttered so softly and with such deep love that Cyril inwardly vowed she should never have cause to regret it, the words must have escaped her involuntarily, for her cheeks were now flooded with crimson blushes, and she turned away her head, lest he should see her confusion.

"Willie, let me ask you one thing. If any one told you evil of me, would you believe it?"

"No," she replied, stoutly.

"And nothing any one said would make you give me up?"

"Nothing."

"And will you promise me never to believe even what your father might tell you without first asking me as to the truth of it?"

"I will."

"Then I am satisfied," and Cyril breathed more freely.

"Why have you asked me all these questions?" then said Willie.

"For the pleasure of hearing you say you can trust me, which you do, do you not, my darling?"

"I do, Cyril; I trust you as—as I trust in God."

Such a confidence was surely worth keeping, worth preserving. It is not often such perfect faith is felt even by a girl of eighteen for the man she hopes will one day be her husband. Doubts will arise, and will too often bear that bitter fruit, jealousy, which poisons so many lives and mars so much happiness. But Willie at that moment, with Cyril all to herself, speaking every now and then fond words— words that promised all truth and fidelity— thought nothing could happen, nothing could be said or done, that would break that pure belief she had in him.

Every trial and trouble is only to be weighed by comparison, and few would imagine that Willie's troubles were worthy even of the name; yet because she had never endured greater they fell heavily on her. It was a great sorrow, a great trial, with all her love for Cyril, all her faith in that love, that still he persisted in his resolve of travelling during the winter. She did not know that his obstinacy on the point arose from a want of trust in himself, not so far as his love for her went—he felt unwavering there, not for a moment did he imagine he should falter in his affection,—but he feared the temptation that other girl's love might prove to him; he feared that for the mere sake of distraction he might be drawn over to Shelton, he might be induced, from pity or good nature or for his own amusement, to get entangled in a web of trouble that might be hard to get free from. He felt his greatest safety was in absence; and though he could not explain this to Willie, he put the matter so before her that, however hard would be the parting, she felt the necessity for it arose from his great love for her, the impossibility to be so near to her and yet so apart.

And this arose from her father's obstinacy, and so the feeling of anger grew stronger and stronger; and yet what could she do? Where was her remedy? She was as powerless as a bird taken from the nest is in the school-boy's hand. The only way she had of showing her resentment was treating her father with coldness and indifference. She resolved never to speak to him about Cyril, never mention his name in his presence. And when he was gone she would then seek his mother; she could talk of him to that fond, doting mother, who never tired of hearing or speaking of him herself. And she could write to him, and have her letters addressed to her at Treherne. And she and Cyril talked all this over, till poor Willie's troubles ceased to appear so enormous; and the time would soon pass, and then he would come back, never to leave her any more. Then they made promises to one another, and, though they knew of their mutual love, yet there was great pleasure in exchanging vows; and so, happy in the present, they endeavoured not to dwell on the future, which was shrouded over by the cloud of separation. They were too young to think of death, or any other of those crushing sorrows that later on one becomes familiar with, and looks on as every-day occurrences. The young rarely think of the possibility of their hopes being withered; all is fresh and green, and their confidence not easily shaken; it takes more than one rude shock of the earth's trials to brush off the bloom that hope lays so thickly on youth; and well it is so! God knows, the blessed film is but too soon removed from our eyes. Let the young revel in their short-sightedness; they will see and feel and learn soon enough that all is illusion, happiness a chimera, trust in our fellow-creatures vain, and the world one huge, gigantic deception.

CHAPTER XVIII.

Cyril Treherne did not return with the Stanmore party : he and Willie agreed that it would on the whole be better not ; and though good-natured Charley thought "Treherne an ath," and " Papa Thorpe another," it seemed notwithstanding as if the pain would outbalance the pleasure. Moreover, Lady St. Aubyn had but faintly echoed her son's warm invitation, and there was that uncomfortable silence when she spoke that it was very clear the whole thing was likely to carry annoyance with it, and Cyril wisely thought it scarcely worth risking the disagreeables that would inevitably arise if he went.

Cyril and Willie agreed they were to meet once again before he left. Mrs. Treherne was to write over to Mr. Thorpe and ask him to bring Willie to spend a day or two at the Court before Cyril left. If he refused, Cyril

was to write and ask permission to go to
Yardley Wood. Supposing he met with a
denial, then — why, then they must—they
hardly knew what, but clearly meet.

However, when Mrs. Treherne's letter arrived,
—which it did about a week after the Thorpes
left Stanmore,—Mr. Thorpe passed it across
the table to Willie. They were at breakfast,
and Willie, having read it, handed it back without a word, but with a throbbing somewhere
between her heart and her throat, which rendered silence the most convenient.

" Do you wish to go, Willie ? "

Willie had to swallow an imaginary lump
before she could get out the somewhat indifferent answer,—

" As you like."

" As I like ? "

Then the father's heart softened, and yearned
again for the time when he and his child were
one in thought and feeling, hopes and wishes
—a time never, never more to be ! A vain
desire, a vain hope, for the child was now no
longer a child ; the clinging confidence of those
happy days, when, without her father by her
side, without her hand in his, all seemed
doubtful and dangerous, was gone for ever !
Another now occupied the whole heart, which

then had hardly a corner that was not entirely devoted to him, and with a love, though of rapid growth, so deep rooted that it could stand all the storms of time and not be destroyed, though its very strength should sap away her life-blood.

"Willie," said her father, at last, when he had gained sufficient command over himself to speak calmly, "my dear, dear child, have you lost all affection for me, because I felt bound to adopt a certain line of conduct that runs counter to what you, in your youth and ignorance, wish? You have now, for upwards of a week, been estranged from me so completely that I feel as if I were alone here; worse than alone, for I see you, but never hear you speak. And yet from the moment your mother implored me, in her dying hour, to fill her place towards you as well as my own, I have—I can safely before God say—done all in a man's power to shield you from sorrow, and direct your course so that no harm could come near you. My whole life, from the moment she was taken from me, has been devoted to you. And now, at this critical point in your existence, if I am a little unyielding, is it not from my great love for you? Is it not that I desire to feel assured that the man I give you to is worthy of you? Surely it is not asking a great deal when I said one year must elapse before any decisive step should be taken. A quarter of that time has already gone, and already has a mist arisen that I must have cleared."

"I do not understand you," said Willie.

At her father's appealing, affectionate words she had begun to soften towards him, and to think she had been somewhat ungrateful; but at the mere mention of a mist—she knew he alluded to the Snape affair—she grew hard again and defiant.

"No, child, and I am not sure I wish you to do so; only I would have you trust my judgment as of yore, and believe that all I say and do is wholly and solely for your good. I can have no ulterior motive for my actions but your happiness."

"But you do not know what makes my happiness."

"I know what you *fancy* does; but that is because you are too young to judge for yourself."

"That is a matter of opinion."

"Not quite," said her father, somewhat in her own tone. "However, we have entered on a discussion that I fear, if continued, will bear no good fruit: it arose from this letter. What answer do you wish me to give?"

Mr. Thorpe's tone was not one to trifle with. He clearly was vexed at having made so little impression on his child; and so Willie felt if she wished to go she had better say so, or assuredly her father would take her at her word if she said she did not care about it. As ungraciously as possible she said she desired to go. So Mr. Thorpe wrote and accepted the invitation.

It was the third week in September, and Cyril was to be off by the end of the month. The shooting-party that was originally proposed had been knocked on the head, owing to the disjointed state affairs had fallen into, and to the unforeseen engagements of those who were invited. The Prendergasts stayed on at Stanmore, thus preventing the St. Aubyns from coming; and though Frank Delafield, Captain Mayne, Major Kingsford, and one or two others came over for a day, there was no regular party staying in the house. Indeed, Cyril himself ceased to desire it, now that he had decided on leaving home till the spring. He had had a hard tussle with his mother; she entreated him, with tears in her eyes, to give it up; she had a presentiment—all women have on such occasions—that evil would ensue from it,—she was sure some terrible calamity would result; but her words fell on a deaf ear, on an ear that had already resisted the pleading of one it had cost him something to refuse.

"Go away from here if you like, travel as far as you choose, but give up going to sea,—don't have any more yachting!"

But Cyril was firm. His inclination for a sea life was too great for him to resist such an opportunity, the last, perhaps, he might ever have. His vexation and annoyance at Mr. Thorpe's obstinacy was as lessened as it could be by his anticipated pleasure of spending four or five months on the broad, open sea, pitched about by every light wind, not caring where it carried him.

Once or twice the great brown eyes of Cherry Mason seemed to rise before him with their wondering expression, and reproaching him with his broken promise, but he drove the vision and the temptation to go and see her and bid her farewell away. Better not run any risk; he had barely escaped from the results of his one stolen visit; and though he had neither seen nor heard any more of Snape, he by no means felt sure he should not. The days were passing quickly, and Willie would soon be with

him, so there was not much time for him to
spend in regrets for the poor little girl that had
tended him so carefully, and who would have
given herself up to him, body and soul, if he
had cared to take her.

Willie looked forward with eager pleasure to
her visit; but when the time came, and she
was at Treherne, the knowledge that it was but
to precede the bitter parting, that a few hours
would see him she loved best taken from her,
marred all happiness in the present. Not
alone going away, but going to regions unknown to her—places of which she had read
but knew nothing. An unknown land is
always more distant to us than one, perhaps,
actually further off that we do know. Paths
we have trodden ourselves we can tread again
in memory; we can follow in the footsteps of
those who are going the same journey. Whilst,
on the other hand, we can but use imagination,
as we picture the scenes we read of, and try to
follow in the right track; but we are miserably
wrong always, and our fancy utterly de-
ceives us.

"And you are quite determined to go by the
coast of Spain to the Mediterranean?" asked
Willie, as on the last evening they were to
spend together they were strolling down the

beech avenue of the plantation that, by passing through, led to a pretty terrace walk overlooking Sandcombe Bay and Bolt Head.

"At this season it is the best direction to take. I can't well go to Norway," he said, smiling.

"No, I suppose not"; and Willie sighed. "Where will you touch? I mean where can you write from?"

"I can stop where and when I like. Darling, you need not fear, you shall hear often enough; and remember the long, long letters I shall expect to get from you."

"But I shall not know where to address to you."

"I shall tell you that in each of my letters."

They had reached the plantation now, and beneath the thick foliage the twilight faded away into darkness, though the pathway was still visible.

"How dark it is!" said Willie.

She never as a child could bear the dark, and she nestled up nearer to Cyril as she spoke.

"You are not afraid, my own little Willie, are you?" and he placed his arm around her. She looked up; he could see her sweet face beaming with trust and love as he bent his own nearer to it. "The moon will soon be up;

besides, in a minute or two we shall be out of this on to the terrace."

"I am not afraid now," she murmured, yet clinging to him as she spoke; and then, with a start, she said, "Oh, Cyril, what is that?"

"What is what, darling?" and they stood still a moment; but all was silent, not a leaf stirring in that calm autumn evening, not a breath to disturb the birds at roost. "I hear nothing; you must have fancied it; besides, it is impossible any one should be here at this hour."

So they went on; but Willie's steps quickened till they reached the terrace, and then, with the broad, open view before her, she became brave again.

"I am so glad we are out of that wood, Cyril. I never could bear the dark; and I am just as foolish about it as ever."

"We will not go back that way. It must have been a frog or a toad we disturbed, rustling amongst the leaves already fallen. Come and sit down here a little. See, the moon is getting up; how yellow she is! We shall have a fine day to-morrow."

"And to-morrow, Cyril, we part!" said Willie, sitting with one hand clasped in his, his arm around her, and her small, well-shaped head, with its coils of rich brown hair, resting on his shoulder. "Oh, why is it we cannot have all we like in this world?"

"Ah, why, indeed!"

Neither considered that, to a certain extent, they had, in this case, partially created their own difficulties and troubles, at any rate so far as their separation went. Cyril need not have gone away, even though he could not have his own way with regard to Willie so entirely as he wished. We often make matters worse than they need be by not endeavouring to make the best of them.

"I have prayed, Cyril, morning and night, that nothing should ever part us, and yet, by this time to-morrow, we shall already be far away from one another; what, then, is the use of praying? And yet I pray on, and cannot help it; it is a comfort, even though I feel I shall never have my prayers granted!"

This was a subject Cyril found difficult to argue on; he had been so bothered by his mother in his more youthful days with prayers and reading good books that now, having ceased to be under her influence, he rarely gave the subject a thought.

"I shall pray for you, darling," he said at

last, "pray that this time next year you may be my own little wife, and—"

"And that we may never have a quarrel as long as we live," added Willie, gaily, as Cyril seemed to stop.

"There is no fear of that," he replied, turning his head away as he spoke, as if listening.

"Do you hear anything?" she asked, nervously.

"Don't be frightened, dearest. I fancied I heard a rustling behind us. It must be fancy; no one—unless, indeed, one of the servants is out, which is not improbable—could be in the grounds. See, Willie, how beautiful is the reflection of the moon on the sea; look at that long stream of shimmering light, like frosted silver."

"Ah, I shall look at that when you are away, and then I shall think of to-night—how happy I am with you, how miserable without you!"

"Foolish child!" Yet he pressed her closer to him still. Then, after a pause, he continued, "Though your father has forbidden any engagement, Willie, yet you are bound to me, are you not, by all the sacred ties of love— nothing would make you break the silent vows of your heart?"

"Oh, Cyril, do you want me to promise to love you always? Do you not know that nothing, no one, could ever change me? Do you not feel certain that no human being could ever separate me from you?—that I love you with all the strength of my soul; love you with such a love as sometimes frightens me, it is so intense?"

She cowered down, and hid her face on his breast as she stopped speaking, as if ashamed of her own vehemence, as if she hardly realized the warmth and force of her words till she heard her voice utter them. He raised her head, and pressed his lips to hers in one long embrace.

"My own precious one, I am satisfied!" he said.

Then they rose as if by mutual consent; as they did so there was heard a sharp, bitter cry, as if from some one who had received a sudden hurt; and again all was still and silent. Roused by this fresh evidence of some one near them, Willie begged to go back to the house at once; there was no use in reasoning with her now, as clearly she was right, and she had heard some one. Cyril's face paled slightly, not from fear, cowardice was not one of his faults, but from a sudden apprehension that seized him.

He got up, stretched himself, looked around. The scene was very grand; but he was too familiar with it for it to arrest his attention, and yet he stood gazing for two or three minutes at least towards the sloping grass-grown land that stretched away to the sea. Then he walked with his eyes fixed on what seemed a white object in that direction. On he went, as if destiny forced him, nearer and yet nearer, till he came to within a few yards of it. Oh, if even then he had but turned back! His whole after-life might have gone on smoothly and happily, without the harrowing, miserable days that morning's walk entailed. But it was to be. So at any rate we are at times forced to admit when, do what we may to avert an evil, it still by some inevitable circumstance is brought about.

And Cyril did not turn back. He walked on till he came close up to what, from the beginning, he had felt sure was a woman. She lay there so still that he first thought she must be sleeping or dead; but as he got nearer to her, and saw the nervous, agitated movement of the left hand, which was clutching at something hanging round her neck, he knew she was conscious. Her hair hung about her dishevelled; she had neither bonnet on nor shawl,—both lay beside her. She looked up with a frightened, startled look when the sound of footsteps fell on her ear, and then with a cry—such an one as Cyril had heard the night before—a cry as of pain, she sprang up, but only to crouch down again at his feet.

"Cherry! good Heavens! is it you? What are you doing here? Speak to me, my poor girl."

And he stooped down to raise her up, for she clung to him,—one arm round his leg, the other across her face, which, however, was hidden already, for she was pressing it to his feet; she was sobbing convulsively.

"Oh, let me die so!—die whilst you are with me!" she moaned forth at last.

"Don't talk of dying, Cherry, poor little girl! Come, let me help you up; and then tell me how you came here, and what is the matter with you."

" I can't talk," she said, faintly ; " but let me sit here a little,—and, oh, do not leave me ! "

She looked up,—those strange eyes looking more wondering than ever, yet softer and more pleading.

"No, no, Cherry, I won't leave you ! "

END OF VOL. I.

F. J. FRANCIS AND CO., TOOK'S COURT AND WINE OFFICE COURT, E.C.